DON'T FEAR THE REAPER

A. S. FRENCH

NEONOIR BOOKS

ALSO BY A. S. FRENCH

The Astrid Snow series.

Book one: Don't Fear the Reaper.

Book two: The Killing Moon.

Book three: Lost in America.

The Detective Jen Flowers series.

Book one: The Hashtag Killer.

Book two: Serial Killer.

Book three: Night Killer.

Go to www.andrewsfrench.com for more information.

1 SUFFRAGETTE CITY

Astrid was used to people screaming. Like listening to your favourite Bowie song or a snippet of religious chanting, it existed at the back of her head, regardless of where she was. The rhythm would twist and turn, the instrumental howls occasionally dimming for the vocals or tortured words begging for release. She remembered one particular shriek resembling the guitar part in *Ziggy Stardust*. It was a soothing sound which allowed her to focus as eyes widened and blood dripped onto the floor.

But this was different screaming, more disturbing than gasps of fear. This was the cry of kids enjoying themselves, a concept so alien to Astrid, her hand trembled as the mass approached. The thunder of feet hurried past her, childish voices shouting for joy as they headed for the playground, leaving the mothers, sisters, guardians, and nannies in their wake. Astrid kept the phone close to her chest, switching her scrutiny from the green-eyed redheaded vacuous-looking girl on the screen to the crowd of adults trooping after the children. Her fingers gripped onto the neon, nails biting into the plastic. All the lesser lights of her past paled into insignificance compared to what she was about to do. Once she found her target.

She took a swig from the cup of coffee she'd bought on the way into the park. It was putrid and tasted like snake blood and bile, a toxic medicine she'd once sampled in the hidden streets of central Jakarta. The back of her throat shrivelled, and her eyes shrank. Astrid spat the drink onto the floor and followed it with the cup. Her long black hair swung behind her like a mane as a faint, transient, wistful smile lightened her brooding face.

A hint of mint and sweetness hung in the air, and she thought of sipping mojitos on a beach. She gazed at the suffragette statues as she waited, staring at the long body-consuming outfits they wore and comparing them to her red leather jacket, painted-on jeans and white blouse. She'd never understood why people squeezed into clothes which were far too small for them. For Astrid, her attire wasn't just for relaxation; it sent out an invisible signal to the surrounding multitude: usually FUCK OFF, but today she was in a more approachable mood.

Astrid stared into the crowd, squinting to find what she wanted. She'd always found it humorous, making her eyes smaller to see something when she should have been expanding them. It was one of the few peculiarities of her childhood she'd kept; that and the escape maps stored inside her mind.

It didn't take long before she spotted the woman whose image she'd studied on the phone: Colleen Moore, Dublin born and now working in London as a nanny. A cigarette hung from Moore's mouth, failing to hide her pained expression. Astrid had scoured Colleen's social media posts and hacked the government website which stockpiled data on everyone. The nanny was squeaky clean, and that worried her. Everybody had skeletons in their closet, but not this girl. Perhaps Astrid had enough to go around.

The stress lines etched on Colleen's face made her look older than her eighteen years. Astrid tried to remember what she had been like as a teenager, vague recollections of hanging around with the wrong crowd. Her mother scolding her for getting up to things she shouldn't. But she enjoyed getting up to something she shouldn't. Soon she'd be getting up to all kinds of things she shouldn't; as long as she didn't mess up now.

There was no sign of the target. Astrid shoved the phone back into her pocket, an eternity of resolutions, doubts and indecisions forcing her on. Was it the wrong place or time? Had she messed up again? The last time that happened, people suffered.

She peered beyond the group of adults marching towards her until the target appeared, dragged behind the nanny in Colleen Moore's cigarette-free hand. Olivia, a small blonde-haired girl, five years old, struggled to break away from the nanny. All of Astrid's buried hopes rose from their sepulchres at the sight of the child. Alien emotions massed inside Astrid's guts, resembling ice cream in a microwave. A week ago, she'd strangled a serial killer in Glasgow, yet now her fingers trembled at the sight of this kid.

As they strode past, she wanted to stretch out to grab hold of Colleen and tell her to be gentler with the girl. The other hand would stroke the long hair of the niece she hadn't seen before today. Olivia ran to the swings, smiling at Astrid as she did, and it was the greatest feeling in Astrid's life. It made her forget her parents' hatred of her; forget the times she'd left home until the last one stuck; forget three years on the street; forget the boyfriend who'd turned her into a computer hacker; forget the girlfriend who'd broken her heart and her arm. And forget how much her sister hated her.

Have I the heart to take the kid from this nanny, to keep her from Courtney, to keep the girl from him?

She captured Olivia's smile in her mind and returned to it over the next hour, watching the kid play with a casual abandonment which only the innocent possessed. The adults supervising the children were a bundle of stress balls, rolling through the playground to keep their kids from hurting themselves. They bellowed out instructions to calm down, but it would have been easier to ask fire to stop burning than to get the kids to obey. Stars illuminated their eyes, every muscle striving to move, to run, to jump, mouths endlessly chattering, giggling, screaming. It was a childhood Astrid had never had.

She was Olivia's age when she got her first black eye. Her mother told the doctor her daughter had fallen down the stairs, but Astrid had never fallen in her life. She'd been knocked down many times, but had always risen with renewed strength and determination. And her greatest resolution was to forget, but never forgive what her family did to her. But even time couldn't wash some memories away.

Inky clouds erupted across the sky. Most of the adults packed up their offspring and rushed off before the heavens ripped apart. As the first drops of rain fell, only two children and their guardians remained. Olivia was one of them, climbing the slide, and then slipping down it, oblivious to the weather. It didn't appear to bother her or Colleen, who Astrid assumed was in no rush to get back to Olivia's parents. Astrid couldn't blame her: she still bore the scars from the last meeting with Courtney.

You're my older sister. You should have protected me.

It was the last time they were together, the night Astrid fled from home and never returned. It was over fifteen years ago, but the words continued to linger in the shadows of her mind. That was when she knew her sister's laugh hurt her more than their father's fists ever did. Now, she stood in the park and rubbed at her flesh through her jacket. She'd put all of this behind her a long time ago; it would be easy to leave and follow through on the plans she'd spent a year making. And then she remembered her niece.

A great pang gripped her heart. She was worrying about what the future held for Olivia, troubled at the possibility the man who'd ruined Astrid's childhood lurked in the periphery of Olivia's life. A harvest of barren regrets consumed her as the gang emerged from the shadows, heading towards the swings and the other child. He was a dark-haired boy of about Olivia's age. The adult with him, a woman in her mid-twenties, was as observant as Astrid and rushed to get him before the group arrived.

The gang left the darkness, marching towards the middle of the playground. The two at the front strode with a swagger born from years of giving orders and arrogance gleaned from the fawning of acolytes. They sat in the vacated swings while the other four stomped around in an agitated state. Astrid recognised the movements of people desperate for a fix.

'Come here, kid.'

His voice croaked through the dead frog stuck in his throat. Olivia and Colleen were in the playground, plus the six intruders. Astrid stood, glued to the shadows, and moved towards the entrance. She stared at Olivia, her mind a barrage of memories long since submerged into the darkest parts of her brain. She forgot her past, remembered what she did in the present, and considered if she'd be this lonely for the rest of her life.

Astrid focused on the gang and knew what she had to do.

'Olivia, come to me,' Colleen shouted.

Astrid hid in the gloom, small droplets of rain bouncing off the ground.

The druggie stared at the girl. 'We only want to play.'

His voice was empty as a freshly dug grave, his face constructed from crisscrossing scars and a nose which had gone too many rounds with somebody else's fists. His friends were no better, all hollow eyes, ragged, unwashed hair and filthy clothes. They stank of desperation and anti-life.

She moved her gaze from the grunts towards those who pulled their vagabond strings. The dealers were closer to ordinary humanity, clean clobber and gaudy jewellery hanging off them; apart from the one with the swastikas and white power symbols tattooed on his neck and hands. Astrid touched her skin and admired the shine the new moisturiser gave her. It smelt of fresh peaches. She hoped the swastika man was allergic to peaches.

Olivia ran to Colleen, who scooped the kid up in her arms.

'We won't hurt you,' the intruder said. There was deception buried in the quicksand of his ignorance. Astrid wiped the rain from her cheek.

'Come any closer, and I'll crush your balls,' the nanny yelled and Astrid discovered a new admiration for the Irish girl.

The thug froze. Astrid relaxed as she observed Olivia. Silence engulfed the playground before a raucous laugh startled the birds from the trees. They scattered as she followed the laughter to the neo-Nazi drug dealer, identifying him as the group leader.

'Let them go,' he shouted at the shivering excuse for humanity Colleen had shamed. She turned from him, striding from the playground and towards Astrid, who moved into the last light of the day, cracking her knuckles to attract the nanny's attention.

'Yer shud scarper while dohs scumbags are ere.'

Colleen's accent was so thick, Astrid struggled to get the gist of it. Olivia smiled at the aunt she didn't know, her grin warmer than the sun, no sense of fear anywhere on her face. Being this close to her niece was blissful and confusing, the perplexity of the emotions forcing Astrid to question everything she'd prepared for her new life.

Would I abandon a year's worth of planning for this kid? Is isolation still what I crave?

'Don't worry; they won't be back again.' Astrid returned Olivia's smile with her own.

'Are ye a copper?' the departing nanny said.

'Something like that.'

As the two of them disappeared into the distance, Astrid strode into the playground, focused on the nearest interloper and the cricket bat at his feet. She hated sports. Ever since that day at school when she'd turned up wearing high heels and the teacher made her run around the field in them. The bruises had vanished, but the pain continued.

She stuck in the shadows, inching towards them unnoticed, fixed on the weapon against the slide as the invader bent down. She was behind him with one movement, snatching the bat while he reached for drugs inside his sock. Astrid put her foot on his back and kicked him forward. The force threw him to the ground, splitting his nose against a smiling concrete facsimile of a unicorn. The sound of cracked bone shattered the silence. The other druggies stood entranced while the two dealers remained stationary in their swings. Astrid stepped over the one she'd broken as he rolled around and swore at her. She peered at him.

'Obscenity is the trademark of the ignoramus.' A dark veil covered his eyes. 'You think an ignoramus is a dinosaur, don't you?' She thought about it as confusion consumed his face. 'You know, you're probably not wrong.'

Astrid turned towards the leader in his swing. The two dealers stared at her, dull black eyes peering as if she was an unexpected treat.

'Free hit for the first one to take her down.'

His voice was guttural and abrasive, the words jackbooting from his mouth. The chemical zombies didn't falter and jumped at her as one. Their intoxicated flesh and mushed brains meant their reflexes were no better than five-year-olds trying Zumba for the first time.

Astrid stepped to the side to evade them as they stumbled past her. She swung the bat in an arc, bringing it around to smash the middle thug in the jaw, shattering teeth and bone. She followed through to strike the next one in his cheek, sending him flying into a crazed-looking rocking horse. She turned to see the last thug gazing at her in shock, his mouth wide enough to eat a cricket ball; instead, she jabbed him in the gut with the large end of the bat. His stomach rippled under the force as he crumbled.

They lay broken around her, but the two dealers hadn't moved. Fear possessed the eyes of the smaller one; he was no threat. It was the fascist she had to make an example of.

'There's still time for you to leave here pain free.' She twirled the bat above her head. 'I don't care who you work for or what you do, do it somewhere else.'

She picked a piece of skin from her fingers and dropped it, drawn to the bright green hue of his eyes, the same shade as one of those frogs you licked to get high. She'd tried it once and lost two days of her life. The leader slipped from the seat, his six-foot-four frame looking ridiculous in the child's swing. He had a physique best described as lean, muscular, and honed more on the streets than in the gym. His green eyes glared at her.

'That piece of wood won't help you, puta.'

'No Necesito nada para Tratar Contigo,' she said as she flung the bat behind her. He stepped forward, flexing his impressive arms, so his muscles bulged like Popeye on an overdose of spinach. She imagined cracking his head like an egg.

He didn't make the mistake the others had; no impetuous lunging from him, but short, sharp jabs to get her measure. Astrid moved backwards each time, avoiding the druggies on the ground and luring him to where she wanted to be: in the middle of the playground and surrounded by slides, climbing frames and a rocking horse. There was no space to manoeuvre. He was a big man with long legs who couldn't move well in the area created for little kids.

She dodged his latest jab, his frustration growing with every miss. Her chance came as his leg caught the sharp metal edge of the slide. Astrid moved as he dropped his shoulder, dodging away from his arm and throwing her elbow into his neck. He collapsed on his side, tumbling over the slide, lying face down like a marionette with severed strings. The others scrambled to their feet and abandoned their leader to his fate.

Astrid flexed her fingers. 'There's less in you than meets the eye.'

He muttered something obscene as he pushed up from the cold metal. He followed it with some terrible insult about her parents, which she would have agreed with in different circumstances. Astrid allowed him to stand and flail his fist towards her. She ducked before bringing her foot up and kicking him in the groin. His face collapsed, his eyes, nose and mouth dropping like high-rise flats under demolition before hitting the ground with a crack.

He cried amongst the leaves as the clouds split asunder and the rain spat out a thousand waterfalls. Astrid left the playground, walking past the spot where she first saw Olivia's smile. and headed towards the exit on the far side.

She peered into the trees. Is this what she'd gone there for, to find a childhood she never had? Shadows slipped from the bushes behind her, but she focused on images of Olivia. The surrounding greenery reminded Astrid of their back garden, of her earliest memory, of Courtney's fourth birthday party and the gaggle of kids who turned up to celebrate it. Sunlight streamed everywhere as an ocean of blue overtook the surroundings. A group of older children dressed as Smurfs entered the festivities; it was as if a sapphire sea had swept the green grass into another world.

Then her father approached her, Astrid, all of three years old, and these were the first words she recalled anyone saying to her:

You're incapable of love, so no one will ever love you.

She barely understood what he said at the time, but she knew from his face, from the void in his eyes, what he meant.

You'll never be like your sister. Courtney is everything to us.

Her sister's fancy-dress party was in full swing. He danced over the grass, a coronet of snakes gripping his head. Or did she only dream that part? He drifted from her vision and into the gloom. But he was always there.

Astrid shook the memory from her head. The experience with Olivia had confused the hell out of her. That confusion meant she was oblivious to the people following her from the murk and past the lake. It was only when she approached the exit and two more dark-suited men appeared that she realised her night wasn't over.

———————————

SOME PEOPLE, weak people, fear death. What they cannot understand is how liberating it is. Think of a lifetime of disappointments and regrets vanishing into the next world. It's the deaths of others which are redemptive. Ironically, my first was like giving birth.

The rhythm of the water held me in its sway. The body floating on the river mesmerised me, how the head peered into the liquid arms waiting for it. The tender cadence of the apple-green reeds matched the movement of my heart as the wind moved the grass from side to side, dancers in nature and observers of death. The hair floated out towards the shore, sleeping on the waves as if her spirit tried to find an anchor to the mortal world. It was an image I kept returning to inside my mind, finding comfort in the aesthetic of death.

The dead sleep with their eyes open; the living walk around with theirs closed. They begged for mercy, but were disappointed. They asked for absolution but received no answers. They searched for salvation, but couldn't find it. Some of them desired to cleanse their sins, but no water was available. It was a new life for me, one which tormented me with panic, creating a fear that gripped me in a vice. Revelations greater than most could comprehend possessed me. The dark and relentless fate I'd envisaged for myself had withered into the ether. A fever of enthusiasm surged through me, heading towards a climax which would only reach fulfilment once she'd suffered at my hands. She had to pay for her sins. The water was too good for her. It was for the others; her iniquities would never wash away. She walked by the lake, and it made me think of the different rivers I'd visited, the hunger growing inside me once more.

I needed to get back to the red water.

3 THE SHOP

Astrid gazed at the dark bowl of the sky, all glorious with the blaze of a million worlds so close, but so far away. She used the movement to check the people observing her, surprised they'd kept their distance. The chill of the evening made the hairs jump on her skin, the scent of the park contrasting with that drifting off her new friends: fresh cologne and clean clothes, shaped to equal precision. She strode on, ignoring the shadows, past the manicured topiary, beyond the unicorn, Cyclops and mermaids, stopping at the teeth of the dragons.

You boys are too quiet in your walk, too studious in your movements to be riddled with drugs. So if you're not with the little fascist, who sent you?

Had they come from her father, ordered to complete his revenge after all this time? He had the means to pay for it and was devious enough to have waited until the park exposed her like this. She tried to push his malicious grin into the shadows, but struggled to rid his taint from her mind. Astrid focused on the intruders instead. Perhaps they worked for her sister. Courtney had been happy enough to take their father's money. Her love and supplication for him were opposite to Astrid's hatred.

Others had sought revenge on her before, but this felt different. She ran through scenarios of who they might work for. There was the criminal organisation in the East End whose extortion empire she'd put out of business; the drug dealers in Manchester who'd suffer nightmares for a long time; the human trafficking gang in Sheffield she'd sent packing back to Eastern Europe.

She was running through the permutations when another two men appeared at the mouth of the largest dragon. Darkness oozed from between the trees, inky fingers creeping towards her. Silence filled the park, the aroma of flowers and freshly cut grass drifting in the air. They wore identical clothes, dark suits with grey shirts buttoned to the top, somewhere in their mid-twenties, both with the same extreme cropped ice-white haircut.

'You boys look like quads from a John Wyndham novel.'

Astrid waited for one of them to say something; it wouldn't matter which; they were cuckoos, and she was a bird of prey.

'The buyer needs you back at the shop.'

His voice was low and shaky, nerves gripping his face, his skin pale and tense. His use of the coded language surprised her. With nobody within half a mile of them, it made no sense to speak in riddles. But now she knew who they worked for, she relaxed, releasing the tension in her knuckles and letting her mind drift back to that perfect time in the playground before the thugs arrived. Whatever they wanted, she could get rid of them in an instant; and then she'd decide what to do about Olivia.

I know what I'm going to do. Plans have been made and set in motion; the plane ticket and new passport wait for me at the hotel. I'll keep the photos I took today of the kid, and that will do. It's not my job to look after her. And surely Courtney wouldn't let any harm come to her daughter?

The same thoughts echoed inside her head as the group stood and scrutinised her. The bloke on the right had a repeating facial tic most people wouldn't have noticed, but to her was a rock tumbling downhill. His twin opposite folded his arms, hands moving uncontrollably, his flesh straining against the jacket a size too small for his impressive bulk. The two behind her were motionless, arms glued to their sides like human biscuits wrapped and ready to be eaten.

She hadn't slept for twenty-four hours, her mind in constant need of stimulation. Astrid checked the faces of her new acquaintances, surprised at their youth, before remembering how young she'd been when introduced to this clandestine world.

A gleam of light dropped from the moon and skimmed off the lake. She controlled the hyperactivity in her brain and focused on what she might face in the next five minutes. Inside her mind, she stretched into the corner where she kept her maps. She'd developed a process as a child, compensation for dealing with events far worse than anything these trespassers could threaten her with. Her brain mapped out two different scenarios: refuse their demand and deal with the consequences, or go with them and see what develops.

As the night engulfed them, Astrid observed the tiny neon lights coming from their shirts' top button; everything was being recorded and beamed live to the shop. She chastised herself for falling into code inside her head. Her annoyance grew by the second: not only had they ruined her experience with Olivia, but they'd used her as part of a training exercise.

'Tell your buyer I've got enough for now, and I don't appreciate the hard sales technique.'

The reply came straight from the echo chamber.

'The buyer needs you back at the shop.'

There was something wrong in what he said, within those eight simple words, and she couldn't work out what. The joy of seeing Olivia had affected her reasoning, slowed down her brain.

Never let your emotions cloud your judgement.

That's what they'd said when recruiting her into the Agency, or the shop when described to any outsider. And she was an outsider now, having stepped away a year ago. She was eighteen when her handler spoke those words, and the advice was as redundant as a cassette tape in a teenager's bedroom. She'd already buried all her emotions when she walked into the Agency the first time.

You can walk away, but you'll never leave, was one of their other phrases of wisdom. Technically, what Astrid had taken was a Vacation, and Vacations were of indiscriminate length. Once your Vacation finished, they would demand your return. And then Astrid identified what was wrong with his words.

'Repeat it,' she commanded. He didn't hesitate.

'The buyer needs you back at the shop.'

There it was: needs, not demands or wants. Needs. This twilight meeting with *The Midwich Cuckoos* was a request. It put a fresh perspective on things. Boredom had been threatening to overcome her in the last few weeks, and she needed extra stimulation. A request could only mean Director George Cross wanted her back, and she couldn't refuse him anything. Not when she owed him so much.

He was the one who had made her forthcoming escape a reality; she couldn't have done it without his help. So, had something changed? Was he in trouble? He'd taken significant risks to help her; risks which could lead to both of them ending up behind bars for a long time. Perhaps this gloomy park gathering was his covert way of getting to see her. If so, she couldn't let him down.

'Okay, take me to your leader.' None of them smiled. 'Did the Agency grow you boys in a lab?' None of them replied.

Something must have happened to George for them to come for me. Had he changed the plans we agreed on a year ago?

Something terrible gripped her heart, sending pain into her skull and confusion through her limbs. Astrid kept trying to regain control until she recognised what it was, an emotion she thought she'd consigned to another life a long time ago: fear.

Not fear for herself, but for Olivia.

Astrid strode forward. Inside her head, she searched through her collection of maps, finding the one she needed. The chill crept into her bones and memories as she stared at the first plan she'd ever created, looking at the childish paths heading from the darkness and into the citadel of light. It resembled the Disney castle from the movies she watched every night locked in the family home. Those movies soothed the bruises he'd inflicted along her shoulders and legs. He was smart, her father, the chief superintendent, always knowing the best spots to hide what he'd done to her. He didn't need to conceal them from her mother and Courtney because they didn't care and encouraged the sadism. But he understood how the world would look unkindly upon what he'd done to his younger daughter.

Her neck ached as she shook her head. She breathed out as her feet crossed the grass in the real world and the inside version of herself skipped down the yellow brick road she'd created years ago. It was a five-minute walk in silence from the park to their car, the four of them keeping the same distance in front and behind like pallbearers at a funeral. When they reached the vehicle, the bloke who'd spoken to her slipped into the rear seat and indicated she join him. Two flanked her in the back while the others got in the front. It was a tight squeeze.

Blacked-out windows obscured her view, but there was only one place they'd take her: the Agency headquarters on the edge of the city. She ignored the quads while she delved into her recent memories, concentrating on more pleasant thoughts: the images of Olivia from a few hours ago. Astrid put them on repeat until they came to a dramatic stop outside their destination, an impressive building three storeys high with four more underground. It was perfect for the Agency, miles from the populace as their cover as an IT company. Astrid's bodyguards slipped out of the vehicle, and she followed them towards the entrance.

She thought about Olivia, wondering how safe the kid would be in that home with the sister who hated Astrid for what she'd done to their father.

Courtney hated me long before that.

The chill of the night cut into her cheeks. The rain had vanished, but her skin was still damp. Her escort continued in the same formation, two at the front and two behind. Astrid followed them through the doors, aware that secret cameras recorded her every move. Then she stepped into the lobby of the Agency and knew she'd made a terrible mistake.

4 HOLIDAY DESTINATION

Disappointment overwhelmed Astrid as she entered the building; an unpleasant and heavy sensation gripped her heart. Fleeting touches of something alien and intrusive wormed their way into her brain, and she found it disturbing.

Is this what it's like to care?

It was a curious and unsettling feeling, and she wasn't sure whether she liked it. She headed for the gate, holding up her arms as she stepped through the electronic scanner. One quad met her on the other side of security.

'In here.' He pointed towards an interview room. It confirmed what she'd suspected during the drive: she'd returned to the Agency not as a colleague, but as a person of interest. Inside her head, she kicked herself for forgetting her objectives.

So damn sloppy.

She entered and noticed the circular table in the middle and the four chairs around it. Astrid sat in the first one, removing her phone. If she didn't keep her brain busy, her head would flood with crippling memories. She was diagnosed with ADHD when she was seven. Her mother struggled to understand what the doctors were telling the family, while her father dismissed it as, in his words, mumbo-jumbo nonsense. Astrid failed to comprehend what was wrong with her, only knowing her head was always so full of information that she found it difficult to sleep. Courtney appeared amused with the whole thing and would whisper into her sister's ear, telling her all sorts of nonsense she knew Astrid would find hard to forget.

It took two years for Astrid to find something which helped ease her condition. It was Courtney's tenth birthday party, and their father bought her a portable compact disc player. Astrid borrowed it when her sister was out and used the music to focus her mind; having the sounds so close to her head made it easier for her to drown out the constant din. Astrid used the music as a crutch, quickly discovering a history of tunes which never left her, but it couldn't erase her condition. Her inner voice would drown out everything else unless she found the right triggers to dial it down.

Her hyperactivity exhibited itself in different ways: fidgeting, squirming, needing to walk frequently, mood swings, insomnia, plus violent episodes. Sex and alcohol were ways of escape, but sometimes morbid horrors would assault her senses, and she'd need to use one of her maps to regain sanity. The photos of Olivia on her mobile occupied her emotions until she chastised herself again for being so foolish not to follow the kid instead of ending up in this predicament.

I can't make sure Olivia's okay if I'm in here.

As the door opened, Astrid closed the phone. She leant into the chair designed to be as uncomfortable as possible, the fabric of it sticking into parts of her back it shouldn't. It wouldn't have been out of place in torture rooms she'd visited; torture rooms she'd controlled. She expected to see her mentor, Director Cross, but he wasn't there.

'Thank you for coming, Agent Snow. I'm Director Davis, and these are Agents Lee and Lincoln.'

Astrid glimpsed an undercurrent of scorn inside the director's words. Agent Lee was a blonde woman with the appearance of Tinkerbell in a regulation Agency dark blue suit. Astrid guessed her age to be early twenties. Agent Lincoln was the opposite, in his fifties with a face of crushed leather and obsessive eyes, bald apart from three strands of wispy hair combed across his head. Astrid and Lincoln had a history together, none of which was pleasant.

'Where's Director Cross?' His non-appearance worried her. *She's Lost Control* by Joy Division played at the furthest reaches of her mind.

They know what we did.

Davis placed her hands on the table. 'That's classified information, Snow. We have more pressing matters to discuss.'

'What?' Astrid gripped the chair. Something serious must have happened if this sourpuss had replaced George. Davis gave Agent Lee a nod, prompting the agent to touch her digital screen before showing it to the director.

'You made a trip to Europe last month; visits to Berlin, Prague, Vienna and Budapest.' She said the names as if they were places to avoid.

'You've been keeping tabs on me.'

'Can you tell us what you did in those cities?'

Her lips hardened, turning into a façade of a grin. Astrid struggled to get a read on the woman. The void of her face, her lack of expression and those dull eyes made it difficult to decipher the contents of her head. Astrid picked up her phone and opened the photo gallery.

'I've got pictures if you want to see them. I should warn you some are risqué and may not be suitable for people with sensitive dispositions.' Astrid glanced at Agent Lee, hoping for a reaction but getting nothing.

Davis took the tablet and read from the screen.

'You drove to Manchester Airport, left your car there, and then flew to Berlin. What did you do next?'

'What's this about?' Astrid asked.

'All in good time; if you can answer the question first.'

Davis poured a glass of water while she waited for Astrid's reply.

'I took a train from the airport to Berlin central station. Then a ten-minute walk to the hotel, where I dumped my bag before finding a bar for food and drink. Do you want to know what I had?' The memory of it made her stomach rumble. Davis shook her head. 'After that, I headed further into East Berlin.'

'Why did you do that?'

'The best time to explore Berlin is at night. Everything is illuminated, and there are fewer tourists. I did a circular route from the other side of the station, up to the Reichstag and the Washing Machine.' Astrid paused and waited for one of them to ask, surprised it was Agent Lee with her curious eyes and cute cheekbones.

'What's the Washing Machine?'

'It's what the locals call the building which houses the Chancellor. They think it looks like a domestic appliance.'

'And what did you do then?' Davis didn't appear interested in the tourist version.

'I took photos at the Weimar Memorial, walked through the Brandenburg Gate, and then under the linden trees. There are images on the phone if you want to check.'

'Did you talk to anybody on your evening stroll?' Davis asked while the assistants made notes.

'I spoke to a few tourists who wanted directions.'

'Your knowledge of Berlin is that good?'

'I've been there a few times, which you're well aware of since all the details are in Agency files.'

'And then?'

Astrid dug into her memory for the rest of that first night in Berlin.

'I went to the late-night bookshop, Dussmann on Friedrichstraße, peered into shop windows and stared at the bears before returning to the hotel for a drink.'

'You were there for another two days?' Director Davis never removed those dull eyes from Astrid.

'I took the tube to Alexanderplatz the next day to go up the Fernsehturm TV tower and look upon Berlin from a thousand feet up. You can see across the city, including where the communists split it in half in the sixties. That motivated me to visit Checkpoint Charlie to get my photo taken with some fake soldiers before heading to the Hack-escher Market for traditional German food and beverages. Then I returned to the hotel. The next day I visited where Bowie lived in the seventies and bought some Krautrock CDs; all mundane stuff unless you have the same interests as me.'

'Far from it, Snow; what you've told us has been useful for our investigation.' Davis tried to smile, but the muscles in her mouth appeared to fight against it.

'So, you'll tell me what this is about?'

Astrid was more bored than irritated, looking at her phone to notice it had gone nine o'clock. If she got out soon enough, she could stake out her sister's house. She had an overwhelming desire to leave and ensure her niece was okay, as long as she didn't have to talk to Courtney.

I don't like these emotions. They're messing with my head.

'Do you know Agent Cara Delaney?' Davis stared at the digital screen as she spoke.

'I do. We worked some cases together.'

Astrid lifted her fingers to her mouth, about to bite her nails until she remembered how much of a filthy habit it was. She hadn't seen Cara in a long time. Not after what happened and their traumatic separation.

'How did you meet Delaney?'

'Cara?' Astrid had shut out most of those memories, but some things she never forgot, and her first and last meetings with Cara were always with her. 'I'd just been punched in the face by a people trafficker when I saw her in the flesh for the first time.'

Agent Lee spoke while the other two checked the digital screen.

'This was in Newcastle during the Vertigo operation.'

Astrid placed one hand on the table, allowing the cold of the plastic top to relight the parts of her brain where she locked away those images and sounds she couldn't erase.

'That's right.'

Davis moved the screen so Astrid could see the photos she'd retrieved. 'This was your doing?'

Astrid didn't need to look at them to see the bodies on that factory floor.

'The police had struggled to catch the leaders of a trafficking gang who were operating throughout England, moving people around the bigger cities. They'd caught lower level functionaries in a few places, Birmingham, Leeds, and Sheffield, so someone high up in the government passed the case files on to the Agency.' She peered into Davis's unmoving expression. 'And we caught a break in Newcastle with a name, Vertigo, and a location. All we needed was someone to work undercover at the factory where the gang were transporting people from.'

'This was Delaney?' Davis said.

'Cara, yes. She was born in Newcastle and only left after university. She'd lost her accent by the time she joined the Agency, but she knew the city like the back of her hand and had contacts there. Director Cross showed me her file; I'd read her details and knew what she looked like and understood why they'd sent her in undercover.'

'But something went wrong,' Lee said.

Astrid plucked the images from her head, seeing everything in front of her as if she was back in that factory.

'Cara was undercover for nine months, working as a facilitator moving their product around. The only contact we had with her were the posts she made on an online toy collecting forum.'

Davis narrowed her eyes. 'Toy collecting?'

'She'd done it since she was a kid, so if the traffickers caught her posting in the forum, she was clued up enough to deceive them.'

'But then the posts stopped.'

'Yes. She was supposed to leave something every day, so twenty-four hours of silence was a message for Director Cross to send someone in.'

'Which was you?'

Astrid shrugged. 'They needed someone on the street, someone who appeared to have been living rough for long enough not to arouse suspicion when they broke into the factory for a warm night's sleep. And I had plenty of experience of that. Plus, I'd been stuck in the office for six months and was desperate to get out.'

Agent Lee scrutinised her every word. 'And you got punched in the head when climbing through the window.'

Astrid rubbed at her cheek as if it had only been yesterday. 'He was smaller than me, but I got my leg caught on the window. He pulled me inside and thumped me. When the birds stopped flying above my head, he dumped me in front of some other goons.'

She closed her eyes and returned to Newcastle, the voice of the one who hit her still in Astrid's head.

'She's just some street tramp. What are we going to do with her?'

A tall man strode over and grabbed her cheek. 'She's not bad under all this dirt. We could put her with the others and make a bit of money off her.'

'The Boss doesn't like surprises. We should just get rid of her.'

Then she heard Cara's voice for the first time.

'Leave her with me. He doesn't need to know about this. You two get back to your work. The transport leaves in an hour.'

They grumbled, but Astrid watched them leave. She rubbed at her eyes before staring at Delaney. Her legs creaked as she stood and said the magic words.

'The fog on the Tyne is all mine.'

Cara's eyes darted around the room, checking the door before she pushed her head close to Astrid. 'You shouldn't be here.'

'Someone had to come after you went radio silent. What's going on?'

'There's a shipment being moved to Scotland tonight,

and Vertigo was becoming suspicious of my internet posts, so I had to stop them.'

'By shipment, you mean people?'

'Yes. Thirty women and girls.'

'So we need to stop it.'

'Only if he comes, which I'm not sure he will.' Nine months of watching people being victimised seeped out of Cara's eyes, and Astrid tried not to think of all the horrible things she must have witnessed while waiting to get this close to catching the man they wanted. 'He's the one with all the contacts in Europe and Africa. Without him, all we'll have are more functionaries, and the whole thing will start again somewhere else. Don't you understand that?'

It was at that point, when Astrid stared into Cara's eyes and saw the pain, she felt the first pang of emotion she'd thought impossible to have.

'Of course I do. What do you suggest?'

The click of a gun trigger stopped Cara from replying. Astrid looked up to see the goons back in the room, standing with a third person. He wasn't the one holding the pistol, but by the way he carried himself, she knew who he was even before he spoke.

'I should have known never to trust someone who collects toys, but Beth was so good at her job.' He strode to Delaney and ran his fingers through her hair. Astrid was impressed with how Cara didn't flinch at his touch. 'Are you two coppers?'

Astrid stood straight. She'd learnt an important lesson early in life never to back down when around predators.

'Something like that. If you tell Mr Potato Head to hand over the gun, nobody will get hurt.'

The man she assumed to be Vertigo laughed. 'Have the police changed their methods?'

Astrid cracked her knuckles. 'This operation you've been running, while terrible and a crime against humanity, is impressive considering how you've been able to move around so many victims while staying so far under the radar.'

He shrugged. 'It's all about brains and opportunity. The public has this misconception that the police are clever and trustworthy when both things are far from the truth. So, once you're dealing with stupidity and corruption, and you factor in how nasty some people are, it's not hard to do.' He held up his hands. 'It's not as if I'm the only entrepreneur in this line of business.'

It was her turn to laugh. 'Entrepreneur? Is that why you called yourself Vertigo?'

'It's good, don't you think? I couldn't use my real name, could I? And I've always been a Hitchcock fan since my old man's obsession with those movies.'

Astrid needed to keep him talking while she inched closer to the goon with the gun, lucky that both thugs seemed more interested in listening to their master's voice than watching her.

'Maybe Psycho would have been a better choice.'

He waved his finger at her. 'No, no, that's not right. I'm not a bad person. I'm only doing this for the money, working as a businessman as many others do. I mean, the government makes millions every year selling arms to countries that do far worse damage than I'll ever do. Where's the moral outrage about that?'

Astrid watched Cara's frustration and anger finally burst from her.

'Businessman? You're responsible for the rape and torture of hundreds of people.' Her eyes were fiery red. 'That stops now.'

Vertigo continued to wave his finger. 'I'm going to miss you, Beth.'

He turned his head to speak to the goon with the gun as Astrid reached out and grabbed that wagging finger, snapping the bone with ease. The gunman froze, and Astrid threw Vertigo into him. The sound of the gunfire and the screams were still in her head when Agent Lee's voice brought her back into the present.

'You said the deaths of James Bower, known as Vertigo, and his two associates were accidents.'

Astrid stared at Lee. 'The gunman shot Bower and the other one as he fell. Then, as I tried to restrain him, he shot himself in the stomach.'

Davis peered at the photos on the screen. 'How unfortunate.'

'For them,' Astrid said.

'And this is where your professional and personal relationship with Delaney started?' Lee said. Astrid hoped that was jealousy she heard in her voice and not disgust.

'It was one of those first meetings we always liked to mention at dinner parties or weddings. You know, when someone would ask how we got together, Cara would say it was over three dead bodies, and we'd both laugh. People didn't know what we really did for a living – they thought she ran a toy shop, and I wrote poorly selling books – so they assumed she was joking.'

'And you worked many cases together after that?'

She wondered why they were asking things they knew from Agency records. Davis and Lee continued to scrutinise the computer screen, but Lee peered at Astrid.

'We did.'

'Including one in Berlin?'

'Yes, five years ago. You know this, so why ask?'

'Did you have a relationship with Agent Delaney?'

Davis couldn't keep the disdain from her voice; physical entanglements with other agents were forbidden. Astrid hesitated, but it was pointless to deny it.

'We did.'

'Have you kept in touch since?'

'No. Why?'

'Did you meet her on your recent trip to Berlin?'

'No. Why?'

'Because the police found her floating in the River Spree in Berlin the day after you left for Vienna. When we checked her phone to see where she'd been, do you know what it revealed?'

'No.' Astrid realised she was about to find out.

'Wednesday, the night you arrived, the Reichstag, the Washing Machine, the Memorial, the Brandenburg Gate, the bookshop, your hotel. Thursday, Alexanderplatz, Checkpoint Charlie...' she stopped reading from her digital list and stared at Astrid.

'Need I go on?'

A portent full of potential danger possessed Astrid as she shook her head, calculating how much worse it could get.

I THOUGHT of Snow sitting inside the Agency, imagining how her interrogation was going, wondering if they'd blamed her for my crimes yet. She was no stranger to Death, but then neither was I. As a child, my only friend was Death, my constant companion. Not that corpses surrounded me. She was my imaginary friend, Death. I craved Her approval, Her attention.

The first memory imprinted on my brain involved the shadows sweeping me up inside their long fingers. They consumed me with small cuts every day, biting into my flesh, mind, and soul. Large, dark, luminous eyes followed me everywhere.

My father was the human version of an iceberg, and not only because he was cold and indifferent to what happened around him. Almost ninety per cent of an iceberg is below the surface of the water. And it was like that with my father's personality and what little emotion he possessed. Occasionally, tremors bubbled beneath his cold exterior. Something inconsequential would upset him to the point his eyes bulged, and his voice stuttered sounds beyond the usual grunts.

'You're the child I never wanted,' he'd say to me.

Or, 'I should have dropped you on your head in the hospital.'

I thought that was normal, that it was the same for all the other kids at school.

My mother never stopped him, but maybe she couldn't.

He was an unhappy man born at the wrong time, at the wrong place and to the wrong people. His parents lived in poverty and, from all accounts, treated him and his brother worse than dogs. Was it all learned behaviour, the reason behind his lack of humanity? Did his lack of empathy transmit to me as I got older? Nurture or nature, which was it that played the most significant part in my metamorphosis? Are we all only the sum of those who gave us existence?

Or did free will drive my quest for revenge?

Revenge on her.

Revenge on Snow.

'What happened?'
Sorrow ruffled Astrid's brows, and the sensation irritated her. A week ago, she wouldn't have been like this. Death had been a constant for most of her life; it didn't bother her. But now mixed emotions and memories irritated her.

'That's why we're here.' Director Davis placed her hands on the table while Lincoln tapped on his screens. Lee was unmoving, but Astrid saw something working behind her eyes.

'You believe I had something to do with it?'

They're keeping something from me.

'That's what we're here to discover.'

'How did she die?' Astrid remembered the last conversation they'd had on the bridge in Berlin, the tears in Cara's eyes when she recognised it was over between them. It would have been difficult for her not to understand, considering Astrid told her in direct enough terms.

'I never loved you, Cara. I'm incapable of loving anyone.'

Had she pretended all the time they were together, or perhaps she'd misled herself? If that was so, then maybe these feeling she had for Olivia were just the same, and they'd vanish as well in time.

Would that be good or bad? Was my father right all along?

She pictured Cara's face on that bridge in Berlin. It had been a shock to see a grown woman collapse into a shuddering pool of helplessness. Her tears came in great waves, threatening to burst the river below them. Astrid walked away guiltless then, but the news of Cara's death upset her now. It surprised her.

Agent Lee spoke next, the details flowing out of her without her having to refer to a computer screen or any notes.

'Even though they discovered her floating in the river, she'd been asphyxiated somewhere else. The plastic bag still was tied around her neck.'

It was a terrible way to die. A method Astrid had used many times on assignments; all of them in the Agency files and her memories.

'What sexual relationship did you have with Agent Delaney?' Director Davis peered into Agent Lincoln's digital screen, her eyes focused on the photos from the crime scene.

'What?' Astrid replied, her brain assuming hostile intent in the questions, glancing at the image of a body being pulled from the river.

'Did you engage in perverted or dangerous sexual practices?'

Astrid held back the laughter, the words coming from the director's mouth triggering an intrusive recollection of her parents asking something similar to her fifteen-year-old self. She remembered the lock of horror on her mother's face and the anger on his. Courtney stood in the corner and laughed. It was her sister who had told them what Astrid got up to at night, away from the house and his hard fists.

'You assume she died after we fooled around in my hotel?'

'It is possible, yes?'

'No.' She stared deep into Agent Lee's cold eyes.

'We'll return to this. What did you do after leaving Berlin?' Davis oozed professionalism, her piggish brown eyes reminding Astrid of crushed hazelnuts.

Why are you moving on so quickly? Why not focus on Cara's murder?

She knew why, recognising the technique of bombarding the suspect with rapid information to disorientate them. There it was; she was a suspect.

'I got a train from Berlin to Prague. It was packed until it stopped in Dresden. It took four hours to get there, and then I took a taxi to my hotel.' The driver was a miserable sod who tried to overcharge her, only handing over the correct change when Astrid said what would happen if he didn't.

'You'd visited Prague before?'

Davis flicked things away on the screen with her hand. Astrid assumed she was staring at the files of her earlier visits to the Czech capital: three successful assignments, with only one causality.

'Yes, years ago and not for relaxation.'

The last time she'd killed a man by forcing his head into the river until his legs stopped kicking. The comparison to Cara's death worried her. Were they trying to create a link between the two?

'What else did you do on your visit?'

Davis sounded like stones rolling down a hill, starting quietly before building up speed for a violent ending. Astrid reached into her recent past, dredging up images which swam in a blurred mist before her eyes.

'I had drinks in the Old Town, before visiting an Absinthe bar to finish the night. The next few days were typical tourist stuff: a river cruise; a trip to the castle; afternoon around the Kafka Museum.'

'Which agent did you work with on your last assignment in Prague?'

She didn't need to think twice. 'Michelle Dark.'

A different agent but another lousy memory. Dark's mistake in letting their target escape led to Astrid drowning somebody on that mission.

'Was that a successful assignment?' Davis returned to being coy, running her fingers through hair nobody else would touch.

'Hardly.' She didn't provide the details they already had.

'When did you last see Agent Dark?'

'When that mission finished, and I requested not to work with her again.'

A request was putting it mildly; she'd told George in no uncertain times she'd strangle Dark if they worked together again.

I said I'd strangle her.

Astrid stared at their digital screens and wondered if they had a recording of that meeting. George had guaranteed her confidentiality, and she trusted him with her life, but she wouldn't put anything past the Agency.

'Indeed. She's been on sick leave ever since,' the director said.

Astrid grimaced. Sick leave was a polite way of saying

Dark received a dishonourable discharge from the service; not that they were in the military. She couldn't work for the Agency again, but they'd keep tabs on her at all times. One word or step out of line, such as spilling Agency secrets, and she'd be buried underground for the rest of her life. And it would be a waking burial.

'Are you going to stop messing around and tell me what this has to do with Agent Delaney's death?' Astrid puffed out her cheeks and formed her hands into fists.

'How long did your river cruise last?'

As soon as Davis asked, Astrid recognised where the conversation would end.

'Somebody murdered Dark, choked her to death with a plastic bag, and then dumped her in the river?' Astrid visualised it all before the words came back to haunt her.

I'll strangle her if I see her again.

And she'd meant every single syllable. Her interrogators stared at each other as if Christmas had arrived early.

'And how do you know this?'

Astrid imagined the noose tightening around her neck.

'It's an educated guess. You must realise that me being in the same cities as two murders, even if they're of people I used to work with, is pure coincidence.'

'We considered that until more agents you'd worked with were murdered in Vienna and Budapest. Killed when you were in those cities, both suffocated. Would you call that a coincidence?'

Astrid sighed at the ridiculousness of it all. She moved forward and poured herself a glass of water.

'No, I wouldn't.' This wasn't a trial; if the Agency confirmed her guilt, she'd never see the light of day again. 'Who are the others?' The drink chilled her lips, as refreshing as sandpaper in her mouth. Davis dispensed with the digital screen and went straight from memory.

'Your first overseas assignment with the Agency was in Vienna ten years ago, assisting Agent Andrews with data salvage. Do you remember that?'

'Vividly.'

Astrid couldn't forget it. Sensitive government financial information was being hawked for sale by a former employee, and it took three days of punching their way through criminals to retrieve it. Plus, she broke Harry Andrews's arm. The successful recovery was all down to her since he was in the hospital, getting patched up. The mission made Astrid an instant star in the Agency. The rumours about her partner's injury flew like wildfire on their return, but only the two of them knew the truth. Or so she thought.

'Agent Andrews tried to assault you in his room.'

Davis spoke as if reading out a train timetable, with about as much emotion as a talking clock. Astrid said nothing.

'Other allegations have been made against him.' Agent Lee touched the silver crucifix around her neck. Astrid hadn't noticed the jewellery earlier. 'Twelve women over a period of two years, in Britain and abroad, all while on Agency assignments. When an agent made the first accusation against him, the others followed quickly. We have details of dates, times and locations.'

'Do you have all that stored in your head, Agent Lee?'

She nodded. 'I interviewed every one of them and listened to all their pain.'

Astrid realised why Lee didn't need a digital screen in front of her. The general name for it was a photographic memory, but that wasn't right. The person who had it, correctly called eidetic memory, remembered more than images: they had complete recall over sounds, smells, touch and taste. It was a useful thing to have in the clandestine world Astrid and Lee moved in.

'Is Andrews dead?'

Astrid didn't care. Since the incident, she'd avoided him at work, their careers heading in different directions after the assignment in Vienna.

'Just like the others, clear plastic bag over the head and floating in the river.'

Astrid noticed a glint in Agent Lee's eyes at the sound of justice delivered to Andrews.

'He continued working for the Agency?'

'He was under investigation, on permanent leave.'

'Were the other two on active assignments?'

Astrid was curious to know if they were under Agency observation while they were in Europe. Agent Lincoln cleared his voice, his throat full of a lifetime's consumption of nicotine and moonshine.

'That's classified.' That gruff Geordie twang sounded like a collection of syllables fighting to get away from each other.

'What did you do in Budapest?' Davis asked.

'Crossed the river, visited the citadel at the top of the hill, the usual tourist stuff.' Astrid recalled her assignments in the city as she told them about her latest visit. She guessed who it would be. 'You found Jack Chill in the water.'

It had to be him. The three of them exchanged those same looks again, confident they had their perpetrator.

'Is that a confession?'

'IQs must have dropped while I was away. Either that or your stumbling ignorance is seeking the road to wisdom.'

Astrid regained her composure. 'Considering what happened between us, if there's another body following me around, it could only have been him.'

'Why?' Davis's eyes shrank into her face.

'He sold secrets to the Russians, even believed he was clever enough to do it underneath my nose while we were in Budapest. Shouldn't he be in prison?'

'He got an early release two months ago,' Lee said.

'Let me guess: he remembered he had dirt to sell as long as you released him?' Astrid didn't understand why they couldn't recognise she'd been framed. So she told them. 'You realise this is a set-up?'

'Why?' Davis liked her direct but straightforward questions. 'Why go to this trouble for you? What makes you so special?'

'You mean apart from my wit, intelligence and good looks?' Astrid's insides squeezed together as if ready to explode.

'And four murders connected to you by place and victim?' Davis said.

'It's all a coincidence.' Astrid knew how impossible that sounded. 'Don't you have CCTV footage of them?'

Director Davis's lopsided mouth highlighted her big nose.

'We have no CCTV footage of Cara Delaney in Berlin. It's as if whoever she was with knew how to avoid electronic surveillance.' Davis stared at Astrid, waiting for a response but getting nothing. 'She probably travelled under an assumed name, so we've had no luck there.'

'What about flights to Berlin?' Astrid said.

'There's no record of her taking a direct flight from Manchester or any other UK airport. She may have gone by train.'

'What about the others?'

Astrid didn't hold out too much hope. One of the many notable things about Agency training was how agents avoided locations with cameras or were skilled at hiding themselves from electronic eyes.

'Enough of your questions, Snow; you're the one under investigation.' Davis moved closer to Astrid. A fever of enthusiasm consumed the director's features. 'So tell us: what did you do with their fingers?'

6 AGENTS OF FORTUNE

'What happened to their fingers?' Astrid asked no one in particular, but Agent Lincoln replied.

'All the victims are missing theirs, sliced off below the knuckles. Somebody is collecting trophies.'

He stared at Astrid as if she'd reach into her jacket and throw those fleshy digits onto the table like cadaverous jacks in a game of death the participants had already lost.

Astrid peered at her nails. 'How careless of them.'

'You've worked some serial killer cases for the Agency over the years, isn't that right?'

She ignored Lincoln's question. Lethargy raced up her spine for an assault on the rear of her head. She fought off its pernicious tendrils, straightened her back, and shook the stupor from her mind.

'I like my fingers delicate and warm, ready to stray wherever I command them to.' Astrid forced a smile and waited for them to speak.

Davis pulled her shoulders up and pushed her chest out. 'We have the evidence, Snow.'

'Everything you have is circumstantial.' Astrid spoke

with a confidence she didn't possess. Davis nodded at something behind her, and Astrid turned to see the doors open as four large boards were wheeled into the room. She gazed into the photos and recognised an artist at work, but this one possessed a fearful and malevolent talent which burnt into her retinas. 'And it had been such a glorious holiday,' she said as she stared at the images.

And the victims peered back at her.

An eternity of silence oppressed her. Staring into dead faces was nothing new to Astrid. She'd gazed into cold flesh before, yet these photographs made her uneasy. The fathomless depths of their suffering poured out of each digital pixel.

The victims were barely recognisable from the damage the strangulation had caused: eyeballs extended, filled with blood as if the pressure around the throat had forced them to search for oxygen; the skin stretched and possessed of a dreadful rainbow of unhealthy colours. Vivid purple and red bruising started on the neck, and then spread to cover the rest of the face.

We might be dead, they said to her, *but a worse fate awaits you.*

Astrid wasn't sure what she felt, but it was unpleasant. As the others in the room muttered behind her, a hideous thought planted its claws into her head: what if this was Olivia she was staring at? What would she feel then?

One by one, the photographs on the boards transformed into her niece, Olivia's delicate features devoid of the innocence and vivacity she'd witnessed in the park: there was only pain and death now. It was a fiction she saw, but it didn't make it any less raw, any less of a nightmare. The images were punches in her gut, hitting hard and fast, so they stole the air from her lungs. As she struggled for breath, they landed again, resurrecting long-buried memories of her childhood, of her family, of her father. As the images returned to normal, all Astrid thought about was Olivia in the arms of her grandfather. She wanted to vomit as she turned to her accusers, a newfound sense of urgency searing into her brain.

'Agent Lee, will you inform Snow what we've gathered so far?' Davis asked her underling. Lee's eyes sparkled as she played with the crucifix in one hand and recited from memory.

'Four employees of the Agency killed in the same manner; the bodies disposed of the same way in four different European cities around the same time as Snow visited them. GPS tracking on the murdered agents phones shows they stayed at the same places Snow did. All the agents had worked with Snow, and all were involved in serious incidents with her.'

Davis smiled at her. 'What do you say to that, Snow?'

The invisible fingers inside her guts squeezed hard enough for her to double up, but she fought the temptation.

'You can't tie any of this to me.'

'What did you do during your three days in Prague?' Agent Lincoln prodded at his screen again. Astrid gave them her best bored expression, pursed her lips and glanced at the ceiling.

'I was the perfect tourist.'

It seemed a lifetime ago, even though it was only two weeks. Astrid loved the place, all of its long and winding narrow streets with surprises everywhere she went.

'You never met with Agent Dark while you were in Prague?' Lee was polite while Lincoln glared at Astrid.

'I haven't seen or spoken to Michelle in three years.'

'You recommended Agent Dark be removed from active

duty because of the mistake she made during your last assignment?' Ice dripped from Davis's voice.

'She was a danger to everybody, including herself. Director Cross saw that and did the right thing.'

Lincoln changed the page on his screen and pulled up Agent Dark's personnel file.

'She was placed in a basement office somewhere in northern Scotland, typing out transcripts from serial killers and child murderers. Five days a week, forty-six weeks of the year for five straight years.'

'Sounds like she found her calling,' Astrid said with no pleasure.

'Being an agent was the only thing Michelle desired. Not only did you take that from her, but she also ended up in a living hell.'

Anger bubbled inside Agent Lincoln's voice: this was personal for him.

'What was Michelle to you, Lincoln?'

He didn't bother with her question and repeated the one Lee asked earlier.

'Are you sure you never met with Agent Dark while you were in Prague?'

'No,' Astrid replied.

'Are you sure?'

'One hundred per cent.'

'You never met her in the city and went to her hotel?'

He was the proverbial dog with a bone, gnawing at her words until she faltered, and he'd bury her somewhere she'd never be found.

'No.'

'Then how do you explain this?'

Lincoln pushed the digital screen towards Astrid, who

stared at an image of an empty glass sitting on a stand in a cheap-looking hotel room.

'It's a glass; even you could work that out.'

She gazed straight into Lincoln's lifeless eyes. He paused before replying, waiting to deliver the *coup de grace*.

'It's a glass with your fingerprints on it; a glass with your DNA inside it. Found in Agent Dark's hotel room. Even though you claim not to have seen her while you were in Prague.' If he could have folded the digital screen in half and written CASE CLOSED on top of it, he would have.

'I had breakfast at the same joint every morning. Somebody took it and planted it in the room.' Someone had framed her, and she didn't know why. The three opposite didn't appear to care, getting up to leave. 'Can I call my lawyer?'

Finally, there was a crack in the director's face, the sharp corners of her mouth discovering the strength to push upwards into a grin resembling a seaside clown.

'You've forgotten where you are, Snow. This is the Agency, remember? I'll leave you with Agent Lee to complete the custodial process.'

Director Davis didn't give Astrid another thought or look, heading for the exit while the others gathered their information. Agent Lincoln's shrewd gaze fixed upon her, a staccato cough interrupting his grin as he followed his leader. Agent Lee stared at the table and avoided Astrid's gaze.

'They left me with the rookie?' Astrid said after a minute's silence.

'I'm no rookie.' Her eyes switched from curious to indignant in an instant, her cheeks turning pink.

'How long have you been an agent?' Astrid forced her

mind to work against the lassitude, searching for any information to help her escape from her impending fate.

'Six months.'

'That makes you a rookie.'

Lee put her hands on the tablet and gripped it, summoning some steel into her voice as she spoke. 'I did five years in the military before coming here. I've seen things you wouldn't believe.'

Something flashed beneath the surface of her professional expression, something hidden and secret, which Astrid found intriguing. She tried to identify what it was, but it vanished as soon as it appeared.

'See, more rookie mistakes. You've given me information about you I didn't have.'

'It won't help you with your situation.'

'You don't know that. Everything you give away, no matter how small, can be used against you. What you've told me, I'll add it to all the other observations I've made since you entered this room.'

Astrid's lethargy vanished as soon as her brain started working overtime. They'd decided on her guilt. They'd isolate her for a while, seeking a confession, before transporting her to a secure unit somewhere else. It meant she still had time to devise an escape from the building.

'What observations have you made?'

'You joined the Agency from the military. It was obvious before you blurted it out; from the way you carry yourself. Rigid devotion to commands drives you forward.' Astrid's eyes were a mischievous twinkle, her voice a subtle hint of teasing. Agent Lee didn't respond, so Astrid continued. 'You worked as an investigator at the end of your time in the military, the last twelve months at least. You joined when you were eighteen, left at twenty-three. I'd guess your age now to be twenty-five or six, let's say twenty-five. You've been with the Agency for six months, so you had at least eighteen months between leaving the military to here. What were you doing?' Astrid didn't wait for her to respond.

'You did something simple, something menial where you wouldn't have to take orders, needing a break from such devotion. You needed time to reassess your life. I'd guess you were in the army, and something happened which forced you to leave a career you loved. Then, after eighteen months of recovery, you got bored and applied to the Agency, who snapped up someone with all your talents in a heartbeat.'

She expected Agent Lee to blow a gasket. Instead, she was a blank wall, as if she'd transformed into a younger, more human version of Director Davis. Then she composed herself.

'I've read all your case files, seen all the videos and spoken to most of your colleagues. You're an inspiration to a lot of us here.' It wasn't what Astrid expected to hear.

'Us?'

'You inspire others in the Agency. We admire you. Nobody cried when they found Andrews's body.'

Astrid scrutinised her. Lee had volunteered a lot of information, something agents were trained not to do, complimenting Astrid when she knew it would be on the cameras. The contradictions intrigued her.

Was it because she's such a rookie, or was it all planned to drip-feed enough details to gain my confidence? Was the crucifix an added brief touch of backstory and character detail?

'You admire me?' It was a novel experience for Astrid.

'It's true. And I'm not the only one.'

'Let's stick with you for now.' Astrid warmed to her

task. Lee should have taken her from the room to her incarceration, but she'd delayed it. And there was no sign of security coming to drag her away. She could fight back, but it would only delay the inevitable; Davis had judged and sentenced her already. The only escape for Astrid was if she could think her way out of this predicament. 'How deep are your religious beliefs?' Astrid had plenty of experience with fundamentalists.

'What do you mean?' The younger woman's hands crawled towards her neck, before dropping to her sides again.

'Who comes first, God or the Agency?'

'Why should they be exclusive?'

Smart, to dodge the question with another one: do you care this is being recorded?

'You've read my files, so you know about the things I've done, the people I've killed. How does that sit with your religious beliefs?'

'There are plenty of passages in the Bible which speak about smiting your enemies.' Astrid wouldn't have guessed she was dealing with a fundamentalist at the start of the night, but it was becoming apparent the two women existed at moral opposites. 'You worked for the Agency, and the Agency exists for the good of the nation.'

Astrid burst out laughing, a loud untamed sound rising from the bottom of her belly and erupting from her throat like Vesuvius on fire.

'What's your first name?'

Agent Lee hesitated, glancing up at the hidden cameras.

Is that for my benefit or theirs?

'Laurel.'

Astrid laughed again. 'Your parents named you Laurel

Lee? They must have been hippies. Don't your religious beliefs contradict your work for the Agency?'

'I make no judgements on how others live their lives, as long as nobody gets hurt. If an innocent person is injured, then the perpetrator deserves all the justice they get.' Absolute conviction and moral certainty emanated from her words. She grew in confidence with each passing second.

'Then you're living in a world of personal contradictions which will eventually force your mind into places it doesn't want to go.'

'What do you mean?'

'You work for an organisation which hurts people by design. You say you admire me, yet you know I've killed for this job. You say you admire me, yet here I sit accused of four murders. How do you balance those things? How do you deal with the dichotomy of your convictions opposing your daily duties?'

'Life is full of contradictions, Snow. All we do is handle them and their consequences to the best of our abilities.'

Astrid placed her hands together and grinned at Agent Lee.

'You're wasted working for the Agency; you should get out while you can.' Astrid finished the last of the water, her mind occupying two unique places. One focused on Lee, the other more critical part contemplated how she'd deal with her immediate future. 'What's next for us?'

Agent Lee stood, clasped the digital computer under her arm, and spoke with zero emotion. 'It's time for your isolation.'

I'D LIVED in isolation for most of my life. Not the isolation born of solitary pursuits, but of being invisible when surrounded by others. I hated being invisible, being ignored. I didn't even have enough imagination to have imaginary friends. Now it was a blessing in disguise, and I love my masks.

It was different for her, always the brightest star in every firmament. When she walked into the room, all eyes were pulled from their orbit and circled her. I pretended not to notice or care, but I did; I always did. She illuminated the greatest darkness while I was the smallest pinpoint hidden away in the vast distance of space, at the furthest edge of existence. How could I not be jealous?

And I hated being jealous. In those moments, when I was covetous and resentful, I transformed into my father. Part of me had always wanted to feel sorry for him, for what he became; for if my childhood made me what I am, then surely his upbringing did the same to him. Perhaps it was the imprint which forged his personality and stamped behaviour into him that he could never break away from.

My freedom instilled in me a determination to pursue a campaign of unbridled ferocity, to seek pleasure wherever it lay. No matter the negative consequences on others. This was the true realisation of my existence: to find fulfilment regardless of cause and effect.

7 GIRL TALK

Ten years working for the Agency had prepared Astrid for all eventualities, including escape from the building where they'd trained her. She'd welcomed their interest in her, what they offered, and the opportunity they presented to step away from her criminal career, but she'd never trusted them. Her suspicion of authority possessed every part of her, originating from her father's thick knuckles and emanating from the fibres of the blue uniform he loved to wear. She searched her mind, inside her map room, and discovered what she needed, knowing where Laurel was taking her.

Agent Lee strode towards the door. Astrid had a choice between standing her ground until reinforcements arrived to overpower her or following. Her chances of escape lessened the longer she waited.

'I hope you have a premium room for me.'

There was no need to panic yet. Agency policy for people like her, for the prisoner she was, followed a strict procedure she knew by heart. There would be a chink of light somewhere, an opportunity to escape, and she just had to be ready for it. Now it was imperative to stay focused.

'I need your mobile,' Laurel said.

She was the same height as Astrid, with a similar physical build. Apart from that, she was younger, a lot paler and, now, more nervous, which Astrid found curious since she wasn't the one about to be locked up.

Astrid handed her the phone. Laurel strode from the room, and she followed like a good prisoner. The ceiling lights illuminated the windowless space, flickering at strobe-like intervals to give it a hazy feel, reminding her of a desperate nightclub she'd visited recently. All that was missing was the throbbing head music, weak alcohol and aroma of cheap perfume.

'Are you going to cuff me?'

Astrid held her hands out in front of her, arms outstretched in mock supplication. Laurel glanced across the room at the agents working at their desks and the others looking busy.

'I don't think you're a danger to anyone here.'

'Even with my reputation?' She scrutinised the room and her former colleagues. You didn't make friends at the Agency, but she was hard-pressed to think of anyone here who would go to such lengths to hurt her. 'I'm no danger even though you believe I've murdered four people?'

'I don't believe you killed any of them.'

They took a right along the corridor, and Laurel swiped her security key at the door to enter the lift. She hit the button for the bottom floor. Astrid slumped against the cold metal, staring at the silver walls as the container descended.

'So why am I here?'

'Not my decision, but you know more than you're letting on.'

'That's ironic because I get the same feeling about you, Agent Lee.'

'I've killed no one.' Lee's face simmered with resentment.

Astrid inched closer to Laurel, pushing her legs as near to her as possible. She moved close to her face, wondering if she could get the crucifix away from her. Any bit of metal or plastic she acquired would be useful for an escape. She dismissed the idea as stupidity.

Lee was unmoving. 'We all have secrets, Snow.'

There were small red spots on the lift behind Laurel's head, dotted around as if flicked out in one swift movement. Astrid swallowed the air to gather as much of Laurel's delicate fragrance as possible. Ostentatious trappings of personal grooming were frowned upon inside the Agency, but she tasted the faint hint of the orange blossom in Laurel's hair.

'Do you recognise what connects the people in this building, Agent Lee?'

She thought Laurel was ignoring her question until she replied.

'No. What connects them?'

Astrid placed one hand above Laurel's shoulder, her fingers pressed into the metal.

'They're impervious to the lessons of experience. Mistakes are repeated constantly, like drunks returning to their favourite bar even though they understand it'll eventually kill them. If you've read my files, you'll know of the many mistakes this organisation has made over the years: blunders and errors left unaddressed; faults which are never made public. The Agency is a law unto itself, and its operatives are allowed to work unchecked with no accountability.'

'That's everybody apart from you?'

Astrid found the sarcasm enchanting. 'Well, you said you admired me for my work.' She moved to the rear of the lift.

'And it's not just me. There are a few others.'

Astrid thought of George again.

He wouldn't have let this happen.

'What's your fake job?' Astrid asked.

Each agent had a false identity created for them by the Agency. It included every scrap of personal information you could dream of, from a place of birth, parentage, and upbringing, to the smallest of details such as taste in music, first kiss and fantasy holiday. If you were detained in a foreign place, accidentally caught doing something you shouldn't in your own country, or found dead anywhere you shouldn't be, then nothing would come back to the Agency.

'I work in financial services.'

I should've guessed.

'You have a pet, a black Labrador,' Astrid said.

'What gave it away?'

'There are dog hairs under your fingernails.'

'Your eyesight is that good?'

'Everything about me is that good.'

'They might have come from a dog I'd stroked on the street.'

'You picked them up coming here? No, you drove to work. Perhaps they're from yesterday. I doubt it. Your skin is perfect, and you smell like fresh orange petals. Your hygiene is too good to have stray dog hairs under your nails for too long. Those are from before you left your home today.'

'Impressive,' Laurel said.

'So, you'll let me stew here for a while?'

The drama upstairs was the warm-up, letting the POI

know what the Agency had on them, hoping they'd break straight away and confess to everything. Suspects rarely did, so the next step was to confine them in a cramped cell for an indiscriminate amount of days, festering inside a compartment which only contained a bed, a toilet and a table; not even a chair to sit on.

The lift hit the ground with a thump.

'I don't know what will happen to you now.'

There was sadness in Lee's voice which dropped little melting ice cubes around Astrid's heart. Laurel exited first, walking without waiting for her to follow. To return to the top floor and out, Astrid needed Laurel's Agency card, to get past everyone on that floor, and then through the central security in the building's lobby. She calculated the odds, and they weren't good. She followed Laurel down the corridor. Inside her head, a tiny version of herself was setting fire to a lot of outdated maps.

'Why do you think they left you with me, Laurel? You're a rookie, a devoted fundamentalist, babysitting a sinner like me, a dangerous killer.'

She stopped halfway down, opened the thick metal door with her security card, and waited for Astrid to enter. Astrid walked up and peered inside. Her last chance of escape would be gone once the door closed behind her; until they came for her again.

'Because once you finished your Vacation, I asked for this assignment.'

'I didn't end my Vacation. I had no intention of returning, but I was asked, or tricked.'

Laurel stood in the doorway, obscuring Astrid's new residence.

'No intention of returning? Everyone comes back.

There's no leaving the Agency; we all know that. You had no choice but to return.'

There was something only Astrid and one other person knew.

'Director Cross signed off on it. No higher authority than that.' That was when Cross was the director. 'What happened to him?'

Laurel Lee's eyes were half-closed when she spoke.

'I'm unsure. Director Davis was in charge when I arrived at the Agency.'

'You must have heard rumours or whispers?'

Laurel moved to the side and gestured for Astrid to go inside as she answered the question without answering it.

'I'll save those details for another time, after you've settled here.'

Astrid frowned: nobody ever settled into an isolation cell. She stepped into the room and stared at the table, looking at the half dozen colourful pens laid on top of it. Laurel moved next to her, as close as they'd been all this time, a slight gap between them. Astrid picked up a pen.

'This is a nice touch.'

'These were your idea,' Laurel said.

'The whole point of the isolation cells is to make the occupants focus on why they're there: to simmer in their solitary confinement of mind and body. They're given nothing to stimulate the brain, a form of sensory deprivation to force an unbarring of the soul.'

Lee smiled at her. 'It doesn't sound like too much of a hardship.'

'One day, I checked on a visitor we'd had for three weeks, a period in which he had no contact with another human being. I found him lying face down on the bed, sobbing into the pillow. He'd used his blood to write on the walls, telling us everything we wanted. He scratched into his arms to find the ink he needed for his story. He couldn't just tell us; he had to bleed and suffer for his redemption, which is when I suggested the Isolation Protocol to Director Cross. Leave our visitors in seclusion for a long time, and then drop the pens in the room for them. Sure, some of them doodle or scribble nonsense, a lot scrawl obscenities, but after six to eight weeks of loneliness, enough of them give the Agency what it wants.' She'd stopped using the word us when referring to the Agency.

'That's just one of your many achievements.'

'But it looks like they don't want to wait around for me to crack.' Astrid rolled the pen between her fingers. 'You've read my files, so I'll assume you've seen my psych profile. You're aware of my ADHD, of my hyperactivity, about my lack of sleep. There's no need to isolate me for weeks because my brain will start the process as soon as you leave. Considering how easily I get bored, how long before I begin on the wall?'

Laurel didn't answer, leaving in silence. Astrid sat on the bed, stared at the blank walls, and pondered her question.

Will I go mad before I get a chance to escape?

WHAT IS MADNESS? My life was serene and wonderful until she came along. At first, I thought it was a good thing, to share my existence with another, with someone like me, but then it changed to one of an unbearable lightness of being. Was it her smile that drove my sadness, her strength that created my weakness and her popularity which made me feel so alone? With her around, there wasn't enough love for me.

It all started with her, which meant it could only end with her.

The falling Snow.

8   SHADOW OF THE REAPER

Astrid attempted to condense the day's events into a semblance of sanity, but all she came up with was the sight of her niece as she walked into that playground. Olivia's fate connected to hers. She hadn't gone to the park just to gaze upon her niece for the first time, but to ensure Olivia's safety; safe from her grandfather. She pressed her fingers against the wall, hoping they would stretch into her brain.

'*You can trust Courtney to keep her daughter safe,*' a whisper said to Astrid during her sleepless nights before going to the park. But it lied, for how could Olivia's mother protect her daughter from him when she'd failed to protect her younger sister?

Astrid picked up the yellow pen to sketch Olivia's face on the wall, to have something to hold on to beyond her memories. She wasn't worried about revealing anything too personal about her life. The Agency knew of Astrid's niece because they were the ones who'd dropped the bombshell about Courtney.

'Your sister is pregnant.'

Astrid had spat her drink over the floor when Director Cross told her. She'd always assumed Courtney was barren. The only emotions Astrid saw from her sister were negativity and hatred, so how she'd snared a father for a child baffled her.

'Are you spying on my relatives?'

She'd said it in jest to distract herself from the feelings she couldn't quite understand. Why should she care about her sister's baby?

'We keep eyes and ears on all our agents' families; you know that.'

George spoke with one of those warm smiles, which meant Astrid should consider her new relatives' imminent arrival. She'd done her best to ignore the news for as long as possible before doubts poked at her skull. Five years she'd waited, filling her time with Agency assignments and fleeting romances; she never checked on her sister's life and refused any opportunity to discover anything about her niece. It was two years after the birth when she finally saw Olivia's name, and that was by accident when she found a report written by George. Or perhaps it wasn't an accident, and that email came to her account deliberately. To her surprise, she'd grown closer to Director Cross the longer she worked for the Agency, and she was aware of his concern about how she'd isolated herself from the others

Once Olivia's name was imprinted onto her brain, her restlessness drove her to discover more about her niece, searching out photos online, finding the name of her school and friends, and tracking down information about the nanny. Once Astrid started the whole process, she understood it wouldn't be long before she had to see the kid in person, and it couldn't be with Courtney around. One of them would likely kill the other, and she wasn't sure who would get the first blow in.

So, twenty-four hours before leaving the country forever, Astrid had made a choice; but it wasn't only about seeing her niece. She'd been in the park to question the nanny about Astrid's father's involvement in Olivia's life, unsure how she'd respond if she learnt he'd returned. She'd have to speak to Courtney at least, a continuation of their last conversation years ago.

Why did you let me suffer? Why didn't you help me?

Astrid had asked those questions before, calmly speaking to Courtney when they were both teenagers. Her sister's violent response, Astrid's cracked cheekbone and dislocated socket healed a long time ago, but the pain was always there, and prevented her from saying what she wanted.

Why did you lie about me? Why did you encourage him?

And:

Why do you hate me so much, Courtney?

Those words, those feelings were locked away with all the other terrible memories in the shadows inside her head. She knew the only way to get rid of them was to face them. Seeing Olivia would lead to facing her sister; Astrid realised that before she set foot in the park. So she constructed her plans, unfurled a road map inside her head which led to Courtney. The plans of escape from the Agency neared completion; all she had to do was finish the others concerning Olivia and Courtney.

But then everything changed in that playground.

She'd pushed those plans to one side once the racist and his thugs appeared. Astrid had no choice but to react the way she did, but her actions that night distracted her, fooled her into thinking she was returning to the Agency because George needed her. Olivia could wait one more night, and the reunion with Courtney was something she was glad to delay. The plans still lay inside her head: speak to her sister and ensure Olivia's safety. Astrid only had to escape from her current predicament, which meant figuring out who'd framed her.

Astrid picked up the purple pen and moved to the wall near the sink, searching into her memories, considering who hated her so much. She drew the letter A on the concrete and stepped back from it, staring at the thin lines; it represented the Agency. The obvious choice would be somebody she'd worked with: an agent would have the resources and the motive if they wanted her out of the way, the irony being they were unaware she was on the verge of leaving.

But which agents? It must be more than one for something this complex and stretching over so many cities and countries in Europe. Who knew she intended to travel abroad? Only George and she trusted him with her life. Perhaps he'd let something slip in this building, an innocuous comment, a careless mistake. It wouldn't have been too hard then to find her holiday itinerary; she'd booked everything online and in her real name. But why murder those people? Sure, she'd fallen out with all of them, but there must be specific reasons to target those four. She placed that problem in one corner of her mind and considered the killer's identity.

Beside the A, she wrote R for Ramon Sheen, the man who'd rescued her from a life on the street and integrated her into his criminal fraternity. She'd dumped him and left the gang, and he'd never forgiven her for both things. He claimed still to love her: Valentine's cards arrived every year, even though she kept her address a secret. It was over ten years since Astrid had seen him, but his family lived and died for the vendetta, so he would never forget. Perhaps his loss had festered for all this time until he couldn't hold it in any longer. He was smart enough for a complex operation like this, and he possessed the resources to stretch across the continent. Would a broken heart transform into revenge so horrible and devious, become so twisted he'd plot and plan for so many years?

And then there was Lawrence Snow. If anybody hated Astrid enough to frame her for multiple murders, it would be her father. She wrote the letter L next to the other two. She tried not to think of him, but it was as Lawrence and not her father when she did. He had the connections, motivation and determination to pin these murders on her.

Why wait all this time? What she'd done, exposing his crimes against her to the world, ruined his career. Courtney and their mother stood by him, which was no surprise to Astrid, but his life with the police was destroyed. But some believed his protestations of innocence or just didn't care about what he'd done to his younger daughter. Yes, he'd lost his high-profile job, and it damaged his reputation, but some continued to help him. Maybe it had taken him all this time to gather his resources to frame her; plus, she'd been well hidden and protected inside the Agency.

The question of time also related to Ramon. It would have been a lengthy period to wait for either of them to come after her. Astrid dwelt on the problem for a minute before pushing it to one side. She hadn't eaten for most of the day, but her body was past hunger. She needed to turn her brain off, and there were only two ways which worked for her: her favoured choice was sex, but she wasn't getting that here. She might fantasise about Agent Laurel Lee all she wanted, but it wouldn't switch off the freight train of information screeching through her mind.

So she had to try something else. First, she stood and placed her hands on the wall next to where she'd written the letters. Astrid flexed her fingers against the concrete, before pulling them away and squeezing her nails into her palms. She stopped before breaking the skin. Then she turned towards the bed, stretched one leg on to it and bent her knee half a dozen times, repeating it with the other leg. When she felt warmed up, she jogged on the spot until the sweat trickled down the back of her neck. Then she twisted her body to each side, using the motion to shake her thoughts until they came together. When she'd had enough physical exercise, she lay on the bed.

Astrid stared at the empty walls and scanned for the hidden cameras in the room. She tilted her head to the side so she couldn't see the letters; gazing at them would have meant she'd have focused on who had framed her all night: that process was for tomorrow. Her gaze melted into the empty wall, her focus meditating on a single precise open spot; all the thoughts of the day, of the Agency, the murders, her family, and eventually, Olivia, disappeared into that emptiness. Then she retrieved an instrumental soundtrack from her inner jukebox, a collection of Eno tunes, and allowed them to wash over the events of the day. She lay on the uncomfortable bed, letting her body succumb to sleep. Her dreams were fitful and strange, drifting in and out of the ordinary and bizarre like waves caressing the sand before rushing away.

As she slept, one image repeatedly returned: a body

floating face down in the water. She wanted to reach in and turn it over, to see their face. But she was too afraid. Too afraid it might be her face, not dead but alive, and the realisation she'd submerged her emotions all these years for nothing.

And afraid it might be Olivia in the river.

9 RIDERS ON THE STORM

Sometime later, she woke and gazed at the walls. While she'd rested, somebody had left water and food in the cell. Two tired-looking sandwiches stared at her from the floor. Astrid picked one and bit into it with relish. Pale ham and plastic cheese fell down her throat, desperate to silence the grumbling at the bottom of her gut. It tasted terrible, grit and cardboard masquerading as nourishment, but was a banquet to her withered insides. She drank half the water in a gulp to remove the flavour. Then she turned her attention to the wall, glancing at the purple letter A.

Astrid took the red pen and started doodling, sketching a face half Picasso and half Dali, in style, not in homage. She'd always wanted to be an artist after a teacher introduced her to Hieronymus Bosch, but her parents frowned upon the idea, forcing her to concentrate on maths and science. She became the geek everybody ridiculed; until she smacked the biggest bully to the ground, pushing his thick nose into the dirt and rubble. None of the kids bothered her after that. Some of them whispered about her behind her back, mentioning how special she was, but meaning it as an insult. She wasn't the only kid in the school with ADHD, but she was the only one not taking medication for the condition. Her father didn't believe in using pharmaceuticals for solving health issues, and it was the one thing she agreed with him on.

She probed her memories and sketched the faces of the murdered agents on the wall: Delaney in red because Astrid broke her heart; purple for Dark because she'd made a mistake; Andrews in black for a rapist and sexual predator; and finally, Chill in yellow because he was a traitor. The Agency wouldn't return to her for weeks, but the cameras watched her, and she wanted to give them something to dwell on. And it helped to stay focused.

More nourishment came later, pushed through the vent: a stretch of grey plastic pretending to be meat, plus some tired green mush which might have been vegetables in a previous life. Another jug of water arrived with it, the drink reminding her of the rivers and the bodies. The murderer knew about her trip to Europe, knew which cities to visit, which meant they might have hacked into her computer. That thought consumed her sleep that night.

The second day, she returned to who'd framed her. Astrid focused on her family first. Her mother and sister hated Astrid, but they weren't capable or desperate enough to devise something so complicated, which left only him. Lawrence was in his seventies. Would he have the strength to strangle four people? He would; his hate would provide him with all the fuel he needed. Part of her hoped it was him, but she thought it unlikely.

Ramon and his gang were a more obvious choice. She'd ended up in prison because of them, failed to steal what they wanted, but she couldn't see this being their work. It was more than a decade ago, and none of them were the sharpest tools in the box.

No, it had to be somebody she'd worked with at the Agency, so she focused on that. Astrid spent the rest of the day staring at the letter A, trawling through memories of every assignment she'd undertaken for the Agency.

On the third day, she wrote her favourite song lyrics on the walls. To make it enjoyable, she did each artist in a different language. The Smiths in English; Bowie in German; Joy Division in Danish; PJ Harvey in French; the Sex Pistols in Spanish; Nina Simone in Urdu; and, to keep herself amused, the Stooges in a bastardised version of American English.

By the end of that night, Astrid was surprised with how creative she'd been; and how she'd staved off the boredom so far. She fell asleep, wondering what she'd do next to keep her mind active, but she didn't have to worry too much as they came to her the next day.

———

LATE IN THE AFTERNOON, when the mush masquerading as food arrived, the door opened and in walked Agent Lee. Astrid continued to lie on the bed and stare at the ceiling.

'Only four days; you must miss me.'

She wanted some fresh clothes, but didn't bother making a futile request.

'I have important news for you.' Ice seeped from Laurel's voice, and it disappointed Astrid.

'I'm all ears.'

'There's another body, this time in the Manchester canal.'

Astrid sat up with her mind full of a thousand possibilities.

'So, that proves I'm innocent, right?' She hated herself for sounding so desperate.

'I wish it were true. But the pathologist puts the time of death to about six weeks ago.'

Astrid sighed. 'When I was there before my flight to Berlin?'

'That's what they say.'

Astrid slumped back onto the bed and stared at the ceiling again. 'It's another agent?'

'I'm afraid so.'

'Who is it?' Astrid couldn't be bothered to guess.

'Agent Joe Storm. Do you remember him?'

She'd never forgotten Joe since he saved her from a life of crime. She lifted, confident she'd found something to dispute their accusations.

'Joe rescued me from prison; why would I want to kill him?'

'The theory is you resented him for bringing you into the Agency, and this was payback.'

'After ten years? Are they crazy?'

Her patience was worn as thin as her nerves as she picked up a group of the pens and smashed them against the wall. Small shreds of plastic splattered over the table like tiny ink-stained children birthed from the hand of destruction.

'I'm sorry, Astrid; I thought you should know. The media have also connected the five murders and have given the killer a name: the Reaper.'

Laurel closed the door and left as Astrid stared at the blank parts of the wall and remembered Joe Storm. She picked up the black pen, searched through her memories until she found the one she wanted. In it, she was confined, like now, but in a different environment. Whereas her current one was sparse and clinical, the one from her youth was the hustle and bustle of a detention centre. Staff wandered around, ever vigilant to visitors passing things to inmates they shouldn't, while most of the prisoners were furtive and agitated. Astrid was a picture of serenity, staring at the unknown man who'd come to see her: his long aquiline face, sculpted cheekbones, neatly brushed short inky hair and narrow eyes which gave nothing away. He made her an offer that day which she couldn't refuse.

She kept the image of him in her mind and drew it on the wall. When she'd finished, Astrid sat on the bed, pushed her shoulders against the concrete and gazed at her work, pleased with what she'd created. After staring at it for five minutes, she returned to it, using a different coloured pen for each letter, and in her best cursive handwriting wrote one word: Reaper.

———

BY THE END of the week, she was surprised at how refreshed she felt, both mentally and physically. The cell was small and sparse, but it gave Astrid room to continue her exercise routine: sit-ups, press-ups, running on the spot. It made her think of Joe Storm again and her early days at the Agency when they'd concentrated on getting her fit.

The work she'd done on the wall recharged her mental batteries. It surprised Astrid in the discovery of talents she'd long thought lost. She switched from focusing on who'd framed her to the method: why strangulation and why dump the bodies in the rivers? The last part might be a forensic countermeasure. Why did this Reaper strangle the victims when there were easier ways to kill people?

And what happened to the missing fingers?

———

I WANTED to feel the power flowing through my hands, their lives flowing into mine. Would the experience make me feel alive? I have to admit that, at the start, the deaths were a means to an end, her end, but as I went along, they took on their own objective. Murder took on its own life.

The Manchester one was the worst because Storm had a family, and that made me uncomfortable. Families always make me uneasy; I never know how to act around them and those who put the family at the zenith of achievement in their existence. Still, my plans had to begin somewhere, and a journey of a thousand steps starts with one, so they say. Joseph Storm was the start of my voyage.

It was easy to get him out of the house: a promise of secrets too scandalous to be shared anywhere else but a derelict warehouse on the outskirts of Greater Manchester. I beguiled his weary soul with the lost and clandestine treats. His reputation in recent years was a man of notorious melancholy and sombre disposition. This changed when he met someone new.

He appeared older than I expected, with thin greying hair and thick dark bags under tired eyes. I guess that's what a new wife and family will do to you.

'I can't be gone too long,' he said to me. 'It's my youngest daughter, Ella, she has football practice tonight, and I said I'd watch her play.'

An attentive father; a loving father. What a rare beast

he was, and there I stood, ready to take him away from that child. In the long run, I'd be doing the kid a favour.

'Don't worry. You'll be back in plenty of time. Perhaps I'll come with you.'

Yes, I could watch kids enjoying themselves and marvel at what I'd missed out on in my life.

He was excited as he entered the building, more about our location than anything else. I don't think he remembered me; he just wanted to see the spot where Joy Division first practised as a group. It was nonsense, a lie I'd told him over the phone; music addicts like him were always ready to believe anything if it fuelled their fantasies.

'I can't thank you enough for finding this for me.' His eyes glazed like the heavens above. 'This is all going into a book I'm writing.'

'Think nothing of it. The whole point of life, I believe, is for every man and woman to help each other.'

I was possessed of calm and premeditated prudence as I led him to the corner of the building, stepping over animal droppings and discarded beer cans. His anticipation grew as I played the knowledgeable tour guide, his face all excitement and giddiness, so he transformed from a responsible adult worn down by the trials and tribulations of life into a fitful boy full of dreams and hopes.

'It took me a long time to realise that work isn't worth it apart from the money, and if I couldn't find something outside of it to engage my brain, I'd go mad.'

'Isn't that what your family is for?'

He pushed his hands together. 'Yes, they're great, of course, but we all need something else to fuel our reasons to live. It might be something simple as a hobby that everyone else dismisses as trivia, or going to a football match at the weekend, or visiting the cinema, or anything, really, but there has to be a spark up here,' he tapped at the side of his head,' that gets the juices flowing. Don't you think?'

I smiled at him. It felt crooked on my face, and I wondered if he thought I looked like a demented frog. That's what my father always said on those rare occasions he found me happy.

'Absolutely. Being with you in this place is what really gets my heart beating. That and how this will make others feel, knowing you'll have met your destiny inside this place.'

His smile was warmer than a faulty microwave, and his exhilaration fuelled mine. I didn't revert to a mythical earlier life, but projected forward to the future when I would ascend into the person I'd been denied all these years.

'So where is it?' he said to me.

I made him kneel by pointing to the spot where Ian Curtis had allegedly scratched his name into the wall; in reality, I'd struck the letters there earlier in the day. It was sad to see him scrambling around in the Manchester grime for the scrawled notes of a man who'd been dead for more than forty years.

When he was down there, I pushed my right knee into his back, keeping him pressed into the ground.

'What? What, are you doing?'

'Don't worry; you'll be joining your hero soon.' I kept pushing him down, watching the dirt swirl up into his face as he struggled against me. 'Think of your daughter now, take an image of her and keep it there, so it's the last thing you see as you leave this world.'

Then I slipped the bag over his head, pulling the corners inwards as he struggled to breathe. He tried to push back against me, but I had too much leverage. I stayed like that for ten minutes, long after he'd stopped thrashing, making sure the job was done. I wondered if he'd died happy because he thought he'd witnessed the writing of one of his heroes. Or if he'd thought of his daughter.

'If you'd never met her, you'd still be alive,' I said to his cold flesh. 'If you'd left her inside the jail, none of this would've happened.'

It was good to speak to him and not expect a reply. I wasn't invisible anymore. Once done, I rolled him onto his back, pushed up his hands and removed the knife from inside my jacket. I'd practised for a week on cats and puppy dogs. His blood smelt of burnt copper, the flesh starting to rot and giving off an aroma that reeked of decaying fish. I popped the fingers into a plastic box and tried not to breathe too much of the local air.

Then I waited until dark and dragged him to his car. He was a tall man but not very heavy, underweight for his height, so it wasn't too hard to get him into the boot. The drive to the most isolated part of the canal was accompanied by the second Joy Division album playing in the CD player. The moon had disappeared from the night sky, only a tiny sliver of it sticking out from behind an ebony cloud, as I let him float away from the bank, making sure he was weighed down properly.

I left the car and took a slow walk back into the city centre, concentrating on the flight to Berlin and the next part of the plan.

And the woman I'd meet at the airport.

I hadn't had a date in a long time.

10 FRANK

On the eighth day, it amazed Astrid to receive another visitor. It was far too soon for her transportation, and from the sound of the footsteps coming down the corridor, it wasn't Laurel. These feet were heavy and laboured, with a lopsided gait indicating someone at least two stone overweight.

As her unknown guest approached the door, a violent cough spurted from their lungs, showering the outside of the cell with what Astrid imagined were the contents of the Agency's poorly provided canteen. They paused and sputtered for a minute with another violent expulsion from their chest. She recognised the sounds of a lifetime of heavy smoking all too familiar from her childhood. Added to the weight, it meant whoever walked through the door would be close to a heart attack.

The security clicked and the door swung open. Astrid lay on the bed, her bare feet touching the aged metal at the bottom. The room had become uncomfortably warm in the middle of the night, so she'd kicked the skimpy sheet onto the floor. Astrid was naked and peered at the emptiness of the ceiling. For two days, she'd contemplated how to reach the top of the cell and sketch something there. The pristine whiteness of the surface annoyed her.

He coughed again, his brooding presence cumbersome next to the bed, his cheap aftershave and deodorant doing a lousy job of covering his natural aroma.

'You should put some clothes on, Snow.'

The words spluttered from his mouth, sending an enormous chunk of phlegm onto the floor. Astrid was unimpressed.

'Make sure you clean that up before you leave.'

'I don't take orders from you, Snow.' He didn't bother with Agency formalities, the words falling out of his mouth like the dead scrambling from their graves, his breath reminiscent of fresh cadavers. She kept her eyes closed, imagining what to create on that ceiling. It would be her Sistine Chapel. 'Get up.'

It wasn't a shout, but he didn't hide the aggression in his voice, two words heavy with anger. She wondered if the Agency had changed its techniques and inserted something new into a system that had worked so well.

She opened her eyes, body rooted in the bed, and turned to where he stood. He wore a faded black suit with food stains down one side, his legs trembling, his body reacting against the short physical activity he'd put it through. She didn't need to look at him to know he had to be an Agency desk jockey, somebody with years of service, unhappy or resentful to be off active duty. Which meant it was somebody she knew.

Astrid rubbed her cheeks. 'Did you bring a bottle of wine with you?'

'I said, get up.'

She didn't recognise the voice shredded through nicotine-scarred lungs. Astrid slid down the bed, enjoying the power in her chest and legs, strengthened by her new exercise regime, feeling happier than she should. She wished there'd been the luxury of a full-length mirror in the room. When she was younger, Astrid's parents had taken great pleasure in reminding her how unhappy they were with their younger daughter.

Why can't you be more like Courtney? What's that muck on your face? Don't twist your body so much.

They told her she had a horrible physique, and nobody would ever like her.

No man will kiss something so ugly. Who would want you as a wife?

Astrid believed their words, for how would anyone love you if your parents couldn't? She spent years avoiding her appearance, covering up mirrors and turning away from anything with a reflection. Only when Astrid was free from home and living on the streets did she regain her self-confidence.

She got off the bed and ignored him, contemplating whether to stay naked and embarrass him, or use her apparent vulnerability for manipulation. One thing she'd learnt before joining the Agency was putting people off balance always helped her. As she considered this, the room's temperature dropped, forcing her to grab her top and trousers and get dressed.

Astrid didn't recognise him, a tall man, about six feet four, with a bulk of muscle and fat fighting for control of his torso. His complexion was terrible, covered in red blotches, which might have come from too much alcohol or eczema. His eyes sparkled with life as if transplanted from someone much younger. His hair was thick, dark and styled like Elvis before he joined the army. It was also dyed. She guessed his age as early fifties; if he sorted out the obvious imperfections, he could be attractive. Not that Astrid was averse to physical shortcomings; flaws added to the desirability. He had a fiery exclamation of wrath and disdain, which marked him for some strange and mysterious doom.

'There's no wine, then?'

'You don't recognise me, do you?' Astrid had to admit she didn't. 'I've changed a bit since we last met at Cara's birthday party.'

His voice, thick with nicotine, was irritable and bitter. And then it hit her: the party two days before they broke up. Her mind went into reverse: the birthday party in Soho; the bar where a group of them were celebrating; Astrid smiling even though it was over, but she didn't want to tell her then. Perhaps it might have been easier there; somewhere Cara might have had more self-control than on the bridge in Berlin. The tears and the begging which came later were embarrassing. At the party, Cara had introduced her to an older man, a tall, dark, handsome bloke with a physique to shame Atlas. His tone was deep, masculine and pulled at the heartstrings.

'This is my brother, Frank.'

Astrid had shaken his hand and ignored the spark between them. Now she sensed sparks coming from him once more. Only these were different; angrier, but just as dangerous.

'Hello, Frank; you're looking good.'

She grabbed a pen from the table and considered stabbing him through the eye with it.

'Did you kill her?'

He hadn't noticed his sister's portrait on the wall, that short bobbed black hair and the mahogany brown eyes that appeared alive even when drawn into emotionless stone.

Astrid took the red pen and doodled something underneath it. The hatred and loathing dripped from him in waves.

'Are you part of the investigation, Frank?'

She filled her words with saccharine and drew a bunch of roses on the wall. She'd given some to Cara on her birthday; that last birthday they'd shared, a tumultuous one of contrasting emotions.

'Director Davis gave me a special dispensation to visit you, considering what you've done.' He coughed again, even louder this time.

'What have I done exactly, Frank?'

Astrid stood back a little to get a better view of what she'd drawn, unhappy with what she saw, his foul breath hot on her neck.

'You're a murderer; you've killed people.'

She held the pen in front of her, trying to get a perspective on the canvas she was creating. 'That's old news, Frank. I've been killing people for the Agency the best part of ten years.'

She recognised what she'd missed; something needed adding to the petals. She didn't look at him and took the yellow and black pens for the next part.

'That's different; you were defending your country. What you've done now; they were innocent people.'

He'd regained a semblance of calm, but didn't hide the anger in his voice. It was the same 'it's for the Agency' defence Agent Lee had used earlier. Astrid didn't believe it, had never thought it, but many in the organisation did, including the bloated man with her. She took the black pen first and attacked the wall again.

'Don't be so naïve, Frank; the Agency kills innocents all the time. They just invent ways to excuse their actions;

excuse *our* actions.' She finished with the black and started on the yellow.

'The five people you killed were innocent. Cara was innocent. Why did you kill them?'

Astrid completed her additions and stepped back. Getting close enough to Frank, she smelt the ripples of sweat swimming down his cheeks and dripping onto the floor. She ignored him and peered at her handiwork: a bee and a wasp staring at each other across the roses. She liked the extra colour it added to the scene, and turned to him.

'I'm sorry for what happened to Cara, Frank, but I didn't kill any of them, and there are no innocents in the Agency.'

His accusations didn't upset her. There was no bitterness in her voice, just genuine sympathy for his loss. She'd never loved Cara, even though she'd foolishly told her she did many times, but she cared for her. Astrid appreciated that now.

'Are you sorry you broke her heart? Sorry you tore her to shreds and dumped her like a used rag?'

Beneath the icy light of his desolate stare, his anger rose again, fists clenched. Her mind worked at a thousand miles a second, seeing a way out.

If I goad him into attacking me, let him injure me enough so they take me outside for medical help, then anything would be possible. Perhaps I could sneak a few of these pens into my pockets for weapons.

A map unfurled inside her head, and she plotted her next manoeuvre. 'Relationships end all the time, Frank; people survive and move on instead of sitting in the corner, crying.'

She resurrected those memories of his sister at her emotional nadir: Cara sending Astrid videos of herself sitting in the dark and pleading for another chance. She'd watched the first two before deleting all the others unseen.

'You killed her years ago, Snow, not last month, and I'll watch you rot away inside a cell for the rest of your miserable life.'

He stepped towards the door without taking his eyes from her, getting ready to leave her alone again.

'I'm innocent, Frank, and everyone here knows it. I don't understand why the Agency is desperate for this, but the consequences will be on their heads. Don't be foolish enough to get involved with their destructive games.'

Her words didn't affect him. 'What happens when you run out of space, Snow? That hyperactive mind of yours will crack. All you'll have left are the memories of the terrible things you've done.'

Frank glared at her, waiting for her to crumble, waiting for her to answer. She supplied him with one, but not the one he wanted.

'Wasp or bee?' she said.

'What?' Confusion covered his puffed cheeks as he spoke.

'Do you know the difference?' Astrid wasn't looking at him anymore, fixed on what she'd drawn. He had one hand on the door, ready to leave. 'Wasps are aggressive; bees are mild-mannered unless attacked. Which one do you think I am, Frank?'

Frank Delaney stood in the doorway and ignored her question while she waited for him to leave. He lingered there, seemingly with something else on his mind. Then he reached into his jacket and removed something. She stared at him as he threw the bits of paper at her. Astrid didn't attempt to catch them, letting them hit her in the face and fall to the floor.

'Maybe they'll help your brain overload.'

He closed the door, and she listened to his feet shuffling down the corridor, hearing the wheeze in his chest and a lifetime of service on his shoulders. Only when he'd gone did she peer at what he'd left at her feet, surprised to see the images staring at her.

She bent her knees and picked up the first postcard, smiling at the image of the Beatles' statues near the Cavern Club in Liverpool. She turned it over and read the short message Cara had written for her brother.

The Fab Four for your collection.

Astrid left the other postcards on the bed, glancing at the photos of the places she and Cara had visited. Liverpool was their first operation together, searching for a suspected spy working in a music venue.

'We get to work and go to gigs simultaneously,' Cara had said to her. 'It can be our first official date together.'

Astrid ran her finger across Cara's naked back. After Newcastle, they'd spent every night together in Astrid's one-bedroom dump of a flat.

'Doesn't this count?'

Cara laughed at her. 'I don't know what you were like with your previous paramours, Ms Snow, but I expect to be wined, dined and shown a good time if you want to hang on to me.'

Astrid stared across the room at her small collection of CDs, with the Bowie next to James Brown and Kate Bush up against Nina Simone.

'You haven't told me much about you, Cara. What music do you like?'

'Well, we've been quite busy, haven't we?' She sat up in bed. 'I'm fairly eclectic in my tastes; some days, I prefer a quiet, contemplative tune in a language I don't understand, perhaps some Sigur Rós, and others it has to be hot and heavy, with Prince breathing hard into a microphone.'

'You won't be seeing Prince in Liverpool, not the real one anyway.'

Cara got her phone and flicked through the screen. 'We have to go to the Cavern so I can get some photos for my brother.'

Astrid nodded. It was still that time when she'd do anything Cara asked.

Liverpool had been great, but they never found any spies.

Frank Delaney had done her a favour with the postcards. She reached down and grabbed the others, hoping they'd ignite the memories to keep her mind occupied.

The second one was of a giant replica King Kong standing next to a town hall. Leeds. It was their first time away that wasn't work.

'I want to go to the Brudenell Social Club,' Cara said.

'I saw The Fall there,' Astrid said. 'It was packed, and the sweat dripped from the walls. Some bloke tried to grope me, so I squeezed his balls until his face turned orange.'

Cara laughed. 'He probably enjoyed it.' She sipped at her raspberry gin and tonic as they sat in the pub around the corner from Astrid's place. 'I met Mark E. Smith once in a bar.'

Astrid bit through a cheese and onion crisp. 'Did he sing to you?'

'No. He challenged me to a game of pool.'

'Did you win?'

'Of course. He was pissed out of his bonce. But he did tell some funny stories.'

They spent that night swapping war stories of famous people they'd met. Two days later, they were in Leeds for the weekend, dodging football supporters and hanging on to various Hen parties.

Cara pointed at a group of women walking down the street, carrying giant inflatable penises. 'I'm surprised they can get away with that in public.'

Astrid laughed. 'At least they found a good use for them.'

She shook the image from her head and admired the front of the next postcard, a photo of *Proserpine* by Dante Gabriel Rossetti taken inside Birmingham Museum and Art Gallery. Their shared love of art was one more thing that cemented their attraction to each other.

'Why is the middle of the country classed as England's second city?' Cara had asked as they stood in front of Tony Hancock's statue.

'Because they have the best football team,' Astrid replied.

Cara stared at her with wide-open eyes. 'You like football? That's grounds for divorce.' Her grin warmed Astrid's heart, though it was warmth which would melt into nothing over time. 'At least support a proper team like Manchester Athletic or whatever they're called instead of Birmingham.'

'Aston Villa.'

'What?'

'Aston Villa. That's who I support.'

'Never heard of them.' Cara dragged her away from the statue. 'Now you can buy me a drink.'

It surprised Astrid how quickly the memories returned. She'd had other lovers since then, but Cara was the only one she'd loved; or thought she'd loved until she realised love was beyond her.

And then she'd seen Olivia. But that was a different

kind of love. One that pulled at the heart when she least expected it: a love that couldn't be abandoned.

Or could it?

Thinking about it made her head throb, so she studied the remaining postcards.

Edinburgh, where they'd got into a fight with a group of drunken kilted Scotsmen.

'At least it's easier to kick them in the balls when they're wearing skirts,' Cara had said after leaving two of them on the floor.

Astrid laughed as she wiped the blood from her knuckles. 'You'll upset them even more, calling them skirts.'

As police sirens approached, Cara wiped away Astrid's blood and kissed her bruised fingers. Then she examined the wounded they'd left on the ground.

'I don't know about you, but I found that strangely erotic.'

They laughed together as they ran from the sirens and back to the hotel.

Cambridge. It was a working trip, protecting a Russian emigre from possible retribution, so there wasn't much time for sightseeing. Astrid read the back of the card.

Because I know you like university towns, brother.

Astrid put it with the other postcards and stared at the last one, unsurprised to see it was from Berlin.

Berlin. Where dreams go to die.

Or at least where she'd told Cara it was all over between them.

'Why?' It was all Cara said for ten minutes.

Astrid had kept her reply simple. 'It's run its course, Cara.'

Then it was, 'It's not you; it's me.'

Until Astrid ran out of patience. 'I don't love you, Cara.' And to make it worse, 'I never did.'

She left her sobbing on that German bridge, never to see her again in the flesh.

Astrid threw the postcards onto the floor of her jail.

And now I can't get those murder photos out of my head.

GETTING in and out of the buildings, moving around the different cities, without being seen was impossible. A virus of video cameras and surveillance systems infected even the smallest of towns. Luckily, I'm an expert in deception. And I've always enjoyed dressing up, so simple disguises such as hats or glasses were easy to utilise while I moved around the heart of Europe.

Manchester was cold and wet, a typical British summer. The homeless and the needy paved its streets. I hadn't been there for some time, but its stern visage was a welcome sight to my eager eyes. Before my appointment with Agent Storm, I'd been apprehensive, wandering through the city, nervous about what I was about to do; anxious that everything would go wrong. But death gave me a new life and resurrected my broken soul. The buzz of adrenaline which surged through me when I choked him didn't abate once he'd breathed his last, staying with me even when I met up with my new love.

'You look nervous,' she said to me on the plane to Berlin, believing it was because of our forthcoming illicit assignation. In reality, my body shook because I needed to take her life as soon as possible. The journey from the airport to the train station was an eternal agony for me, worrying if this newfound desire for entropy would make me reckless;

perturbed that the yearning would sabotage my long-held plans.

'It won't be long now,' she said as she grabbed my hand while the lift took us to our hotel room.

'No,' I said. 'It won't be long.'

11 ENDLESS ART

By the tenth day, Astrid had covered half the ceiling with a swirl of colours, sketches and words in many languages. The centrepiece was a giant fox with text underneath written in Mandarin. Either side of it were small drawings of faces, more like caricatures when she stared at them from the bed. Astrid was a perfectionist in everything she did, but she'd had trouble with some faces. A lot of them were from her past, and she'd struggled to remember what they looked like.

She scribbled some words in Urdu underneath a few of them before lying back and staring at the space she'd left. Including the floor, there wouldn't be enough to get through the next few days unless she eased off. But that meant slowing her brain, which was impossible. She'd contemplated a solution before the Agency presented her with one on the eleventh day.

Astrid realised Lee was outside the cell before she activated the security lock. Laurel was too silent for a rookie. A whiff of lemon and honey from her perfume, and Astrid was alert. She smiled as the door unlocked.

'You're a talented artist,' Laurel said as she entered the room. 'What does the artwork signify?'

Astrid moved from the bed. 'Who says it has to signify anything; art for art's sake and all that.'

'I studied art at college. My tutors said everything artistic represents something.'

Astrid tossed out her hooks. 'Is that why you joined the army? For a proper education?'

Laurel ignored the questions, inching closer to the centre of the room for a better look at Astrid's work.

'The fox seems familiar, as do some surrounding sketches.' Laurel's hands were on the wall, fingers moving across the artwork. Astrid laughed.

'We both know the Agency have photographed all I've done from every angle, blown it up and pored over every inch.' Laurel had left the cell door half open. Astrid moved closer to it, peering through the gap to see if guards waited for her outside. The corridor was surprisingly empty. 'How many agents are there who read Mandarin or Urdu? Just a few, I bet, but they have computers to translate what I wrote, right?'

'There are bits of your text they can't translate, the important parts which add meaning to the sentences.'

Laurel pushed up on her toes, stretching like a giraffe to get a better look at the ceiling. She seemed oblivious to Astrid peering at her like a cheque waiting to be cashed. Astrid laughed again, quieter this time as if she wanted to keep it a secret between the two of them.

'Doesn't it worry you, Laurel, that even though I'm stuck here, isolated for over ten days, I can still outwit the thousands of people the Agency uses?' Astrid wasn't bragging, only curious as when Agent Laurel Lee would have her epiphany about her employers.

'You're no ordinary woman, Snow.' Her eyes sparkled as she spoke, and Astrid wanted to take a bath inside those clear blue waters. Just the thought of it made her realise how terrible she must smell.

'Okay, I'll explain everything, but only on one condition.'

Laurel paused for a second. 'Which is?'

'Take me for a shower; I must stink like holy hell.'

They smiled together, and Astrid was curious why the woman with the crucifix hanging around her neck wasn't offended by her choice of words.

'I didn't want to mention it, but you do reek a bit.' Her professionalism disappeared into puddles of laughter.

'Thanks, but I'm sure it's much more than a bit.'

They both grinned again, Astrid noticing how easily Lee had given in to the request. That's when she realised Laurel was there to take her away. The watchers had finished with their observations. Agent Lee pointed at the large animal in the centre of the wall.

'You're very talented.'

Astrid wondered if Laurel was speaking only about the art as she gazed at her work. Inside her head, she had a gigantic map containing all the directions plotted for where her life might go from now. Most were grim and desperate, but two strands provided hope. The Agency's attempt to deprive her of stimulation had backfired. She permitted herself a delicate smirk as she replied.

'That's Reynard the Fox; from Chaucer and European folklore.' Laurel shook her head, which disappointed Astrid. 'He was a trickster in a world of anthropomorphic animals, deceiving his fellow creatures for his gain. Do you know who the sketches are?'

'Some; we ran them through facial recognition, but didn't get them all.'

'That's my fault, but not a deliberate attempt to deceive. I struggled to remember what they looked like.'

Lee switched her gaze from the wall to Astrid. 'They're all agents you've slept with?'

Astrid fell onto the bed and creased up with laughter. 'Jesus Christ, Laurel, is that how bad my reputation is?'

The convulsions decreased, and she was back under control, though her stomach and jaw ached. Astrid didn't remember the last time she'd laughed so much.

'I'm sorry, Snow, it was only a guess.'

Lee appeared crestfallen by her *faux pas*. Astrid pushed herself off the bed, stood up straight and inched closer to the other woman. She wanted to plonk both hands onto Laurel's shoulders and give her a lecture, only stopped by the thought of those who would sprint into the room and pin her to the floor if she did.

'I've slept with two of my colleagues.' Astrid peered at Laurel. 'Possibly three.'

'You don't know?' Laurel's voice trembled.

'It gets confusing sometimes, but it doesn't matter. They were all mistakes, and I learnt valuable lessons from them. Plenty of others wanted to and tried, all of whom failed.' Astrid pushed her shoulders back and put both hands on her hips. 'No, my badly drawn boys and girls are all agents I've worked with, about thirty of them.'

Laurel appeared puzzled, lowering her eyes and staring at the head sketches. 'You've only worked with thirty agents?'

'All people I've worked with and pissed off.'

'Oh.'

'You believed it would be more?'

'No. I never thought that at all.' Laurel crossed her arms and clenched her fists.

'Okay, enough flirting; take me to the shower.'

Astrid walked past her and out the cell before Lee replied. She stared at both ends of the empty corridor, picturing a smaller version of herself running down her map of possibilities as if at the centre of a board game. Where she stood now only led to jail, another cell, worse than the one she'd spent the last eleven days inside.

'I didn't flirt with you.'

Laurel closed the door behind her, and they went to the lift. Astrid said nothing until they were inside and it was moving up.

'But I flirted with you.' Laurel turned a fresh pink. Astrid could touch her in this confined space, and nobody would do anything about it, but she didn't, getting tantalisingly close enough to hear Lee's increased breathing. 'Is there room for two in this shower?'

Astrid grinned, planning on how to get out of the building as the younger woman's skin transformed into a vibrant red.

THE SECOND ONE was harder than expected. After Agent Storm and the unforeseen pleasure of choking him, I believed everything else would go smoothly, but I didn't anticipate how attached I'd get to her. We took the flight to Berlin with assumed names and fake passports and shared the hotel room for three nights like a new couple. I'd spun a story of my recent fortuitous inheritance, a long-lost aunt who'd fallen from the Eiffel Tower while attempting to take an elaborate and extravagant selfie.

'Lavish and ravish,' she'd said between raucous laughter and intoxicating champagne.

'Have you visited Berlin before?' I asked.

The mischievous glint in her eye sent a shiver through me. 'I've had good times and bad times here.' She reached over and took my hand. 'But, as the song says, life's what you make it.'

The sex was fantastic, the best I'd had for years; she had no inhibitions, open to all my suggestions. I didn't remember the last time I was so happy, my mind shifting into dangerous thoughts and wondering what it would have been like if we'd met under different circumstances. Berlin is beautiful at night, the lights shining around the Branden-burg Gate and the Reichstag, illuminating them to where they weren't mere buildings anymore, but constructs straight from the Twilight of the Gods. I expected the Valkyrie to swoop down and whisk me away. How joyous that would be to feel the lips of a Hell Maiden against mine. And I remembered the history of where we were, holding hands together as we stared at the bullet holes in the Reich-stag; feeling our hearts tighten at the memorial for those who'd died under the Nazi occupation; walking solemnly through Brandenburg and down the street of lime trees.

The joy on her face told me she was as happy as I. She talked tentatively about plans for us. And that's when I grasped why I was so pleased: I understood we had no future together beyond Berlin; knew she'd die at my hands; knew I was in complete control. The realisation was euphoric, and when she gazed into my eyes, she saw it too, knowing it was all for her, but mistaking the reason.

On the third night, I suggested a romantic interlude at a secluded spot by the river. She thought I meant sex, but I had something much more pleasurable in mind, the anticipation of it more magnificent than any orgasm.

'You've made me feel loved again,' she said as I readied for her death. 'I never thought I would, but there's something about you which lifts my heart so I can forget the past.'

She was kidding herself; none of us could ever forget our past. We might fill our heads with new experiences, cram our brains with drugs and alcohol, but those memories which forged who we are would never leave us. And that's why I was using them to recreate myself in the image I should always have been.

I slipped my hand into my pocket and touched the plastic, the greatest prophylactic ever. I told her to kneel and close her eyes, the moonlight reflecting off the water and providing me with enough illumination to slip the bag over her head. She was easier than Storm, not struggling at all as if she'd given up on life and our trip away was a brief prelude to her voyage into the next world.

'It's better for you this way,' I said as the light dissipated from her eyes. I perceived my actions not as banal evil things, but as precious moments of relief for those I blessed with my touch. They were still only cogs spinning towards my goal, but now I had a greater understanding of the gift I had; the gift I delivered.

When it was over, I slipped her body into the river, and it floated like a Viking funeral without the fire. I smelt her fragrance of lavender in my hair and on my lips as she drifted from me. Her fingers were in mine as she disappeared out of sight. It had become a ritual.

A ritual I'd never sacrifice.

12 DRESS YOU UP

They took the ride to the next floor in silence. Laurel did her best to avoid Astrid's gaze by staring straight into the scratched metal. Astrid speculated on how the marks had got there, imagining the prisoners throwing themselves at the door in desperation, clawing at the freedom they wouldn't see again.

They stepped out on level two and a hive of activity. A dozen agents sat at desks, staring at digital screens, moving between workstations while looking busy, or standing around chatting. All the men wore similar clothes: dark-coloured suits, white shirts and regulation ties. The women were just as conservative: the same blouses, half wearing trousers, half in plain skirts which ended below their knees. The Agency frowned upon anything above the knee. On her first visit to the building, not long past her eighteenth birthday, Astrid had marched through its doors wearing a sleeveless top and bright red miniskirt. The security had palpitations that day, as did most of the agents.

Astrid smiled at her former colleagues as Laurel led her to the facilities; might it be someone here who'd framed her?

'You remember where the showers are?' Laurel said.

'Unless things have changed.'

There was no escape through the back, no window to crawl through. She pushed the door open and found the area empty, with no chance of fraternisation. In her time with the Agency, she'd never used the private showers before, always preferring to get home and relax. And delouse. To wash away the smell and grime from those she dealt with. She removed her clothes, dumped them onto the floor and walked into the first cubicle.

'I'll be right outside,' Laurel shouted through the whiteness surrounding Astrid.

She pressed her head against the tiles and turned the water as hot as possible without burning her skin. It came shrieking from the shower like a tormented banshee.

There was no soap or shampoo, the Agency likely fearful she might choke or poison herself. She smiled as the water pounded her skull, amused at how little they knew her. She switched back to her current problems: how to get out of the building and find the killer. As the scorching water pummelled her neck, Astrid twisted her head to scan the room. The Agency was either generous or lax with the amount of freedom they'd given her. Or they were over-confident.

She turned the shower to the highest it would go, the pressure so strong it could peel the paint off the walls, and stepped out and into the rest of the washroom. She moved quickly, checking the other cubicles. A brush or comb, perhaps a discarded earring, any of them would help with her escape. A pair of scissors would be perfect. But the showers were spotlessly clean. She stepped away from them and towards the toilets, pushing doors open and running her fingers under the bowls and delving into the cisterns. Nothing. The escape map in her mind was shrinking by the second. Some exquisite refinement in the architecture of her brain told her not to panic. Other opportunities would be on the horizon.

'We have to go.' Laurel banged on the door as she shouted. Astrid waited two minutes before turning the water off, enjoying what might be her last minutes of freedom. As she strode from the showers, she didn't think about towels or clean clothes. She stood there naked and wet, wondering if her appearance would affect Laurel. Hoping it would for several reasons, but Lee's face was unmoving. Towels draped across her arms. 'We haven't got much time.' She held out two cream coloured towels.

'You've got plenty of time.'

Astrid shook her body like a dog crawling from a bath, her lengthy hair flying around her head, splashing Lee and getting her immaculate suit wet. She was only a few feet away from Laurel. She assumed the good religious woman would avert her gaze, but she didn't, never taking her eyes from Astrid's athletic physique and the way her skin glistened under the fluorescent light. Laurel handed her the towels, but didn't leave.

'I need something to wear, unless you want me to parade around naked?'

How wonderful that would be.

'There are fresh clothes for you outside. We have to go.'

Astrid took the small towel to dry her hair. She did a cursory brush with the cloth over her head before doing the same with the larger towel across her chest and stomach. The water cooled against her skin as she dried from the bottom of her foot to the top of her thigh, all the time keeping her eyes fixed on Laurel's unmoving face.

'Okay, let's get this started.'

She threw both towels at Lee and walked outside to grab the regulation Agency garments she expected, surprised to see a set of her own clothes waiting for her: skinny jeans, orange blouse, and matching cream coloured underwear. Laurel exited without the towels.

'I went to your house for those.'

Astrid stared at Laurel and reconsidered her initial thoughts. Earlier, she'd blushed at mild flirting; now, she didn't flinch at Astrid's nakedness: the woman was a curious enigma.

'Did you have a good nosey around?'

'No. Other agents had searched your house.'

'Of course, they had.'

'How do you even get those on?' Laurel asked as Astrid pushed her legs into the jeans.

'The tighter, the better.' Astrid buttoned her blouse. She tried the pockets of the trousers, expecting nothing, and was unsurprised when she was right. The jacket she'd been wearing when they'd brought her in, with its many zips, would be useful. 'I expect I'll be getting my jacket when I leave.' Laurel ignored her and removed a set of handcuffs from her pocket. Astrid sighed. 'I guess it's time, then.'

She held out her arms, her mind racing through the chances of escape: now, in the building, zero; when she reached her destination, zero. Her only chance, slim that it was, would be during transportation.

Laurel brushed her skin as she slipped the restraints on to Astrid, the cold metal of the cuffs sending a tiny shiver across her flesh. They walked through the main office again, turning at the lifts, then down a corridor towards the exit.

'It's time to go, Astrid.'

Astrid stared at her; Lee wouldn't be the problem. The two armed guards posed the biggest challenge. The Agency always used ex-SAS as their muscle. They would sit opposite her in the van, weapons pointed at her chest, their eyes never moving from her. Her escape might be possible if they were overconfident and didn't realise who she was. Another potential route appeared on the map in her head.

She formulated the plan as they stepped out of the room, an idea quickly consigned to the rubbish heap when six guards walked towards her. The Agency was not messing around. As the security surrounded her, she thought again about how that glass with her fingerprints on it ended up next to a dead body.

GETTING the glass was easier than I expected. The ferocious hot weather helped. They said on the news it was the hottest in southern Europe for more than a decade, so she sat outside for breakfast on both days. It was a little cafe specialising in Czech dishes, not the commercial western junk dotted around the main road: the unappetising burgers, deep-fried chicken and underground sandwiches. Not like the place I frequented, opposite her and across the street, with its American menu of limited options, zero taste and a million calories.

She spent forty minutes there each morning, no more or less, partaking of scrambled eggs, toast, local tea and the cafe's homemade lemonade; the empty lemonade glass I took and left in Agent Dark's hotel room. As soon as she paid and wandered off down to the river, I was across the street, sitting at the same table, slipping the evidence into my bag, dark shades and hat keeping my features away from the sun and anybody who might stare at me too closely.

My confidence had grown after Berlin, so I got a ticket

for the same journey to Prague she took, sitting three carriages behind her in first-class. She was in with the proles. I had no fear she would wander through the train and find me there, but the thought of it made my skin shiver with tension and excitement.

First-class wasn't worth the extra payment, all you got was more legroom. The four-hour journey allowed me time to dwell on what I'd achieved in Manchester and Berlin, and to look forward to what was to come.

I was only a few hundred feet behind her at Prague station, able to get close enough to hear her give the address of the hotel to the glum-looking taxi driver, smiling to myself when I found it was near mine. Agent Dark stayed further away, but that was for the best, limiting the chances of her stumbling into anyone she shouldn't, apart from me.

13   HEART OF GLASS

Astrid took faltering steps down the stairs to the garage. They didn't use the lift because it was too small. The only sounds were boots hitting the concrete and the cogs inside her head working through the gears. She stumbled between two slabs of Agency meat, a security protocol reserved for only the worst prisoners. Enough cold sweat dripped from her bodyguards for her to guess they'd waited around all day.

'You guys stink.' She wanted a reaction but got nothing.

How well trained are you?

When they reached the bottom, Laurel pushed the door open. Astrid searched the dark corners of her brain to find her escape map torn into a thousand pieces.

The van was just ahead, back doors wide apart and waiting for them. Two guards climbed into the vehicle, checking the insides. Laurel followed them with Astrid, then the rest of the security. Astrid sat next to Laurel, with four guards opposite, while the other two were near the door. She considered escape, but it appeared impossible. If she was lucky, she could wrestle a weapon from one of them, but there wasn't enough room to do anything beyond injuring one guard.

Kids will ruin your life.

The flash of Lawrence's voice inside her head sent electric tendrils into her stomach, so she lurched to the side before Laurel could catch her. She tried to push the memory into the abyss at the pit of her gut, but it was hopeless, an image of his face burning through the back of her eyes.

'I should've killed him when I had the chance,' she whispered into the metal stuck to her head. If she'd done that when she was fifteen, how different would her life have been?

'What?' Laurel said. The van jerked forward and pulled away. Lawrence continued to grin at her from the shadows of her mind. Astrid unglued her face from the wall and turned to Laurel.

'I said I'm innocent.'

At least of these crimes.

'I'm sorry.' Laurel spoke as the van picked up speed.

'Sorry for what?'

'The way they treated you in there.'

'Which part, being stuck in isolation for eternity or the façade you put me through?'

'All of it, and...' Laurel hesitated, watching the guards staring at them through their masks and security goggles.

'And?'

'And I think you're innocent.'

'I'd prefer an automatic rifle.'

She shot the guards a mischievous smile. Lawrence lived inside her head, whistling some awful nursery rhyme which signalled him taking his belt to her. After a time, she'd grown to prefer the belt to his fists; it seemed more impersonal. Now she had a complicated relationship with leather.

'Why would anybody do this to you?' It was the question on everybody's lips.

'Either somebody hates me, or...' a thought struck Astrid like a lightning bolt.

'Or what?'

They hit a bump, and everyone jumped a few inches in the air. She ruminated on what a perfect opportunity it would have been if there weren't so many damn guards there.

'Are you convinced by the investigation into the murders?' She continued to stare at the men opposite her. The shunt in the road indicated their reflexes were lacking for professionals. It gave her a tiny slither of hope, helped by the fact Laurel appeared to be on her side. 'Be honest.'

'It's as you mentioned. Most of the evidence is circumstantial. And I don't think Agent Lincoln is qualified to be part of it. Or me.'

'Lincoln hates me because I turned his advances down a long time ago.'

'That seems... overly sensitive.'

'I might have broken his nose.'

'Oh.'

'So, either somebody detests me with a passion, or we have an Agency-wide conspiracy, and someone wants me gone.'

Astrid's mind returned to Director George Cross and the plans they'd devised a year ago. Her friend's warm smile pushed the image of Lawrence and his vile whistling from her skull.

'Why would that be?' Laurel said.

'I've made plenty of enemies over the years, so it's difficult to pick out a name, but a few things could narrow it down.'

As they talked, a smaller version of Astrid scrambled around inside her skull, throwing maps into the air to find something to help. The Agency had two secure units close to the main building, each an hour away in opposite directions. It meant the best opportunity would be thirty minutes into the journey when they were equal distance from any backup. It was bad enough with six of them in the van, but reinforcements would be the end of her.

'What would narrow it down?' Laurel shifted in her seat.

'Whoever it is, they're ruthless, clever and with access to plenty of resources.'

'Are they working on their own?'

'Considering the logistics of what happened in Europe, I wouldn't rule it out, but it seems unlikely. Five murders with no clues, and then the worst investigation team, no offence, gathered for the case, and all when Director Cross has disappeared.' Astrid struggled to identify who hated her so profoundly.

'Is it possible your father is responsible?'

She would only have been more shocked if Lee had suggested Santa Claus as the designer of her current fate, not because she hadn't considered Lawrence as the culprit, but because Laurel had too.

'I haven't seen him in over ten years.' Astrid's voice was dry, the back of her throat craving water. 'Why and how would he do this now?'

Every one of Astrid's words was thick with scepticism. Dozens of lights illuminated the van, but it was as if darkness hovered below the roof. Her shoulders stiffened as her eyes narrowed, ready to broach a subject difficult to talk about.

'Maybe because of what happened between the two of you.' Laurel dodged around the specifics. Bitterness crept over Astrid's face.

'You think he hates his younger daughter because...'

She wouldn't make this easy for Laurel. It wasn't easy for her, so why should it be for anyone else?

'He's a callous and conscienceless brute,' Laurel said.

Astrid laughed at the words, surprised to find humour in anything connected to him.

'You're quoting me now?'

Laurel's voice wavered. 'I remember it from your file. It was the only thing you told the Agency therapists about him.'

'They didn't want to know; most of them, anyway.' A crop of disappointments grew in her memories, but she scythed them down swiftly. 'All they cared about was getting me into the best shape as quickly as possible to work for them. I was eighteen, my childhood over, and none of it mattered anymore. They told me to forget the past and concentrate on the future. So I did.'

'You can never abandon your past, Astrid.' Once again, she observed something lurking behind the younger woman's eyes. 'Your father lost his career, his reputation. He could have blamed you for that.' Laurel pushed beyond her hesitancy.

Astrid laughed louder than she wanted, a raucous noise originating from the pit of her stomach. It was a cold laugh, enough to chill the bones. None of the guards reacted.

'He did blame me for it. Twenty-five years as a copper, respect and admiration everywhere he went. And then he lost it all in an instant because of some girl and her wild accusations.'

A flame of scarlet crept in a swift diagonal across Astrid's cheeks. Her voice was shaky, nails digging into her palms. She cursed herself as more submerged emotions rose from the shadows in her mind.

'It wasn't just some girl. It was his daughter; it was you.'

'Well, thank you, agent. I'm glad I've got you around to keep me informed about my life, especially now it's all gone to shit.'

'I'm sorry.' Laurel looked like a child saddened by the death of a pet. 'What about the people you worked with before you joined the Agency, the criminal gang who left you to rot in prison?'

Memories of Ramon Sheen drifted into Astrid's head as something hit the vehicle, sending ripples through the van like a bowl of jelly. Then a large object battered the side, throwing her and Laurel into the guard opposite.

Her training kicked in, holding up her arm so it received most of the force as she fell into the synthetic fibre protecting the man. The cuffs hung loose on her wrists as instinct took over. She grabbed his jacket and threw him to her left, where he nose-dived into the guards at the door. Her attention switched to the right without a moment's hesitation. Grabbing hold of the confused man's weapon, she pushed it into his chin. He let go of it. Astrid turned the gun on to the last two guards and shook her head at them.

'Throw your guns down.'

There would only be a split second before the others behind regained their composure. Astrid didn't know what was happening outside, but she was aware this could be her only chance to escape. Before she acted, they were hit again, the vehicle spinning and rolling over. She was dizzy as her eyes scanned the van's insides while they continued rotating like a motorised guinea pig ball.

She tried to grab hold of the sides as people kept on falling around her. Laurel flapped at the bulky arms of the nearest security guard. There was a pause as they moved, before the final fall and crash which smashed a massive dent into the side of the van. Eight bodies tumbled over as if inside a drunken washing machine.

Astrid reacted before anybody else, throwing both arms over her head for protection, landing next to Laurel, whose eyes were glazed. Lee moaned as tiny bits of blood dripped from a cut above her eye. Astrid had no time for concern, using the confusion to check on the rest of the guards. Before she could react, the back doors opened.

'Follow me.'

It was a voice thick and heavy behind the mask, a male physique underneath the uniform of dark clothes. 'And bring Lee with you.'

Astrid's senses recovered before anybody else's. Grabbing hold of Laurel, she dragged the unsuspecting agent with her. She climbed over displaced guards and jumped out the van. A large black SUV waited for them, doors open, its front dented and a crack in one of the side windows.

'This could be the Reaper?' Laurel snapped awake and wiped the blood from her eyes.

'I'd rather take my chances with him than stuck in a high-security prison.'

Astrid didn't give a second thought to Laurel's safety and pushed her into the SUV. She was about to follow when a shadow loomed behind her in the reflection of the window. She moved to one side as a clenched fist missed her by inches and struck the car with a thump. Astrid swivelled her hips and brought her arm into the neck of her attacker. The guard dropped to the ground like a stone.

Before she could praise herself for her quick reactions, something hard hit her across the knees. She smashed her hip against the concrete, rolling to the side while a bloke stuck to her like glue. He'd lost his gun, but had a knife pointed at her throat. Aiming to plunge it into her, but he hesitated. His wavering was his undoing as she lifted her arms and grabbed his wrist. She pushed it back, bone snapping as the wind blew around her head. She flung him from her as he cried, lifting up and towards the van.

Astrid jumped into the car, falling into Agent Lee. It sped off before the back doors closed, and the Agency van disappeared in the distance. She peered out the window, hoping to get a sense of location, but the gloom meant they could have been anywhere on the outskirts of London.

'Who are you?' Laurel was more curious about their new friend's identity than Astrid, who focused on overpowering him if she needed to. Her safety odds had improved considerably in the last five minutes, but the danger was still present. The driver didn't answer, cutting back on the speed as they entered a part of the road with more traffic, and more cameras.

'Are you okay?' The bleeding hadn't stopped, and Laurel's face had turned into an unpleasant shade of light red where she'd struggled to keep the blood from her eyes.

'It's just a small cut; I'll be fine.' Astrid wasn't too sure, noticing the tremor in Laurel's hand as she placed it on her cheek to wipe away the blood. She peered at her, searching for stability but finding slight traces of shock in her pupils.

'We have to get somewhere safe; she might need medical attention.'

The mystery man ignored Astrid's words and kept

driving. Outside the window, the sign for the M25 heading south whizzed past them.

Laurel handed Astrid the keys to the handcuffs. 'You need these.'

Astrid smiled as she pressed her fingers into her wrists. 'If you don't tell me where we're going, I'll kick the doors out and we'll jump.'

The car hit sixty miles an hour, but she didn't care. His heavy sigh echoed in the back as she caught the smell of a recognisable aroma.

'We have to avoid the toll roads, so it'll take longer than it should; about ninety minutes. Will she be okay?'

Laurel had drifted into sleep, her chest rising and falling in a constant rhythm. Astrid removed the last of the blood with the sleeve of her previously white shirt. She knew Laurel would be okay with a bit of rest, laying her head on her lap in the back of the car. She returned her attention to the driver, his body odour and breath revealing his identity to her.

'Is this revenge for your sister, Frank?'

14 DRIVE

She stared at the back of his head while Laurel slumbered in her lap. Frank Delaney had one hand on the wheel while the other removed the mask. He sped past a police car on the motorway without a care in the world. Astrid peered into his grim reflection in the mirror and wondered if she'd have to thank or kill him.

'They'd get suspicious if I slowed down.'

'Is this a kidnapping or a rescue?'

'You'd rather be in the back of that van?'

His laugh annoyed her. She stared into the dark through the window, catching the occasional glimpse of road signs and the countryside.

'You should head to the centre of London.'

'Are you crazy?' Delaney weaved past a lumbering truck and glared at the driver.

It'll be just my luck, he'll crash after getting me out of that van.

'I need to get to my sister's house as soon as possible.'

The gloom inside her head was as oppressive as the weather battering the car. He slid the vehicle across the road and into the outside lane. If he was trying to keep them inconspicuous, he wasn't doing a good job.

'Your sister hates you. Why would you want to go there?'

Astrid observed his face in the rearview mirror, all scrunched up and wrinkled like a used potato skin.

'It doesn't matter why. You need to do it before I drag you into the back with me and we end up smashed in the middle of this road.' Her voice was calm, quiet against the howl of the wind outside.

'Don't be stupid. It's the first place they'll be waiting for you. You need to be smart now. You can't go back to your previous life until we get this sorted.'

He was right, but she didn't like it. 'I didn't kill Cara.'

'I know,' he replied. 'That's why I broke you out.'

She leant closer to him, hands ready to spring around his neck if they needed, no thought given to the fact he was driving at sixty miles an hour.

'If that's the case, why visit my cell?'

The perspiration dribbled down his head as the sweat living under his armpits escaped into the air.

'You're clever, the best the Agency has, apparently, so you tell me.'

He appeared to be enjoying himself, which she found disturbing. Attacking the van was reckless and reckless people got you killed.

'You set yourself up with a nice alibi, showing the Agency your anger, pretending to hate me. Nobody would suspect you for this after that performance.' His foresight and planning impressed her.

'I wasn't pretending. I hate you with every bone in my body for what you did to Cara.' His face in the mirror turned red.

'Why break me out then?'

'Because you're the only one who can discover who killed Cara, and you can't do that in the deepest sub-basement in an Agency prison. Once in there, you wouldn't see the light of day until ready for hip replacements and a nurse to wipe your arse.' They picked up speed as his tension increased and the weather paid a visit, rain bouncing off the tarmac and attacking the car with relish. 'I'd do anything for Cara, even this.'

When she and Cara had been together, Astrid had thought they made for strange siblings: Cara's fragility and lack of confidence contrasting with Frank's self-assurance and vitality. But Astrid dismissed their differences as nothing more than two people brought up in the same household taking diverse personality paths in life. Astrid had her experiences with Courtney to understand how easy that could be.

Frank Delaney loved his dead sister so much he'd do anything: attack an Agency transport; risk his career and his freedom. And work with somebody he hated. Astrid thought of the love she had for a child she'd never really met. She'd enjoyed that fleeting moment in the park, but she needed to ensure Olivia was safe. Now she was free, wasn't her niece's safety more important than her own?

Lee shifted in her lap and Astrid hoped she wasn't concussed. Her wound had stopped bleeding, seemingly only a scratch. She stroked Laurel's hair and gazed at the crucifix hanging around her neck.

'Why did you force Agent Lee to come with us?'

Would the Agency view Laurel as a victim or a fugitive?

'She'll be useful. She's not as innocent as she seems to be.'

With that vague comment from their saviour, Astrid

glanced outside the window as the sign to Crawley disappeared behind them.

'What makes you think I didn't kill Cara and the others?'

She wondered why he'd take her side. He laughed as the rain grew heavier and danced across the road.

'You're not so sloppy. You wouldn't leave such an obvious piece of evidence in the hotel room in Prague. The Agency has plenty of video footage of you in Europe; it's not complete, sometimes they can't track you, but you're just another Brit tourist abroad.'

He splattered his sentences with the occasional harsh cough, threatening to chuck his lungs all over the floor.

'So why the sham with Davis? Why dump me in the cell and get those idiots to interrogate me? And what's happened to Director Cross?'

'Cross disappeared, and nobody knows where. I assume none of them tried too hard to find him. He had plenty of enemies in the Agency, and Davis took his position before anybody could react. I think she hates you.'

'I'd never met the woman until I walked back into the building. What have I done to make her hate me?'

Delaney laughed like a drunken hyena. 'Who knows with you, Snow? You have a knack for upsetting people.'

She didn't argue, more concerned about their immediate future. 'Where are we going?'

There was enough grit in her voice to lay a driveway. Astrid hadn't forgotten his refusal to answer the question the first time she'd asked. She scrutinised the bald spot on the back of his head and the scratch marks across his neck. They looked like they'd come from human fingernails. Laurel murmured something unintelligible in her lap.

'We're heading to the other side of Crawley, to the Delaney family home.'

His words made Astrid remember Cara again.

'I'm sorry about your sister.'

'Why?'

She thought it a strange question.

'I'm sorry because she's dead.'

It was something which shouldn't need saying, but she did anyway.

'She was dead inside once you broke her heart. You weren't sorry then.'

He appeared ready for an argument.

'What happened to you, Frank?'

'What do you mean?' His eyes never left the road, but he glanced at her in the mirror.

'You were a rising star in the Agency, and Director Cross had big plans for you. You were handsome, charming and had a physique men envied and women admired. And now look at you, stuck behind a desk, overweight, with bad skin and poor hygiene. Changes like that don't happen without a trigger.'

'Shit happens.' His blood-red eyes stared at her in the mirror.

'Apparently.'

Is that my future? Now I've allowed emotions into my life.

Thoughts of Olivia consumed her, skirting around the periphery of her mind until she let them in; welcomed them in. The world passed by outside as Astrid considered how soon she'd be able to get back to her niece. To make sure Olivia was safe. It was her priority, but she appreciated her effectiveness would be limited until she dealt with her problems, which meant relying on Delaney whether she liked it or not.

He drove on; with so much tension in his fingers Astrid thought he'd snap the steering wheel in half. Maybe he'd scratched the back of his neck so hard, he'd drawn blood in an agitated state?

'What did you do before you joined the Agency, Frank?'

Cara had never spoken much about him, but she knew they were close. She found positive family relationships to be curious things, mythical creatures like dragons and monsters. And then she remembered that monsters were real, and they lived within families.

'I signed up straight from university.'

Of course, he did. Something else he undoubtedly resented about Astrid, if he needed any more reasons: the girl recruited from prison; the runaway.

'What did you get your degree in?'

Looking at him, she guessed it would be something like sociology or journalism. The weather worsened, the road turning into a night river, water jumping off the wheels as Delaney pushed the car even harder.

'Media studies.'

She didn't contain her laughter. Her body rocked so much, Laurel spluttered into consciousness, lifting her head with a jerk.

'Where are we?' She rubbed at her eyes. 'Why am I in your lap?'

'Don't worry, Agent Lee, I'm only looking after you; nothing untoward happened.'

'What?' Laurel stammered.

'Laurel, have you met Agent Delaney?' Astrid's smile was mischievous. Lee regained a measure of control and stared at the man in the driver's seat. 'He told me how his extensive familiarity with eighties teen movies got the Agency recruiters begging him to join. He hasn't said why he got so large and putrid.'

Disapproval was etched across Laurel's face, giving it a stern Victorian look, which Astrid didn't like. It ruined her pretty eyes and transformed those touchable cheekbones into tight canals of harshness.

'Is this why people fall out with you: because of your obsessive need to belittle others?'

'Oh my dear, you ain't seen nothing yet.'

Astrid stretched her legs, the ache in her bones from the recent physical exertion attacking her with renewed vigour.

'Why am I here?' Laurel glared at Astrid, but the question was for Agent Delaney.

'You'll help us find who killed my sister.'

He gripped the wheel as they slowed because of the traffic ahead.

'And how will I do that?'

Laurel put her seatbelt on, dragging it across her chest and shifting in the back. The car didn't move, allowing Delaney the opportunity to turn and peer at the junior agent.

'You'll tell Snow everything you forgot to say at her sham of an investigation.'

Laurel lifted her hand to her scalp, feeling the scar. Astrid wondered how the three of them would last more than twenty-four hours without tearing each other apart.

'Would you care to enlighten me as to what he means?' she said to Laurel.

Agent Lee placed her fingers on the cut before glancing away from Astrid's scrutiny.

'Davis told me she'd discovered something about you and Cross, something secret.'

Laurel's voice was calm but hesitant, her fingers shaking as dried blood peeled off her head.

'Would you like to elaborate?' There was only one secret she shared with George.

'I don't know any more. Davis wouldn't tell me the specifics, only it was treacherous, and you and Cross would be locked away because of it.'

Weariness seeped through every word, and Astrid empathised with how tired Laurel seemed. She relaxed into the seat as the darkness drifted by and wondered if that's why George had disappeared. Did he realise the Agency was on to them?

Was that why the Reaper had framed her?

———

IT HAD UNNERVED ME, realising how much the act of murder increased my libido. The last night in Berlin, my mind and body high on the adrenalin, I'd scoured the city's most salacious spots. Money burnt in my pocket when I picked her up at a bar so run-down, it was amazing the walls hadn't collapsed. She claimed she was twenty-five, but it was a lie; the wrinkles on her face and neck throbbed like rings inside a dead tree. It didn't matter; I just needed a sexual release.

'Let's go back to your place,' she said with a cloying voice. A smile revealed several rotten teeth. I laughed and told her no, I wanted to do it in the alley behind the bar. She didn't seem opposed to the idea, no doubt having done the same thing many times before. So we stumbled outside, high on speed and the smell of gasoline, stepping over broken bottles and used needles. I pushed her against the wall, hands over her breasts, my breath burning into the back of her head.

'Do what you want to me,' she said. I grinned at the invite I didn't need, my fingers clawing for the tops of her legs. Somewhere behind us, a dog barked while a police siren screamed in the distance. I hoped they were rushing towards the river and my earlier adventure.

And that's when my hands stopped creeping downwards and headed in the other direction. They were around her neck, my mind wondering where the plastic was as my fingers worked without their usual release. My nails dug into her flesh until the blood congealed underneath them, only stopping when a drunk came crashing out of the bar and landed at my feet.

As I let her go, she spat up a mixture of blood and phlegm. We stared at each other, both recognising what I was; what I'd become. She fled with a face consumed by terror, all bulging eyes and quivering lips. It was only as she disappeared from the shadows that I recognise I'd orgasmed.

'What an interesting development,' I said as I headed away and thought of her again; dreaming of the one I hated.

15 OUR HOUSE

Twenty minutes later, Astrid squirmed in the seat, fingers fidgeting with the seatbelt she wasn't wearing. 'What's the name of the village where your house is?'

The sound of silence was interrupted by the rain bouncing off the car as he got them closer to their destination.

'Pease Pottage.' His eyes were fixed on the road.

'How did a media studies degree help you become one of the country's secret weapons, Frank? Did your intimate knowledge of British TV soaps make you a wiz at the Agency? Or was it your specialist knowledge of terrible Britpop music that got you the cosy desk and lifestyle?'

Astrid couldn't control her thoughts, her mind rambling in all directions, heading towards images of Olivia and Lawrence until she pushed them towards her current saviour. Delaney ignored the questions.

'It won't be long now.'

They passed a motorway station, then on to Horsham Road. Delaney drove past a pub and stopped at the bottom of the street.

'Don't you live in London?'

Astrid couldn't imagine having to do this commute twice a day.

'This is the family home. Our parents lived here. And then Cara did after you dumped her.'

Astrid wondered at what point in their new partnership he'd stop reminding her of what had happened to his sister. She stared at his face, his inability or refusal to hide his hatred, and she understood he'd never stop reminding her.

They got out of the car, the early morning darkness transformed into the new day as the street lights sputtered at their arrival. Neighbourhood cats crept along the edges of the pavement, eyeing the visitors with scrunched faces and grave suspicion. Delaney strode up the drive, and they followed him.

Astrid glanced at Lee. 'How are you feeling?'

Laurel forced a smile through her sleepy face, the tiredness evident on her weary features as eyes drooped and words dripped out in a querulous tremble.

'Don't worry; I'll be fine.'

She didn't look fine to Astrid. Laurel's skin had lost its sheen as soon as Delaney rescued them, while the cut on her head had turned into a violent shade of purple around its edges.

The rain ceased pounding the land, leaving a bouquet of fresh water and dampness drifting around them. Some of nature's tiniest creatures crawled along the ground and skittered into the muddy grass. Astrid gazed at the house through a fresh mist. It was separated from the others on the street, but had the same appearance as its concrete brothers and sisters: long and narrow with a garage on the side, it stretched back like a giant shoebox. It was three storeys high with a small attic at the top, a conservatory as an extension.

Astrid glimpsed its dirty windows as they approached the door. The front garden was pierced with weeds, looking like the poor relation to its neighbours with wild bushes, impressive trees and vividly coloured flowers.

Delaney slipped the key in the lock and pushed the door open. It was the smell that hit Astrid first, an overpowering aroma of detergent and cleaning fluids. She couldn't see anything clean as dust lay over every surface like grey snow. They stepped over a pile of mail cascading across the floor, a paper infestation ready to creep through the rest of the house. He threw his keys onto a side table and strode towards the kitchen.

'Does anybody want a drink?'

Astrid helped Laurel inside, the younger woman unsteady on her feet. She put her arm around Lee's waist and guided her towards a brown-coloured sofa.

'How long is it since anybody lived here?' she shouted towards Delaney in the kitchen. He returned, carrying a dirty glass and a half-full bottle of whisky.

'Cara lived here, on and off before she went to Europe. This was our parents' home before they died.' He poured himself a full glass before downing most of it in one go.

Laurel shook her head. 'Isn't it a bit early for that?'

'It helps me sleep.' He refilled his glass.

Astrid scanned the room. 'Do you have a laptop I can use?'

He pointed over her shoulder. 'There's one on the table behind you.'

'Why was Cara in Europe?' she asked him while holding onto Laurel's waist.

He took a large drink from the glass, eyes pointing to a picture on the wall of a burly man on a fishing boat. The man in the photograph was an older black-and-white version of Frank, and she guessed he was the Delaney father.

'She'd met somebody new, and they were going on holiday together.' Astrid wanted to ask him if it was only a coincidence his sister was in Berlin while she was there. 'She needed rest and recuperation.'

'Which is what we need now,' Astrid said to him.

He slumped into a chair opposite a TV from the 1970s and finished his second drink. 'You can take the large room at the top of the stairs. Agent Lee can have the one next to it.'

'And you?'

'One more drink and I'll be snoring in this chair. I need to get to work in three hours, or they'll wonder where I am. There's food in the kitchen, and I'll bring some more when I return tonight. You need to stay inside and keep out of sight.' His face looked about to collapse at any second.

'And what happens then?' Laurel kept on with the questions.

'Then we start working out who's behind all this.'

He propped the bottle on his corpulent stomach and closed his eyes. Astrid helped Laurel to stand and grabbed the computer from the table.

'Come on; let's see what luxury awaits us above.'

The stairs were to the left of the main room, short and narrow. She guided Laurel up, holding on to the rail and finding dust clinging to her skin. Laurel relaxed in her arm as they moved beyond the first bedroom and towards the one Delaney had described. She kicked the door open and sat Laurel onto a bed which didn't appear to have been slept in for quite some time. It was the only piece of furniture there.

'This must be Frank's childhood room.' Faded Nirvana

and Blur posters hung from the walls, while stacked up in every corner were towers of collected memorabilia: records, CDs, videotapes, books and magazines. The layers of dust made Laurel sneeze loudly. 'Do you want to get undressed?'

Laurel said no before lying down and pulling the covers up to her chin. 'I'm fine.'

Astrid doubted it. 'Try and get some sleep.'

She closed the door behind her. Down below, Frank Delaney's snoring shook the dust from the ceiling. She headed into the bedroom, which was a kitsch nightmare of pink flamingo wallpaper, with paintings of cats knitting and dogs playing cards, and a carpet containing hundreds of small images of Vladimir Tretchikoff's blue-faced *Chinese Girl*.

On the wall were a few framed family photos. She moved towards one, peering through the glass at a middle-aged couple and their two children: Cara and Frank and their parents. Cara must have only been five or six in the photo. She stood to one side as if placed there as an afterthought, peering from a sepia-toned past. Astrid turned her gaze to Cara's mother in the photo, struck by how much the older woman resembled the grown-up daughter Astrid had pretended to love. Then she looked at the image of the young Cara. How responsible was she for her murder? Was faking an emotion the same as lying? Had Astrid's deceit ruined Cara's life?

She turned from the photo, her mind an explosive mixture of ideas falling into each other. The neon clock to her right said six-thirty in the morning. Her body demanded rest, but her mind requested sharpness while Delaney was downstairs. She'd only close her eyes once he'd left. If he was returning to the Agency, he'd have to leave by seven-thirty to beat the traffic and get to his desk before the working day started. She wouldn't get any sleep before he left. He may have rescued her from Agency custody, but she didn't trust him.

Astrid opened the laptop, glad the internet worked without any prompting for a password. The first thing she did was check the news sites for updates on the Reaper case, which all said the same: ongoing with no new leads. She touched her face, running fingers over her lips. Did she really want to do the next bit?

Of course, she did. She closed the news sites and brought up the most popular social media pages. It wasn't hard to find her sister's profile on Facebook, Twitter and Instagram. Courtney was married, but she'd kept her family name.

Was it because she loved Lawrence so much?

She stared at a recent photo of her older sibling; Courtney had his eyes and their mother's face. In the image, she had the same grin Astrid remembered from when Courtney watched him beating her sister. Looking at the photo stabbed at her gut, a chunk of bile swirling around her like soap suds inside a hyperactive dishwasher. She forced her nails into her skin to stop her punching that irritating digital grin from the screen. Her head throbbed as if a thousand tiny Irish dancers were jigging inside her brain.

Contrary to popular belief, ADHD didn't mean she couldn't focus on things, but it meant she had a compulsion to gather up as much information as she could inside her head as a way of concentrating on specific issues. It was like piling wood on top of more wood to flatten the piece at the bottom; the more details in her head, the easier it became for her to isolate what was most important to her. She'd once described it to Cara as having a never-ending jigsaw inside her mind where, when she focused fully, the pieces would come together at some point, and everything would stretch out before her in perfect illumination.

Astrid returned to the computer screen, jagging her finger into Courtney's pixelated head and flicking it to one side, moving through her sister's interminable selfies. She couldn't find any images of the mysterious husband or Olivia.

She was disappointed not to find any photos of her niece, but at least there weren't any of her parents either. Courtney's Twitter account was a banal litany of posts about trashy TV shows and D-list celebrities. Perhaps it was a good thing Olivia wasn't on Courtney's timeline. It was better not to have any pictures of the kid online, not with all the perverts lurking on the internet. Astrid had worked enough child abuse cases to recognise where the dangers lay. She pictured Olivia's smiling face running around the playground once again.

I could hide in the shadows outside the nursery and get a glimpse of Olivia there tomorrow.

Large bellows rising like ash spewed from a petulant volcano erupted from downstairs and ripped that crazy idea from her head. Their host had awakened like the Kraken.

Astrid dragged herself from the bed. She crept towards the door, pressing her ear against the flaking wood and listened to Delaney moving around, hoping his noise wouldn't wake Laurel. He spluttered and spewed for a bit longer, talking to himself, before she heard the unmistakable sound of him grasping his keys and leaving through the front door. She walked to the window, pulled back the chintzy orange-coloured curtains and peered through the glass, watching him get into the car and drive away.

She flopped onto the bed, finding respite in the comforting grip of the darkness. She formed an idea as to what she'd do next with Laurel and Frank.

But could she trust either of them to help her?

When Astrid woke, the neon numbers to her side flashed seven o'clock in the evening. She was stunned she'd slept for twelve hours, unable to remember the last time she'd spent so much time asleep. Her body was much better for it, but her bones creaked because of the contours of an unfamiliar bed. She got up and strode towards the door. A delicious aroma drifted up from the kitchen, the smell of fried food which triggered rumbling inside her stomach.

The thought of hot greasy sustenance made her smile as she went to check on Laurel, unsurprised to find her room empty. Astrid slipped into the bathroom and peered at her face in the mirror. The blue of her eyes had lost some of its sparkle, her hair was unwashed and unkempt, with a passing likeness to something a murder of crows would design to inhabit. She threw hot water over her skin, burning her senses awake, before running her fingers through her twisted strands and shaping it into a facsimile of respectability.

Behind the bathroom mirror was a cabinet. She was

reluctant to open it in case she found something of Cara's, but she was in desperate need of deodorant. Astrid dragged it open, finding it empty and appreciating that was one reason Frank Delaney emitted a particularly pungent masculine odour. She grabbed hold of the soap, ran her fingers under the tap, and scrubbed under her armpits hoping it would do the trick. She dried herself and strode downstairs. In the kitchen, she was greeted by the sight of perfect domestic bliss, Delaney with a frying pan in hand while Lee was busy mixing eggs and onions into an omelette.

Laurel grinned at her. 'Hello, sleepyhead.'

It seemed as if they were living everyday suburban lives and weren't on the run from some secret conspiracy. Astrid ignored her and stared at the food: bacon, eggs, toast and mushrooms so large, a family of gnomes could live inside them.

'It smells good.'

'He's even made me some veggie sausages.'

Laurel thrust the plate of pale-looking fake meat underneath Astrid's grimace. She laughed at her as Astrid grabbed a seat at the table. Her senses told her to concentrate on the food, but the analytical part of her brain overrode those and stared at Delaney as he placed a fresh orange juice next to her.

'What happened when you returned to the Agency?'

He joined her at the table. 'Food first, then we'll talk.'

The first taste to hit the back of her throat was heavenly, the crispness of the bacon crunching between her teeth and crumbling down her throat. She plucked a piece of toast from Laurel's fingers and pushed it into the bright yellow of the egg gazing at her. She ignored Laurel's complaint and washed the food down with a slurp of juice.

'You'll make somebody an excellent husband, Frank.' Astrid regretted the awful things she'd said to him earlier. It was another new emotion to add to her resurrected list. She was undecided if she liked the person she was becoming. She noticed the large plaster over Laurel's cut. 'How's your head?'

'It's fine; just a scratch. Frank patched me up.'

Astrid sat back and shovelled the eggs into her mouth. It didn't take long for all three of them to finish, Delaney announcing the end of the meal with a large burp which sent Astrid and Laurel scampering into the living room.

'Nice,' Astrid said to him as she searched for the TV remote, wanting to check the news for any mention of last night's activities. She was also interested in the media reports about the search for the Reaper, wondering if the Agency had already provided a scapegoat and the case was over; they'd done similar things before.

She found the device stuck down the side of the sofa as she slumped into it. The furniture had seen better days, with washed-out flowers growing out of a design worn thin. The ugly green border around the cushions reminded her of a vomit-inducing dress an ex-paramour had presented to her as a belated birthday present.

Astrid turned on the TV, amazed to see it start without being wound up from the back, and then sprinted through the news channels. There was nothing about the collision with the van and very little about the Reaper case, apart from a rolling ticker-tape style news announcement on one station saying it was ongoing. Delaney came into the room and stared at the screen. She turned towards their rescuer and host. She should have been grateful, but couldn't be when the trust wasn't there. After all, he did say he hated her. She muted the sound, but left the TV on the news channel.

'What happened when you got to headquarters?'

'I went to work. I have cases to work on.'

He stood in the doorway between the living room and the kitchen, the extra layers of flesh around his stomach hanging over the top of his trousers like drunken sailors preparing to abandon ship. His indifference annoyed her, and she resisted the temptation to get off the sofa and wring his neck.

'If you broke me out of the van to help you track down your sister's killer, you better start telling me something useful, or I'll be out of here, and you'll be back on your own. Or did you get the two of us here so you could play at happy families?'

Delaney glared at her with no attempt to hide his resentment, his face all twisted and stern; the frivolity of the kitchen had withered away. She was in no doubt he hated her, but he'd said he needed her, and she chose to believe that for now.

'They don't know who attacked the van, but they were in the process of formulating a theory you had a partner before the escape. Now they're convinced of it.'

'Apparently, I have two partners.'

She stared at them as if they were a tiny angel and devil she'd once seen in a cartoon when she was a kid, one to sit on each shoulder. She buried the memory swiftly, keen to push back any childhood recollections.

'They're going to let the Reaper investigation continue while they search for you, before pinning it on some unfortunate who'll kill themselves. Some killer they already have in custody. They can't have you or anything to do with you appearing in the media.'

'What about me?' Laurel asked.

'They believe she kidnapped you. Some of the security witnessed Snow dragging you out the van, so your innocence is guaranteed for now.'

'I am innocent.' A fire burnt behind her resentful eyes.

'How many do they have searching for us?'

'Everybody,' Delaney said. 'And that includes me.'

'Excellent. That's our first bit of good news.'

Laurel narrowed her eyes. 'Why?'

'Full mobilisation won't last for long; it can't. They have too many other things to do. If we can stay out of their reaches for a week, they'll pull people from the search, sooner rather than later. The longer Frank can get access to the investigation, the better for us.'

Delaney gave Astrid a crooked smile, reminding her of a drug dealer she'd once busted; he would give you just enough to get you hooked, and then when you least expected it, you'd be sucked so far down into the darkness, you'd never get out.

'Tell me what you have, Frank.'

She crossed her legs, relaxing after the food. Delaney dropped his shoulders, choking a cough in his chest before it was born.

'The crime scene evidence from Vienna and Budapest is in, being examined by Davis and a bucketful of assistants.'

'Anything helpful in what they've gathered?'

She wanted to hear if there were any more staged scenes or fake glasses.

'So far, there's nothing that ties you to those two murders. But none of them seems too worried about that.'

'Why aren't they concerned?' Laurel asked.

'Because, rookie,' Astrid grinned to show she was being playful and not hurtful, 'all they need is the glass with my fingerprints and DNA on it from Prague to make their case: a case they're only making for themselves, remember. The glass connects me to Michelle Dark's murder, which has an MO the same as the other four; that's all they need to convict me in their private kangaroo court.' There was no animosity in her voice, only recognition of how the Agency worked.

Frank drifted back into the kitchen in an apparent attempt to avoid Astrid's gaze. She glanced around the room, looking for any sign Cara Delany had once lived there. She'd been tempted to check on Cara's room while Frank was at work, but her extended sleep had scuppered the idea. And she wasn't sure why she wanted to look at a dead woman's things.

A notebook sat on the coffee table, casually open, with a set of names scribbled on one page. Astrid picked it up and recognised them. There were two dozen of them, names of the people she'd sketched on the walls of her cell at the Agency. Her eyebrows arched as she stared at Laurel.

'I plucked them from memory, the ones we could iden-tify from your artwork.' There was no emotion in Lee's face or voice.

'That's some memory you have.' She was suitably impressed and understood why the Agency recruited Lee. Laurel nodded.

'It's not perfect, but I can remember an image in so much detail, clarity, and accuracy, it's as though it's still in front of me.'

'I'm sure it'll come in handy when we track down the killer. Do you still have your pen?' She scrunched up next to Laurel on the sofa, smiling inside when the younger woman didn't object.

'Sure.' Laurel reached down the side of the sofa to rescue the pen.

'What do you want me to write?'

They gazed into each other's eyes, distracting Astrid's thoughts which should have been focused on discovering who was framing her. She stared at Laurel's crucifix, and it jogged her back into the moment.

'Cross out all the male names and add these three female ones.' Astrid dictated the words to her.

Frank Delaney entered the room, towel in hand as he dried one of the glasses. 'Why remove those names?'

Astrid settled into the sofa and allowed the tension to evaporate from her body.

'Because whoever's doing this is a woman.'

17 THEORETICAL GIRLS

Laurel and Frank's eyes glazed over in stereo, lips turned upwards in confusion.

'What?' Laurel said.

Frank frowned at Astrid. 'And how did you work that out?'

She picked up Laurel's notes and stretched her legs until her feet rested on the table. Once Laurel had scratched through the male names and added the ones she'd given her, there were seven left on the page. Astrid got the remote and switched the TV set off.

'You might want to sit down for this, Frank.' Astrid gave him a twisted smile, like the grin of someone about to divulge their most treasured secret. He pushed the cushions off the chair next to the TV and stared at her. 'The murders and the Agency's deliberate incompetence in investigating them are two different things.'

'You don't think there's a connection?' Laurel replied.

'I believe somebody wants me to think there is, so I'll focus on the Agency and who wants to frame me. But it doesn't make any sense. As useless as I believe them to be, in general, there are still some skilled people there.'

She peered into Delaney's bloodshot eyes before turning to stare at Lee.

Frank laughed at her. 'You're too kind, Snow.'

'If somebody high up in the Agency wanted to frame me, there'd be evidence pointing towards me at all the crime scenes, not only in Prague. Even if it's a rogue agent acting alone, they would've had plenty of opportunities to leave evidence incriminating me.'

'Maybe they're cleverer than you, Snow.'

Frank's shirt peered out of his trousers, and there was a sauce stain underneath his chin. He must have sprayed himself with something citrusy as a smell of lemon hung around the room.

'I think the Agency's smartest agents are all in this room, Frank.' Astrid grinned at Laurel and ignored the scowl on his face. 'No, a single individual is behind this, and influential people at the Agency are using it to smear my name and incarcerate me. They got lucky with the timing.'

'Why?' Frank asked. 'What makes you so special?'

Astrid sighed and told him what she'd already revealed to Laurel. 'I wasn't coming back to the Agency; Director Cross signed off on it.'

'Maybe that's why Cross disappeared. If they were on to his deception with you, he'd have ended up in a cell as well.' He peered at the two women as if he'd discovered something significant in their investigation. 'They probably think Cross is your partner, and he helped you escape from the van.'

Astrid could see why the Agency had stuck Frank behind a desk. 'Let's hope they believe that. The more they follow the wrong leads, the better it is for us.'

'The Agency would find you if you left,' Laurel said. 'I've read the files about the ones who tried to quit. It never ended well for them.'

'Not me.' There was no arrogance in Astrid's voice, just absolute confidence and self-belief.

'Snow's right,' Frank piped up.

'I'm right about which part?' She was curious as to why he'd switched from disagreeing with her.

'You're too good for the Agency. If one agent could disappear from them, it would be you, especially if Director Cross protected you. They couldn't allow that to happen. Once you sign up for the Agency, they've got you for life; the only way to leave is in a wooden box.'

Laurel rubbed at the mark on her head. 'Why couldn't they bring you back into the fold, keep you there?'

'Isn't that what they did?' Astrid gazed at the stain on Frank's chin, getting hungry again. 'A deep cell underground is a pretty permanent place to keep somebody. If Frank hadn't busted me out of the van, I'd be sitting in the shadows for the rest of my life.' She acknowledged her debt to him with a nod. His scowl morphed into a grimace as she asked him another question. 'Do you know what happened to Director Cross?' It was too much of a coincidence for him to have disappeared before Astrid got entangled in this mess.

'Nobody knows. One day he's at work, the next he isn't.'

'The Agency searched for him?'

'Of course, they did. They found nothing.'

'So much for them being able to find anybody who tries to leave their orbit,' Laurel said.

'They might not be trying to find him.' Astrid peered at the plaster on Laurel's head, feeling a strange kind of emotion for her. 'Or they might know where he is. And

Frank could be right: if they knew what he'd planned with me, George would be locked away as we speak.'

Frank nodded, the skin below his chin rippling in a most unattractive fashion. 'They didn't waste any time in getting somebody new in.'

'And Director Davis replaced him?' Astrid asked.

'It's her empire now.'

Laurel sat up. 'Why did you say it was a single individual behind the murders?'

'I don't think there could be two people who hate me so much.' She allowed herself the luxury of a chuckle.

'Don't be too sure,' Frank said without a trace of humour. His ire couldn't knock Astrid from her upbeat mood.

'There's too much controlled anger in those five murders for it to be two people. It's one person, and it's a woman.'

'Go on, then, enlighten us,' he said. Astrid found it amusing her apparent saviour would sing her praises one minute, the next make obvious his disdain for her theories.

'You've both seen the crime scene photos, right?' They nodded in unison. 'Any marks on the bodies of Andrews and Chill?'

'Yes,' they both said together.

'Small bruises on their backs, as if somebody pushed against them to hold them down during strangulation?'

'How did you know?' Laurel asked.

'Don't worry; I didn't do it, or any of them. Don't you think it's strange the three men have the marks while the two women don't?' Astrid removed her legs from the table, scratching the top of her ankle before a bout of cramp ensued. 'I saw the photo of Chill's body. The bruise was small, too small to be from a man unless he's on the short side. And if our suspect has two hands on the plastic bag over the victim's head, which they must have, it's safe to assume they held them down with some part of their leg. It can't have been their foot as they wouldn't have been able to reach their head then, so it must've been their knee; same with the other men.'

'Okay; why not the same MO with the other two murders?' Frank said.

'Because generally, women don't think other women are going to kill them. We're always suspicious around men, but another woman we trust; mostly.'

'It must be someone with a similar or larger physique,' Laurel said.

'Absolutely, so it was easier for them to overpower the victims. There was no need to hold them down; hence, there were no marks on those two bodies.'

'That's all guesswork.' Frank didn't sound convinced.

'It's an educated analysis, Frank. It's what I'm good at. You know this. It's why you broke me out of that van.'

'I don't buy it.' He jumped from his chair and stormed into the kitchen.

'He certainly dislikes you. His sister must have taken your breakup pretty hard.'

'She did.' Astrid tried not to think about it, a brooding look on her face as she grabbed hold of the TV remote again.

'What must it be like to love somebody so much?'

The sadness in Laurel's voice startled her. Staring at the other woman and recognising the pain in her face, Astrid didn't know how to answer so switched on the TV and searched for news about the Reaper. Laurel stared at the names she'd written, with a far-off look in her eyes.

Astrid ceased the pointless changing of the channels,

stopping on a cartoon of a frustrated cat trying to smash a small grinning brown mouse. The moggy chased its prey around an old-fashioned kitchen on an endless loop of a desperate pursuit which would never end, no matter how many times they played out the same scenario.

'You could go back to the Agency, Laurel.'

'And what would I do there?' The anger in Laurel's voice pleased Astrid; as long as she used it positively, it would be much better than wallowing in sadness. 'We have Frank on the inside; there's no need for two of us there.'

How quickly this has turned into 'us' and not just me.

'Are you not concerned about your reputation, of what might happen to you the longer you're with me?'

Why are you still with me, rookie, when you could be back in your safe everyday life with the Agency and your dog?

A million and one theories rattled inside Astrid's head, and every single one of them wanted to pull her deep below the murky waters of her current predicament.

'They think you and your partner have kidnapped me; I'll be okay for a while. You never know, I might return there as a conquering hero. We both might.'

Astrid laughed at the thought of it combined with the sight of the frustrated cartoon cat getting a creampie stuffed into his startled face.

'My theories didn't convince Frank; how about you?'

'I examined all the evidence they had. Your analysis appears sound to me. But then what do I know? I'm only a rookie.'

Astrid stared at Laurel, expecting to be greeted by a morose vision of unhappiness, but was pleased to see the other woman grinning at her, blonde hair shimmering in the light of the digital screen. Some pots and pans were thrown into cupboards as Frank completed his domestic duties in the kitchen. Astrid nodded his way, pointing towards the racket coming from the other room.

'What do you make of him?'

'I don't know him at all. I've seen him in passing at headquarters, but we'd never spoken until I woke up in the back of the car.'

'Do you trust him?'

'I don't know who to trust.' Laurel gazed at her. 'If you were going to disappear from the Agency before, why don't you do it now?'

Astrid ignored the flashing psychedelic lights coming from the TV and shuffled closer to the younger woman, cutting out the space separating them on the sofa.

'Someone is trying to destroy my life, and I'm not the type of person to stand by and let that happen.'

'Why do you think they're doing this?'

She answered while flicking through the news channels again. 'I don't care why. I'm just going to stop them any way I can.'

Frank trundled back into the room and glared at them. 'We need to talk about what we're going to do next.'

'That's simple.' Astrid turned off the set. 'I'm going to find Director Cross.'

18 VIENNA

Vienna is a beautiful city; a place bathed in imperial grandeur with a pastel palette of Baroque and Renaissance architecture which is wondrous to behold.

To do such a dreadful thing in such a beautiful place was a shame, but Harry Andrews was a terrible man who deserved everything he got. I had to humiliate him first, make him pay for all those women he'd hurt. It was easy, really. Point the gun at the head and issue the command. The weapon sleeps at the bottom of the Danube now.

'What do you want?'

It seemed a strange thing for him to say, considering I was pointing a gun at him. Only when I gazed into his eyes did I realise he wasn't afraid. His arrogance stopped him from worrying about his situation.

I waved the weapon at him. 'Take your clothes off.'

My finger on the trigger removed any reluctance he might have had. He stood there in an undershirt and pants an old man would wear.

'I've got money if that's what you're after.'

The mania in my eyes must have told him I was a

druggie in search of a fix. If that was the case, he wasn't far wrong. I pointed the gun towards the shirt, and he pulled it over his head. There were fresh scratch marks on his chest.

'Did your last victim hurt you?'

He ran his fingers over the scratches and grinned at me. 'Is that what this is about? You're a friend of the family?'

He shivered in the room as I wiped the sweat from my forehead. 'Yes, something like that.'

The fear seeped through his skin, dripped from his eyes, eroding the person he thought he was, consuming all the arrogance and confidence which drove him through his existence. The contortions were visible in his stomach, my invisible hand crushing his insides in anticipation of what was to come. His breathing was fast and erratic, coming in great clumps before disappearing for seconds as he struggled to come to terms with his imminent future.

For one moment, I recognised a promise of resistance in his startled eyes until I pushed the revolver against his skull. Any hope of defiance was crushed against the blackness of his soul. I made him strip naked before forcing his head against the flaking plaster of the wall. Whatever he'd paid to rent the property was far too much.

My knee was pressed tight against the bare skin of his back, the plastic in my left hand, gun in the right and glued to his cheek. I thought a man of his violent proclivities would protest more, would put up a fight, but all he could do was piss over the floor as I slipped the bag over his head. I dropped the gun onto the ground and got both hands on the bottom of the bag, forcing my leg even harder into his back as my fingers grabbed hold of the plastic.

As the life slipped away from him, his hands grasped at his throat, struggling to pull upwards as my knee pushed down. As I pulled hard on the plastic, his head tilted in the air, and my eyes followed his as they focused on the wall and the last things he'd ever see. I'd thought about placing photos there of the women he'd attacked, but dismissed the idea as too risky. Taking no chances of leaving any evidence behind, instead, I placed random postcards of Vienna's sights on that spot on the wall: the Belvedere Museum, St Stephen's Cathedral and Schönbrunn Palace. It was ironic a man so ugly on the inside would see such beauty as he breathed his last.

It's a cathartic experience, taking another's life, a cleansing of the soul. I wanted to defile his body, burn every part of him so he'd disappear from existence. But I couldn't; it had to follow the same pattern as the others, be part of the larger plan.

Once it was done, I removed the postcards and dumped them into a rubbish bin as I wandered towards the Österreichische Galerie Belvedere. The museum was open for another hour, giving me plenty of time to visit some old friends. The lateness helped thin out the annoying tourists and their selfie sticks. I glared at a few of them, picturing my technique for thinning out the herd. Once the plan was completed, plastic bags would be neither practical nor safe for when I continued. I needed to think of new methods.

As I considered using an array of knives in future endeavours, my eyes were drawn to the glitter of my old friends. A gun would also be essential to get people in position. I could still use the plastic bags on the odd occasion. It would be a sweet memory, homage to the grand plan.

I stared at my old friends, her face permanently turned away from his. A long time ago, I believed they were deeply in love, the way he embraced her in that field of cloth and gold; they were bound together, through choice, as one being – one entity.

My interpretation had changed over the years; now, I saw her as an unwilling victim of his oppression. Rather than the embodiment of true love, they were the quintessential symbols of death. Head turned away or eyes closed, pale skin contrasted with the opulent gold and green of life surrounding them. She was limp; she was passive; was she alive?

I stared at them until it was time to leave. Ushered outside, I was thinking about life and death. Dreaming about what I'd do once I returned home.

THE JOURNEY to Brighton was a straight drive down the A23. Frank gave Astrid his car while he took the train to London and returned to the Agency.

'How do you know where his home is? Only a few people at the top of the Agency hierarchy know where a director lives.'

Laurel fiddled with the seatbelt as Astrid ignored her question and cruised down the road. Laurel was uncomfortable wearing the same clothes for more than a day and had repeatedly told Astrid that as they readied to leave the Delaney household.

'I'm sure Frank has kept all of Cara's clothes upstairs in her room; ask him if you can borrow some.' Laurel declined, and Astrid was glad. She shuddered at the thought of seeing Laurel wearing her dead ex-girlfriend's clothes. 'You'll have to make do with what you're wearing, then. George might have something at his place.'

They drove past a sign for Mud Mania, and Astrid grinned at the thought of getting dirty.

'His full name was George Cross?'

Laurel appeared bemused, her pretty eyes creeping upwards as those delicious lips headed south. Astrid kept on smirking.

'Yeah, he wanted to change it but never did. His parents were dedicated patriots. They were none too pleased when they discovered what they called his alternative lifestyle.'

On their right was a large billboard advertising Hot Tubs. Laurel scratched at her stomach as the car slowed because of the traffic.

'How do you know where he lives?' Laurel asked again.

'Because he told me, and I've been there before. He was my friend.'

Astrid didn't know why she'd slipped into the past tense when she mentioned him. She kept her eyes on the road. It was warm outside, so she turned on the air conditioning.

'What happens when we get to Director Cross's house?'

Laurel pulled at her trousers and scratched under her shirt. Her constant frustration began to annoy Astrid.

'I take one of George's computers and hack into the Agency system and see what they have on me.' She was pleased with the idea, but Laurel frowned. 'Why the long face, beautiful?'

Astrid always enjoyed flirting, more so with women than men. She'd found that men expected it to develop into something else. For them, it was an aperitif guaranteed to lead to an entree as a gateway to the main course. But for most women, it was an end in itself, something frivolous that could just be a bit of fun.

'All your files have been moved from the main server.' Laurel passed on the information as if updating somebody about a loved one's death.

'Why?' It was disappointing to hear. She could think of any number of reasons, but wanted to know the official line.

'I was told it was a new security protocol issued by Director Davis.'

'And the files for the five murders?'

'They were still on the server before I was dragged away.'

'That will have to do then.'

Astrid sped up as the traffic cleared in front of them. She turned off the main road and headed to the retail park.

'I thought we were going to Brighton?'

Laurel sounded puzzled. Astrid kept on driving before pulling into the underground parking for their little diversion.

'We are, but I can't put up with you twisting and scratching in those clothes for much longer; it's driving me crazy. We can get you some new apparel here, assuming you have cash on you?' It was the one thing that might scupper her impetuous plan. Laurel frowned again before checking her pockets.

'I've got a card and about fifty quid in notes.'

'The card is no good. They'll trace you with it. Fifty is enough for a cheap and cheerful outfit.'

'You said we didn't have the time.'

'It can't be helped.' Astrid frowned. 'You're distracting me too much.'

She's distracting me in more ways than one.

'Aren't you worried someone might recognise us?'

She parked the car in the first empty spot.

'You'll need to keep some cash for the parking charge on the way out,' Astrid said before answering the question. 'They're looking for us, but they're not looking for us; officially, anyway. They can't have any photos in the media or with regular law enforcement in case an ordinary Joe or

Josephine picks us up. They wouldn't trust me not to blab. And I know a hell of a lot.'

The Agency was the clandestine government organisation the public could never know about; the people who broke the strictest laws in the state's name. Not that any government official could ever be connected to the work the Agency did. But Astrid knew enough to bring the government down and put many well-known high-profile public figures behind bars. Perhaps that's why she'd been set-up as the Reaper.

They got out of the car together, Astrid's senses assaulted by the aroma of damp concrete and dried piss. It was dark, but Astrid found the parking machine, striding towards it without a care in the world. She came back and stuck the ticket up against the glass of the windscreen where even a myopic parking attendant wouldn't miss it. The last thing they needed was Delaney's car in the system because of some trivial parking fine.

'How long are we here for?' Laurel scowled at her.

'An hour should do it. Unless you want to go for a coffee while we're here?'

'You're taking this awfully casual.' Laurel scratched at her leg.

Astrid checked the parking lot to see if they were alone.

'Nerves and excitement won't do us any good; this isn't a date.' Though she was beginning to wish it was. 'We treat this as if it was a normal day out.' She tapped the side of her head. 'As long as we stay cool, the rest is only a matter of detective work.'

They strode towards the lift. Inside it, Astrid considered the last time the two of them had done this, back at Agency headquarters. Not the time squashed against the guards, but the time before when it was only the two of them, and

Laurel had blushed so spectacularly at her suggestions. They went down three flights. She didn't blush now.

'How quickly things change.'

'And yet still stay the same.' Astrid stepped into the illuminated world of materialism. She grinned as she grabbed Laurel's hand and dragged her towards the shiny new clothes adorning the multi-coloured plastic stands.

Astrid had loved clothes from an early age, when she'd experimented with dressing up using her mother's outfits, parading in front of the mirror before her parents convinced her she was ugly. This was when she was still young enough to believe adults would look after her. So she raided her mother's wardrobe, wearing things which were far too big for her, and far too plain and dull. Her mother's tastes in what to wear were like her views on the world: ultra-conservative, more utilitarian than fashionable. It was only when Astrid started shoplifting in her teenage years that she expressed her creativity.

'Do you want underwear first, Laurel?'

She dragged her new partner towards the lingerie department. A glittering infectious smile jumped from her face and on to Laurel, whose skin was warm against Astrid's hand.

Laurel laughed. 'Always start at the bottom.'

'Is this too fancy for you?'

Astrid smirked; the accelerated beat of her thoughts fluttered between sorting clothes for Laurel and what they'd find at George's house. She tried not to think of Olivia too much. Dwelling on whether her sister was in contact with their father was too distressing.

'Too much choice,' Laurel laughed.

Supermarket music bounced off the walls, and Astrid cringed at the retail choice of dull pop tunes.

'Just for once, I'd love to go into a shop and hear something decent coming from the speakers.' She kept an eye out for security guards. 'Anything by Bowie would do.'

Music had got her through a traumatic childhood. When those memories crawled from the shadows in her head, of her mother holding her down while Lawrence whipped her, Astrid reached into her favourite jukebox to listen to *Diamond Dogs* or *Station to Station*. If the scars returned with too much intensity, she killed the pain with the Stooges or the Velvet Underground. Then his slobbering face and her manic glee disappeared into nothing. But nothing could erase the image of Courtney standing in the doorway watching her suffering. At first, Astrid assumed her sister had no choice, that their parents were punishing her as well by making Courtney watch, until she saw the smile on her sister's face and realised how much she enjoyed Astrid's pain. It wasn't long afterwards she discovered the lies her sister told their parents to get her into trouble.

'I had a job in a supermarket once.' Laurel's voice dragged her back from the abyss. 'All the staff had to dress up in light blue uniforms like Smurfs.' Astrid took the image and imprinted it over the one of Courtney's grin. 'I crept into the office one day and changed the piped music for something of my own.'

Astrid smiled at her. 'I'm betting you were a goth when you were younger.' She imagined her all in black.

Laurel laughed again. 'Not quite, but I managed to clear the shop of customers and get fired because I changed the music to *The Queen is Dead* by the Smiths.'

Astrid clutched on to her stomach to stop herself laughing too much; it would be foolish to draw attention to themselves now. She checked the rest of the store; afternoon shoppers and bored teenagers filled the place. She pushed through them all, dragging Laurel to the changing room to discard the clothes which infuriated them both.

She touched Laurel's wrist. 'You go first.' She expected a rebuttal, but received a tender smile instead.

'You do know how to spoil a girl.' Laurel slipped behind the curtain.

'You don't know the half of it.'

Astrid considered how quickly things had changed between them, from Laurel locking her in an Agency cell only yesterday to waiting outside a changing room while the rookie selected new clothes.

An old woman scowled at her before scurrying away to pay for some awful outfits she clutched underneath her arms. Astrid stared at the bottom of the changing booth, peering at Laurel's delicate ankles as she removed her trousers. All the problems stacked up inside her head shifted to one side as she imagined Agent Laurel Lee slipping into her new underwear. It was a brief moment of imaginary joy swept away by the flickering red light of the security camera above her head.

It's worth the risk.

She counted on Agency incompetence stopping them alerting local law enforcement about her escape.

'I wonder what Frank would think of our little shopping spree,' Laurel shouted from the other side of the curtain.

'He'd be fuming.' Astrid grinned. 'Upset because he wasn't amongst the lingerie with us.'

They burst out laughing in stereo, Astrid imaging a life beyond her current predicament where it could be like this all the time.

'Are you waiting to use this cubicle?'

The voice was close to her shoulder, its owner's shadow falling over her head, providing an ominous creeping presence across the floor. She didn't bother to stand, twisting her neck to one side to stare into the weather-beaten face of shop security. Just behind him lurked the scowling woman, shaking her head and pointing at Astrid.

'There's no hanky-panky going on if that's what you're thinking.'

She gave him her widest smile, all flashing teeth and sparkling eyes. The temperature was cool in the shops, yet droplets of sweat ran down his forehead and into his eyes.

'Oooofff course,' he stuttered.

'You must have filthy thoughts.' She smiled at the offended woman.

'No, no, I'm sor-sor, sorry,' he stammered before turning away and barging past the flummoxed old bird.

'What do you think?' Laurel said as she stepped into the light and gave her a twirl.

'You look divine.' She took Laurel's arm and pulled her towards the counter. 'Let's get these paid for and back on the road.' Astrid searched for the security cameras.

'Don't you want to try your clothes on?' Laurel said through flummoxed lips.

'No time,' Astrid said without explanation.

They left five minutes later armed with new underwear for each of them, a couple of shirts and a trendy pair of trousers for Laurel. Astrid had worked it out, so they had enough to pay for the parking. As they entered the underground garage, they laughed like teenagers on a first date, striding arm in arm towards the car.

She let go of Laurel, reached for the car keys and put her hand on the door. The hairs on the back of her head sprang to life: something was wrong. In the reflection of the window was a shadow with its arm around Laurel's neck. She turned to see the nervous security guard with a large kitchen knife at Lee's throat. It had a price sticker hanging off the blade.

'We didn't steal anything, so you might be overreacting here.'

She tried to keep him calm. A trickle of blood slithered down Laurel's skin.

'Put your hands in the air and lean against the car,' he said.

Astrid dropped the shopping bag to the floor with a clatter. 'Well, which is it? I can't do both.'

She stood motionless and stared at him. Any wrong move on her part, and there was no telling what he'd do. The grimace on Laurel's face was enough to tell her he had the edge of the blade too close to her flesh.

'Throw your keys on the floor.'

'What's this about?' She ignored his command. 'Is this some harsh store policy against women flirting with each other?'

She grinned at him, wanting to keep the tone light until he made a mistake. He would, they always did, but she didn't want to get Laurel killed in the process.

He pulled her closer to him. 'You're that serial killer they're looking for, the Reaper.'

'They informed shop security about me?'

I underestimated how desperate the Agency could get.

'My girlfriend's a cop,' he said. 'She got your details last night.'

'Are you looking for a promotion?'

She noticed the nerves creep out of him as he smirked at her. 'They all laugh at me for what I do, her and the bastards she works with. But this will show them, me catching a psycho serial killer on my own.'

'Are you going to kill my hostage first?' She bent down to retrieve the shopping bag.

'Wha-aat?' His stammer returned.

Astrid stuck her head inside the bag and pulled out the lace underwear she'd just bought. 'The woman you're holding; I was going to strangle her with these, but you go ahead. I don't mind watching once in a while.'

She blew him a kiss. It landed on his chin and made his legs buckle.

'She's not your partner?'

'Of course not, silly boy.' She pressed the button on the keys and opened the driver's door. 'I haven't got all day, so if you don't do it quickly, I'm going to have to love you and leave you.'

She turned her head from him, watching his reaction in the reflection of the window. All she needed was Laurel to play her part.

'Please don't kill me.' Laurel managed to sound like a traumatised teenage girl. It was enough for him to drop his guard for one split second. She pushed her back into his stomach with enough force to knock him back against the wall and ran to the car. 'Let's get out of here.' Laurel grabbed hold of the door.

'We can't leave him here like this.'

Astrid strode towards the security guard.

'What?' Laurel shouted.

'Our car will be on the security cameras when we came in. They'll have our registration and be able to track us from here. We have to silence him.'

He steadied himself against the wall and thrust the blade towards her face. She dodged his lunge and grabbed his wrist, twisting it to the side, so the bone snapped in one go.

'Aaaaaaa,' he screamed. Laurel sprinted towards them as he collapsed to the floor. Astrid bent down and picked up the knife.

'You've only got yourself to blame for this.'

She tightened her grip on the blade.

'You can't kill him,' Laurel yelled as she reached for Astrid's arm.

'What do you take me for?' Astrid shook her head. 'Maybe you *do* think I'm this Reaper?' She turned away from the groaning security guard and peered into Laurel's eyes.

'No, no, I was just worried...'

'I know what you were worried about: you thought I was going to kill this bloke.'

She reached down, grabbed his arm and pushed him into the wall.

'What will you do with him?'

Astrid kept him pressed against the concrete with one hand.

'We got lucky. There are no witnesses, but if we leave him, he'll go to the police, or at least cry into the arms of his unfortunate girlfriend.'

'So, what's the plan?'

The security guard started to sob as Astrid dragged him towards the car.

'We'll take him with us for now. We don't need long at George's, and then we can let him go.'

She opened the boot as she finished talking. Laurel didn't look too convinced.

'I... guess so.'

Astrid reached into the shopping bag and pulled out a brand new pair of knickers.

'What a lucky chap you are.' She gagged him with the underwear. 'If you make a sound, I'll slit your throat, do you understand?'

He nodded, and she dumped him into the boot. She slammed the lid and strode towards the driver's side. Laurel's wide eyes startled her.

'This is risky, Astrid.'

'That's what makes it exciting.' She climbed into the car, and Laurel slipped into the other side. 'I was looking forward to wearing those as well. I guess I'll have to go commando instead.'

She grinned at Laurel as she drove out of the shopping centre and returned to the main road.

'This is why many of us at the Agency admire you so much.'

'Is it because of my great taste in clothes and impressive driving skills, or the fact I can lock dopey-looking blokes into the boot of a car?'

She swerved past the vehicle in front and put her foot down. The man in the back rolled to one side and made a hefty thumping sound. Laurel laughed and shook her head at the same time.

'It's because of your strength in the most extreme situations.'

'You're too kind.'

They weren't far from their destination, coming off the

main road and heading to the house. Right on cue, Laurel asked the question.

'How many times have you been here?'

'About half a dozen visits.'

'How do we get in; do you have a key?'

She wondered what Laurel would look like in her new lace underwear, so didn't hear the question as she pulled the car into the first free spot.

'What?'

'Do you have a key?'

'You'll see when we get there,' Astrid said as they got out of the car.

Laurel peered across the road at the row of houses. 'Which one is it?'

'It's none of those. We're a couple of streets away. Did you complete your Agency training?'

'Of course.' Laurel sounded offended by the question. 'Why?'

'Have you had any active assignments?'

'You mean apart from this one?'

'Do you know how to recognise when people are watching a building?'

'Yes,' Laurel said, still annoyed.

'Great. I'm going to need you to check the front while I go around the back, okay?'

'What about our friend in the boot?'

'He'll be okay in there for one night. It might do him some good to stew for a while and think about not playing the hero again.'

'What's next for us?'

'Hold out your hand.' Astrid was amused at the confused look on her face as Laurel did as requested. She took her hand, enjoying the touch of Laurel's skin against her own, and removed a pen from her jacket and wrote on Laurel's palm. 'Here's the address. It's a couple of streets along here, right at the roundabout and then halfway down the road. Walk as casual as you can. Use those observational skills I know you have. There's a pub on the left; if you think everything is okay, meet me by the side of it in fifteen minutes.'

'And if everything isn't okay?'

'You're on your own.' She walked away in the opposite direction. Laurel scowled as she followed her orders. Astrid strode back to the car and opened the boot; the bloke peered at her through petrified eyes. 'Any noise from you, and I'll break your neck. Do you understand?' He nodded, and she shut the boot.

Astrid strode to the bottom of the road. She moved through the afternoon glamour of suburbia, passed the single mothers pulling their kids from the chocolate temptations decorating the shops, and glanced at the old men as they staggered in and out of the local pub. A few of the more energetic specimens of masculinity attempted to whistle at her, sounding like asthmatic steam trains rolling down their final broken tracks. She hated the suffocating constraints of the suburbs and all of their less than beautiful attractions, moving around the small dog attempting to copulate with a much larger version of its species and the middle-aged men who laughed at the canine pornography.

A few yards ahead, a wooden fence separated a large field. She climbed it before dropping onto the grass on the other side. The director's home was two hundred yards away as she ran past the empty cider bottles on the ground. Dogs barked in the distance behind her as she reached the building and peered over the fence. The garden was overgrown as if nobody had paid attention to it for months.

Weeds punctuated the gravel path, and an unkempt lawn greeted her feet as she climbed over, glancing for any sign of life.

The house was in darkness as she crept towards the window on the back door, eyes piercing the glass and finding nothing inside to concern her. She pressed against the glass for a minute, her ears tuned to the ambience inside the house, picking up no sounds at all: it was enough to convince her it was empty.

She ran back to the fence, placed her left hand on top of the damp wood and leapt over it with ease. It was a short jog back to the other end of the field and another jump into the car park at the back of the pub. The baying dogs and humans had disappeared, replaced by a hopeful Laurel Lee sitting on the wall and ignoring the leering loons inside the alehouse.

'Another couple of minutes, and I'd have been inside the pub and smashing glasses over their heads.' Weariness and irritation combined to make a heady cocktail in her voice.

'Did you miss me?'

A mischievous smile danced across Astrid's face and pirouetted towards the younger woman as the sound of somebody murdering *Dancing Queen* on the karaoke escaped from the pub. Laurel bounced off the wall with newfound energy.

'There's nothing suspicious outside the front of the house unless you count the three-eyed raven statues sitting in the neighbour's garden.'

'Great,' Astrid said. 'Are you good at climbing?'

She didn't wait for an answer, and was back over the fence in a flash. Laurel mumbled something under her breath before following her on to the path. She got over in time to see Astrid disappearing over the other side of a fence down the other end of the field.

'I hope you have a key?' Laurel scrambled into the back garden of the missing Director Cross.

'Will a code do?'

Astrid punched the six digits into the electronic keypad hiding inside the small black box on the wall. She kept invisible fingers crossed inside her head and hoped her friend hadn't changed the code. She let out a tiny sigh of relief at the sound of a small clicking noise before pushing the door open.

GETTING into his house was no problem. Jack Chill was the easiest of them to manipulate. Somebody who traded secrets to all and sundry had no qualms over who they took money from. There was no hesitation from him when I said we should meet in Budapest. I'd promised him a substantial fee, half upfront, for all the Agency's dirty little secrets. It was an offer too good for him to refuse.

We met near the citadel, the day after I'd followed her up the same path. The dark glasses and large hat I wore were perfect protectors from the sun, as well as keeping my features away from prying eyes. The oppressive heat had tracked me to Budapest, forcing natives and tourists to seek shelter wherever they could. Hundreds of people flocked towards the calm waters of the Gellért Thermal Baths as I trudged upwards, wishing I could join them.

The two hundred and thirty-five metre walk took me past the peoples of the world as tribes of tourists went by me in all directions, my gaze and strength focused on getting my body up the hill in one piece and to my rendezvous on time.

A crowd gathered around the Liberty Statue, taking selfies and spending more time staring at their electronic devices than observing the beauty and history surrounding them. I moved past them, taking a brief second to look at the monument to those who fought the Nazis and resisted the Soviet occupation. Just around the corner was where I needed to be.

There was a stall selling souvenirs on the right, and to the left, some ambitious entrepreneur had set up a mini archery stand. Chill leant against the citadel wall. He didn't recognise me as I approached, but he saw the hat I wore, adorned with a small badge of a monkey's grinning face, which was the symbol to let him know I was his rendezvous. No words passed between us as I handed him the electronic code with the account details containing the rest of his payment: money he'd never be able to spend. He spent a minute checking the information on his phone before handing me the data stick with the Agency's hidden files.

I slipped the stick into my pocket as he left in the opposite direction, descending into the heart of Budapest. He'd forgotten about me as I waited thirty seconds before following him, moving down the hill towards the Elizabeth Bridge and through the Garden of Philosophy.

He was just ahead of me as I contemplated what I was about to do to Jack Chill.

21 GEORGE

The cold inside the house sent a shiver down Astrid's spine, making her back arch and fingers clench. It also triggered her first memory of the man who should be living there. It was six months of training and frustration before she got her first taste of an active investigation; and her first sight of Director Cross. Something important was happening across London, and the heads of the other intelligence agencies had made their way to the clandestine organisation hidden from the public.

'Is this a COBRA meeting?' she'd asked Agent Storm.

'COBRA is what the public see,' he replied. 'This is CHAMELEON.'

The Agency was a hive of activity; people with gloomy faces and dread in their eyes scurried everywhere. The only expression of calm in a sea of worry belonged to Director Cross. He was a handsome man who could have spent his days lounging around on fashion shoots in the world's most stylish cities, with his warm blue eyes, chiselled cheekbones and distinctive short grey hair. As he ushered his colleagues into a windowless room, she stared at him, and he gave her a smile which warmed her heart. She couldn't understand why she was like that. Up to that day, she'd thought about running away again, fleeing another situation which constrained her. It was that brief expression of emotion from Cross which convinced her to hang around a little longer, to let the Agency provide some direction in her life.

It was another three months before he spoke to her, a cheery 'good morning' as they passed in the hall. By the end of her first year, she was sitting in his office, waiting for her initial appraisal. She'd expected it to be delivered by Joe Storm and was surprised to see the director walk into the room. Their friendship had grown from that moment. Grown enough for him to convince her that life in the Agency would eventually destroy her.

'Once you accept the Agency's invitation, you're there for life,' she told him. Astrid knew of agents who had tried to leave; they got their way, but not how they wanted. They didn't return to a life of freedom, but were spirited away and never seen again to keep the Agency's dirty secrets from an unsuspecting public. That's why George initiated her disappearance from the Agency, until it had all gone wrong for both of them.

Astrid remembered his sweet smile as she flung the door open and marched into his home. Her hand stretched out to turn the light on as she stepped over the pile of unread mail scattered on the floor. Laurel kicked the paper on the ground to one side as she closed the door.

'How long since you were here?'

Astrid continued into the house, decorated with floral prints and brilliant blue paint on the walls. The place smelt clean and fresh, with a hint of his aftershave lingering in the air. But it was only her imagination recalling her last visit to the house, her face pressed against his as they said their goodbyes.

'A year ago, not long before I started my Vacation.'

Apart from a thin sliver of dust across everything, nothing had changed in the room: a medium-sized TV in the corner; table by the side of the wall adorned with plastic roses; small pieces of jewellery; and two porcelain ornaments of a mother and child. Grey carpet covered the floor, with a three-seater sofa accompanied by two single-seaters in the same patterned style of reproduction Art Nouveau. The walls were white and bare, reminiscent of a doctor's surgery. Against the far wall was a large bookcase stuffed with volumes of all shapes and sizes.

Laurel slumped into one of the single chairs as Astrid sprinted up the stairs.

'What are you doing up there?'

She did a quick sweep of the upstairs, checked everything was safe and clear, before heading down carrying a laptop.

'Laurel, can you check the kitchen to see if there's anything edible in there? And put the kettle on while you're at it.'

It was more of a gentle request than a command. Laurel did as instructed while Astrid slumped into the sofa and opened the laptop. She crossed her fingers and hoped it was charged since she hadn't been able to find the cable for it, sighing with relief when it sprang to life. She punched the password into the screen as Laurel returned, holding a couple of dusty tins of chilli beans and a packet of posh-looking rice.

'These are out of date by a week, but it was the best I could find, unless you want some indiscriminate green fruit.'

'Beggars can't be choosers.'

'If you hack into the Agency system with that, they'll track us here. They've improved their search and destroy technology since you took your Vacation.'

The worry in Laurel's voice drowned out the sounds of hunger in Astrid's stomach; neither of them had eaten since they'd left Delaney's.

'Eventually, they would, yes. But I don't need to get into the Agency files. There's a perfectly good database on this computer; it's just a tiny bit out of date. You're not on it, for example.'

The grin transformed into a smile wide enough to catch flies. Astonishment consumed Laurel's face.

'What?' Laurel said. Having a copy of the Agency database outside the building was a treasonable offence.

'One of the first lessons George taught me was never to trust anybody you worked with or for, especially in our line of employment.'

She indicated Laurel should sit next to her. It was so she could show her what was on the screen, but she also had a sudden craving to squeeze her hips next to the other woman. Being in dangerous situations had always played havoc with her libido, and the current perilous state had thrown it into overdrive.

Laurel sat down, clutching on to the two tins of out-of-date chilli beans as if they were comfort blankets. The rice was lying in the middle of the floor where she'd dropped it at the news of Director Cross's illegal and unprofessional activity.

'Is this why he never returned to work because they found out what he was doing?'

'I don't know what happened to George; and I will find out, but I don't think it was because he was collecting information he shouldn't have. If it were the case, they would've found this place and what he has here.'

Laurel stared at the screen. 'How old is the database?'

Astrid scanned the details. 'It's at least a year out of date. He must have prepared this not long after I left; I'm not on it.'

Laurel grasped the significance of that: everybody who'd ever worked for the Agency - current staff, deceased agents, those on Vacation, and all those who'd left in some ignominious way, including imprisonment - were on the Agency database.

'He was going to use this to replace the existing one so you could disappear forever?' Laurel's eyes were as wide as Astrid's grin.

'That was the plan.'

'But people would remember you.' She sounded as if she didn't believe they'd get away with it.

'Of course, they would. But if I weren't officially in the database, they'd assume I'd moved on to another pseudonym, another identity. And if they were brave enough to ask at the highest level, George would say it was need to know only.'

She relaxed into the sofa as the laptop warmed her legs. Laurel dropped both tins of meat into her lap, only aggravating Astrid's hunger for something more than food.

'Why would he do this for you? Risk everything he had, that he'd built over the years, for somebody who worked for him?'

Astrid's mouth quivered for a fraction of a second, highlighting the vulnerability inside her. It was a liability she perceived as weakness, something she'd erased as soon as she'd left home. At least, she'd thought she had. It pained and warmed her at the same time. Fearful it would cost her everything, she was also glad of the new pleasurable sensations it had given her: first with Olivia, and now with Laurel. To feel protective of somebody else, like she did with her niece, or to know that somebody was concerned for her generated a type of happiness she'd rarely experienced before. Before now, George had been the only person she'd cared about. She thought long and hard before answering the question, hesitant to open herself up to anybody.

'Because I was like the child he'd always wanted but could never have. For me, he was the parent I'd dreamt of since I was a kid while my biological father hurt me and my mother laughed.'

And my sister conspired against me, smiling all the time she did.

Wherever George Cross was, she was determined to find him.

Laurel took the laptop from where it sat on Astrid's legs and placed it on the floor next to the tins. Then she took Astrid into her arms, and they held on to each other into the night.

In life, Jack Chill had a ready smile, knowing eyes and the convincing charm of a duplicitous man. In death, he was alabaster white, lips turned from pink to blue like the colour of leaves springing from summer to autumn. His eyes glared at me through the frosted plastic; his last gasps clutched the inside of the bag. They were desperate eyes, ones I recognised from a thousand broken mirrors, a thousand broken dreams.

I leant in closer than I intended, hoping to see phantom words scratched on the inside of the material which had ended him. But all I saw was the last of his spittle stuck to the sides, and of course, it was me who'd killed him, not the unmoving plastic.

An overwhelming sense of despair infected me, and I didn't know why. My body lacked control, and I hated it, not being in charge of my emotions; not controlling who I was. I removed the bag from his head and laid it on the dirty wooden floor of the house he'd rented. He'd been shocked to see me at the door, not realising the danger to him until it was too late and the metal was pressing against his skin. A frigid kiss from my hand touched one of his cheeks while the gun's silver ice caressed the other one.

Pearl-shaped tears rolled out of his wide luminous eyes, his mouth babbling something unintelligible as I forced him to turn from me. I so much wanted him to gaze into my eyes as I throttled him, but I wouldn't be able to catch the full glory of the life slipping from him through the plastic bag. Plus, I wasn't confident that he wouldn't grab me or clutch at his throat if he was facing me.

So I stuck to the method which had worked so well up to then, pushing him down onto the floor, pulling the trigger back on the gun when he plucked courage from somewhere and tried to protest. My knee forced him down while I dropped the bag over his head and pulled back until he stared at the ceiling. I'd perfected the technique, and his thin frame was no deterrent to what I did. I guess they hadn't fed him too well while he'd been inside a cell.

He clutched at the wall, drawing blood from his broken fingernails and cracked skin. The muscles in my arms and legs were tense, forcing his life into mine as his last flailing struggles dissipated into the ether. When it was over, a gloom overcame me, and I didn't know why. Sadness slipped through my veins, and it discomforted me. It certainly wasn't for him, but it left me confused.

I stretched out my feet until they were only inches from his head, my thoughts returning to the others. They were cold, so cold. The life which had dwelt within them had disappeared, and they'd gone from the challenges of this world. No more love for them, and I knew how that felt. But there's still one who loves me, who is dedicated to me.

And then I understood where my despair had come from. Death wasn't kind, and neither was I. I wasn't feeling the pain because of what I'd done, the people I'd killed; I experienced it because the body next to me was the last of it. It wasn't death I'd planned for her; she had to suffer a lot more than that. But I'd grown accustomed to the pleasure murder had given me, and my heart sobbed at the thought of never feeling that way again.

But it didn't have to be like that. I stared into the sleeping eyes of Jack Chill as I lay next to him and dreamt of my eternal sleep.

———————————

ASTRID AWOKE in the most comfortable bed she'd ever slept in, not that either of them had got much sleep. Her body ached and every inch of her tingled with Laurel's delicate touches. The bed was empty, but Laurel's contours were still there, embedded in the sheets like a fabric spirit which had entered into her life, and then flitted away into the atmosphere.

She panicked for a second, her heart gripped by invisible fingers while a voice whispered terrible things into her ears. Sounds drifted in from the other room, the noise of water bouncing off the shower and a voice singing a mournful lullaby.

'Sing me to sleep,' Laurel sang as Astrid crept towards the shower, still naked apart from the multitude of thoughts sprinting inside her head and the palpitations pounding in her chest.

'It's a tight squeeze, but I think I can fit in,' Astrid said from the other side of the steamed glass.

She stepped inside; their bodies pressed against each other again. Unlike the first time in the lift back in the Agency, there was no resistance from Agent Laurel Lee, just blissful consenting acquiescence.

Astrid shampooed the younger woman's hair. Her fingers created a gentle foaming caress through Laurel's locks, and then moved down to her neck. Her delicate touch moved across Laurel's breasts, over that flat stomach and down until she found expectation and desire combined into one. They pushed up against the glass, letting the water wash over their skin and the heat consume them.

Thirty minutes later, they were eating microwaved chilli beans and rice. Laurel clutched at the cross around her neck, and Astrid's curiosity got the better of her.

'Do you regret what happened?'

She told herself she wouldn't be disappointed if the answer was yes, but it was a lie. Those pesky new emotions were playing with her heart again.

'Quite the contrary; it was the best time of my life.'

Laurel held on to the cross as she shovelled a solidified block of rice into her mouth. Astrid noticed her eyes wandering around the room as if somebody on high had seen everything she'd done.

Laurel laughed with a smile which melted any last resistance Astrid had. The sex was great, there was no denying it, but the sensations coursing through her were worrying. Emotional attachments were things she avoided whenever and wherever possible; she had too many scars to want to get burnt again.

First, it was her niece, and now there was this. And she should be focusing on finding who'd framed her, what had happened to George and checking on Olivia's safety. She tore her eyes and mind from Laurel and went to find the laptop she'd left in the other room. Laurel's fragrance was still on her skin, and it was glorious; the touch of her fingers lingering across the nape of her neck. She loved the sensation, but it played havoc with her thoughts.

She turned to religion to clear her mind.

'Have you always been a believer?'

Laurel held on to the cross as she sat next to Astrid. 'My mother gave this to me. She had unwavering faith; I fluctuate between believing and not believing. It's the same with people.' There was melancholy in her face, seeping out through the small amount of shadow she'd applied around her eyes and the unusual vibrant pink lipstick Astrid only just noticed. 'Director Cross has a great choice of products in the bathroom cabinet. I wanted a change from Agency dullness.'

Laurel placed the top of her fingers on those succulent lips, distracting Astrid for a second from the digital screen she was peering at. Astrid's soft lips stretched into a smile which didn't quite reach her glowing eyes.

'It suits you. George would approve.' She stretched out her arm and took Laurel's hand in hers. 'Make sure you bring it with you on our road trip.' Laurel gripped back.

'Where are we going?'

On the screen were the seven names Astrid had filtered through the Agency database, the same female names she'd written on the piece of paper in the Delaney house.

'The furthest away is in the wilds of Scotland; the closest is about ninety minutes down the road in Portsmouth, so we'll start there.'

Her mind worked on that plan of action as Laurel leant in closer, her shoulder pressed against Astrid's arm, their heads separated by the smallest amount of space.

'Are these potential victims or suspects?'

'Could be both, could be neither, but we have to start somewhere.'

Laurel stared at the name and address of their next destination. 'Anne Dvorak; thirty years old and runs an upmarket art gallery in Portsmouth. That's not a bad cover identity to have.'

'Better than I ever had.'

'So, what did she do to offend you?'

Astrid closed the laptop and handed it to Laurel. 'We argued over the aesthetics of contemporary art versus Art Nouveau. I told her Mucha and Klimt had more artistic merit in their little fingers than anything produced in the last thirty years.'

She moved to the living room window, staring outside as her mind jumped back to her last meeting with 'Sophisticated Annie' Dvorak. They were working to find stolen paintings. Dvorak's expertise in that field was supposed to complement Astrid's considerable expertise in everything else.

'That doesn't sound too problematic.'

Laurel relaxed into the comfort of the sofa. Astrid continued to look through the window: something was wrong on the other side, but she couldn't work out what it was.

'It wasn't, until I whacked her over the head with a small recreation of a Damien Hirst shark.' Laurel was a picture of shock and amusement. Then she burst out laughing. 'The idea of me hitting a woman with a small plastic half-shark amuses you?'

'The image of it will never leave me.'

'I had a fierce temper then.'

She peered through the glass. Laurel switched on the TV and searched through the channels. Astrid tuned out the chattering heads on the screen, pressed her head against the glass and listened to find the noise from before; and there it was again, the low growl of dogs preparing to bark. Familiar sounds to her.

'Fuck!' Laurel dropped the computer onto the floor. Astrid didn't turn around.

'I know; it's the dogs from outside the pub.' She spotted them running across the road and towards the house, followed by their owners; the same men who'd ogled her earlier. 'We've got company.' If they weren't from the Agency, then they were brave local thugs.

'No, look at this.'

Laurel's high-pitched voice forced her to turn and stare at the screen. She recognised the scene at once: it was the outside of Frank Delaney's house, joined by many flashing police cars and an ambulance. Across the bottom of the screen ran a ticker tape of information which had one large headline:

THE REAPER STRIKES AGAIN.

Astrid was about to swear when there was a knock on the door, and a group of boisterous dogs barked against the wood.

After Frank, the plan neared completion, but I needed something else to clear my head. The disc I'd gotten from Chill provided me with the perfect recreational opportunity. Now I could let my creativity flow. And nobody would shed any tears for what I was about to do.

I waited outside as he left his hotel. He clutched a copy of today's paper under his arms, walking with the confidence of a man about to do something terrible, and nobody would do anything about it.

The bottle was cold to my lips, the beer not having time to touch the sides of my throat. I dropped the empty into the bin and stepped over the homeless woman in my way, her head bowed, arms outstretched in the hope of receiving a few coins. Change rattled in my pocket as I kept my focus on the target. It needed doing if the plan was to stay on schedule.

It was a thirty-minute walk, through the beaten paths no self-respecting tourist would dare to venture into. He headed deeper into the shadows, expecting their dark blanket to nurture and protect him. Other hunters lurked there, but they avoided him, recognising a kindred spirit as he passed. They did the same with me.

A delicious smile crept across my façade as a chill wind snapped at my bones. These were the same shadows I'd feared for most of my life, but now I fed off their penetrating gloom. He kept on going, beyond those who held no interest to him. They were always blonde, skinny and young; the younger, the better for his tastes; girls with vacant eyes and dreams of better lives in different worlds. As he strode past the ones who didn't meet his requirements, I peeked into their grim faces, spotting a desire to be invisible. I didn't have the time to tell them invisibility was worse than pain. At least with the pain, somebody acknowledged your existence; with the invisibility, it was the same as never being born.

The narrow streets smelt as if all human existence had passed through them. Sweat, blood and tears mixed in with decaying food and never-ending shit. A summer rain had splashed through the gaps in the city's veins, but still, the aroma lingered. Excitement rippled through my heart as we neared our destination, close to where concrete and stone met the river. I reached into my pocket for the tiny bottle, brushing against the plastic. There was a knife in the other one for emergencies. This was the first time I'd practise my future techniques. I was planning ahead, just like she did.

He let fly a bunch of expletives in front of me, frustrated at failing to find what he wanted and running out of room. There were only the two of us there, but he was unaware of me. The hair on the back of his head was straggly and unkempt from where he'd pulled his fingers through it. Before he could turn, I strode forward and kicked him in the back of the legs. He dropped to his knees, cursing as his bone cracked into the concrete. I put my foot into the square of his back and pushed him forward. This time, the crack was his chin hitting the ground before he rolled towards the edge of the river.

I left him to wallow in the dirt for a second, confident he wasn't going anywhere, and he was no danger to me. I made sure nobody else was with us, thinking again how fortunate it was there were no street cameras in this neglected part of the city. I grinned as I approached him, wanting to thank him for making this much easier than I thought it would be.

His head was in the ground, blood leaking from his skull and swimming down to join the river below him. I pressed my knee into his back, hearing his spine buckle as the smell of his piss cut through the air. I stared across the river and wondered if anybody on the other side was peering in my direction. Not that I was worried anybody would see my face; the scarf pulled up to my eyes and the flat cap on my head was an adequate cover. No, it was a new sensation which had recently possessed my waking thoughts and occasional dreams: of having somebody watching me as I ended the life of another human being. I guess it meant I was evolving.

I considered it some more as I tightened the plastic around his neck and over his head. I contemplated the future. He struggled for a couple of minutes, but I kept on pulling for at least five, his strength dissipating and transferring into me. I flipped him over and scrutinised his death mask. There was one last thing to do before I rolled the body into the river.

I took the phone from my pocket and clicked on the camera function.

THE TV SCREEN showed a mass of bodies outside Frank's home. Uniformed officers kept the media and the general public back, but there was no doubt the Reaper circus had descended upon the sleepy West Sussex town of Crawley.

The barking of the dogs jolted Astrid and Laurel from their reverie.

The loud knocking on the door forced Astrid to the window. She pushed the curtain to one side. Outside was one of the men from the pub, the taller of the two, dressed as if he was going to a football match in his tight sport's top and faded jeans. A dark, overgrown beard obscured most of his face.

'They've found us.' Astrid didn't remove her focus from their visitor.

Laurel continued to stare at the TV. 'What?'

'What do you want?' Astrid shouted through the glass. The man gripped on to the leash, holding the dog from the door, and moved towards the window. There was no attempt at pretence.

'The director wants to speak to you.'

His politeness and formality were the exact opposite of his outward appearance. She gazed beyond his craggy face, finding no one else but knowing they were there.

'I'll think about it.' She moved from the window and into the centre of the room, her mind switching to escape mode. Laurel focused on the screen. 'Any news on what happened to Frank?'

She didn't like the man, regardless of the fact he'd rescued them from the van, but she bore him no malice, annoyed he'd become another victim of whoever hated her so much.

'No, they keep repeating the same information about

another Reaper death. They haven't released his name yet. Who was at the door?'

'Davis is here with her merry band of acolytes; she wants to speak to us.'

Astrid let the information sink in and sprinted up the stairs to get a better view outside the house. There would be agents on all sides, preventing any chance of escape. She checked the front first: the bearded man with the dog had retreated beyond the wall, staring towards the house and whispering something under his breath. It wouldn't be long before he'd return, with more than the dog for company.

The street outside resembled the emptiness of deep space; only it was inhabited by stationary vehicles and exquisitely manicured gardens. For a brief second, she imagined the curtains twitching in the bedroom opposite, but dismissed it as nothing and went to check the back, heading towards the room George had said was hers anytime she was in the city. She'd glanced through it when they'd first arrived; now, she walked inside and peered out the window.

The landscape stretched beyond George's garden, over the fence and path they'd travelled to get there, and then what was left behind by the city planners. It was the embodiment of architectural boredom, the back ends of numerous housing estates merging into one amorphous urban beast, where a multitude of concrete, plastic and wood extensions had grown outwards like weeds of humanity hell-bent on destroying the beauty of nature.

There could be dozens of agents hiding there, waiting for them to get desperate and flee over the fence. She took one last look around, smiling at the pile of new books George had left for her at the side of the bed. She was wanting to pick one up, to keep it as a souvenir, when the banging on the front door returned, and there was no more time for stalling. She jogged down the stairs and headed for the entrance. Laurel got there before her, pulled the door open without hesitation, grimacing at the pallid blank face of her boss.

'How nice to see you, Agent Lee; we've all been worried about your safety. Can I come in?'

Years of smoking had made her voice sound like each syllable was crawling over sandpaper to get out of her mouth. Laurel glanced at Astrid for confirmation.

'Take a seat, Davis; let's get this over with.'

Astrid took the space at the end of the sofa while the director examined the room before settling for the seat opposite the woman she'd come to apprehend. She wasted no time in getting to the point.

'We found Frank Delaney's car not far from here.' Davis peered at her. 'With a confused man in the boot who said you'd kidnapped him.'

'Are you here to arrest us for that?'

Davis smirked and shook her head. 'Tell me, Snow, why the affection for George Cross? I've read your files, and apart from your sexual dalliances, you've never shown positive emotions for others; so why this?'

Director Davis held her arms aloft as if the room they sat in encompassed the whole of George Cross. A momentary pique of curiosity crawled across those blank features. Astrid recognised when someone wanted to mess with her head. She didn't mind; the feeling was mutual.

'You shouldn't take your work so personally, Davis; the mistakes you'll make will eat you up inside.'

'You weren't lovers, obviously.' Davis's smirk was out of place on her like an elephant in a china shop. 'Was he a long-lost relative? The father you never had? Or perhaps he had an affair with your old man? Your dad was a cop like

Cross, right? The two of them, maybe, fumbling outside of those tight blue uniforms while your mother was crying in the other room.' The smirk transformed into a grin, creating the first sparks of emotion her pale flesh must have experienced in a long time. 'Of course, your father was a strange one as well.' The director let those words linger while she searched for something in her pocket. 'Don't worry; it's not a gun.'

'It wouldn't do you any good, Davis.' Astrid clenched her fist.

'It must have been hard for him, watching his career and reputation vanish into thin air once you made your accusations.'

It was a crooked sneer aimed at Astrid, words scattered in her direction like bullets from an emotional shotgun. In contrast, she observed Laurel grip the sofa so hard, her fingers tore into the soft fabric. She shot Davis a blank expression, smiling on the inside and amused by the director's blatant attempts to unsettle her. They could have stormed the house with guns blazing, but hadn't.

'You know there's an alarm here connected to the local police station.'

She hadn't discovered where it was, but they didn't know that.

'Cross was always the paranoid type.' To Astrid's great surprise, Davis took an electronic cigarette from her pocket and started to suck on it like a kid with a lollipop. She continued to talk about Cross in the past tense; it was just another tactic intended to upset Astrid. 'George did like his secret life, but his feelings for you were a shock to us all.' The grin was now as vicious as a virus. 'You appear to be somebody difficult to like, never mind love.'

'What do you want?' It was a stalling tactic as she

considered how they'd get out of the place in one piece. She raised her eyebrows to Laurel and nodded towards the window. Davis shifted in her seat, the grin changing into a bitter, sarcastic smile.

'I want you to come back with me peacefully, and we can deposit you in your rightful spot.'

She crossed her legs as an expression of a job on the verge of completion, her plain dark slacks as conservative as her imagination.

'And what happens to Laurel?'

'Agent Lee will return to us as a hero, survivor of the serial killer known as the Reaper.'

The scenario was set in stone, scripted to scapegoat some poor unfortunate, while Astrid would rot away in some unseen underground imprisonment.

'You believe I'm a rogue agent who's been murdering people I didn't get along with? There'd be enough bodies to stretch to the moon if that was the case.'

Her gaze never left the director's stony face, aware Laurel had completed her surveillance of the outside of the house.

'We have the evidence, Snow. You would do the same in my place.'

Davis was good at sugar-coating untruths, but she didn't believe a single word.

'And what happens if I resist?'

She understood the drill: they'd launch tear gas through the windows, and then enter with a shoot first, ask questions later policy. Whoever was to be the Reaper's patsy was likely inside the large black van sitting outside the house. It was the answer she expected, but not what she received. There was a weary drag on the electronic cigarette before Davis replied.

'We have people at your sister's house. Your niece, Olivia, is a cute kid. Just imagine what she could grow up to be; or how traumatic it would be to see her parents murdered in front of her by the Reaper. I guess her grandfather, your father, would get custody of her.'

There was a minuscule amount of time as Astrid processed what Davis had said, her mind sprinting through memories of Olivia's smiling face. She didn't hesitate to jump forward, knocking the fake tobacco from the director's mouth and grabbing her by the throat. She pressed down on the windpipe with all her strength and grinned.

'Since you want me to be the Reaper so much, I'm happy to oblige.'

Somewhere inside Astrid's head, the dogs barked again.

24 COMPUTER LOVE

She pushed the other woman down on the sofa, so deep she thought they were sinking below red ocean waves. Davis was choking, unable to fight against Astrid's superior strength. Lights invaded Davis's eyes, the reflection of the anger flowing from Astrid's face.

Her head was a swirl of contrasting images: her niece with the broadest of smiles; her father with his diabolical smirk; George with his arms outstretched, offering her the emotional warmth she'd never had before; and Courtney grinning at her. A sudden and stinging delight swept through her bones as the life slipped from the woman she'd pressed against the couch. She'd forgotten how good this was.

Hands gripped Astrid's waist, pulling her backwards, a voice shouting at her, imploring her to stop. It was Laurel grabbing her once more, this time in desperation to save a life. They tumbled to one side, fell to the floor together, reminiscent of their shared passion not so long ago. Astrid gave in, staring towards the tiny lights George had placed around the edge of the ceiling, before returning to the anguished eyes of Laurel Lee.

'Are you okay, Astrid?'

Laurel looked as grave as a gothic churchyard, her voice solemn and quivering. Astrid wasn't, but she nodded anyway. Director Davis was prone on the sofa; no more strangled choking noises, only the sound of silence. Astrid had one concern now: making sure Olivia was safe. She needed Davis alive, but was seething about the threat to Olivia's safety.

'I'm fine, Laurel. Get me the laptop while I check if Davis is still breathing.'

She'd formulated a plan and was worried she'd killed the director; she needed her fit and healthy if they were to escape from the house. Laurel scrambled across the floor, grabbing the computer and hurrying back across the room.

'Is she alive?'

Astrid propped Davis against the chair, watching tiny breaths drifting from her mouth.

'She's fine, just winded.'

Astrid had her doubts as she noticed the shades of blue and purple forming on the director's neck, before snatching the laptop from Laurel. She connected to the internet, opened a tab for her secret email account, and one for a social media site she hadn't used in a decade. She needed the email message to do the trick, but the second option was an emergency measure. Laurel went to the director and checked her pulse as Astrid's fingers skimmed across the keyboard.

'What are you doing?'

She continued to type with furious speed. 'Making sure my niece is safe.'

'How will you do that?'

Astrid finished her task and searched for the software George had hidden on the machine, which would obliterate everything on the drive and leave it as blank as Davis's unconscious face. She found it and set its destructive operations in motion: predicted completion was thirty minutes away.

'We need to wake her up.' She pointed at the snoring Director Davis.

'Do you want me to throw a bucket of water over her?'

'No need.' She strode over and slapped Davis twice on the cheek, the second time harder than the first. That blow would have been enough to resurrect the dead, and Davis spluttered back into life. 'You lay a finger on my niece, and I'll kill you.'

Twenty-nine minutes before the computer was clean.

Davis grimaced, eyes narrowed with lips curled.

'I guess you're not as cold and emotional as you'd like to appear, Snow.' Blood crept over her bottom lip, and she coughed out the words. 'Strangulation appears to be your weapon of choice.'

Astrid ignored the taunts and concentrated on the computer screen.

Did the messages get through? And if they did, what would be the response?

Astrid picked bits of skin from under her nails and dropped them onto the floor.

'You're lucky I let you live.'

Davis wheezed through a damaged throat and brittle lungs. She didn't give up on the questions.

'Did you know about your father's disappearance?' Davis spat blood onto the floor, her eyes twitching as she spoke. She had Astrid's attention now and didn't let go. This was news to Astrid. Or it was misinformation. 'It happened at the same time as your sister's pregnancy. It's in the Agency files, but nobody cared, especially with your attitude.' Davis brought her arm up and brushed it across her face. 'The whispers said maybe you'd kidnapped him, payback for what you claimed he did to you when you were a child.'

'I can tell you're lying because your lips are moving, Davis.'

'I knew your father when he worked on the force, did you know that? He was a twenty-year veteran when I joined. Such a shame what happened to him.' She paused in her taunting, glaring at Astrid but getting nothing in return. 'Is that what this is all about, Astrid? Did those images you've suppressed all these years come back and trigger this killing spree of yours?' Davis grinned like the Cheshire Cat. Astrid's face was unmoving, a vast silence creeping behind her eyes. 'How dire and painful must those memories be which slip from the pale shadows of some dim corner of your mind?'

Davis was enjoying herself. Astrid was impassive, concentrating more on her present than her past. The news about Lawrence was curious, but she couldn't allow it to distract her from what she needed to do next.

'He means nothing to me.'

As long as he kept away from Olivia, but she couldn't trust Courtney to make sure of that.

'Why did you go to Frank Delaney's house and kill him? Did you hate his sister that much?'

Astrid was poker-faced while smiling on the inside: they didn't know Frank had planned the escape from the van, continuing to pursue their ridiculous theory she was on a rampage to kill as many agents as she could.

Twenty minutes to go.

She ignored the questions and slipped into the kitchen, touching Laurel on the shoulder as she went. Astrid returned with a large kitchen knife, striding back towards the director as the map inside her mind unfurled to reveal all the escape points.

'How much value do you place on your life, Davis? More than you do for an innocent child, I'd guess.'

Her eyes burnt volcanic red. Eighteen minutes to go.

'You want to march me out of here so you and the new girlfriend can disappear hand in hand.'

The disgust in Davis's voice was palpable; gone was the emotional blankness of before; now, the anger and bitterness seeped through her face.

'It's as good a plan as any.' Astrid nodded at Laurel as she spoke.

'And how far do you think you'll get?'

Davis wiped mucus from her nose before touching the expanding bruise below her chin.

'I'll get far enough to find the real killer. I may even go to your house in Knightsbridge or the flat you have in Camden.'

Fifteen minutes remaining.

The words spluttered out of Davis's mouth. 'How do you know about those?'

Astrid approached her with the knife at her side.

'You haven't done your research on me, have you?'

'You wouldn't dare harm my family.'

Astrid laughed in her face. 'I've sent all your details to some old friends of mine. Anything happens to Olivia or her parents, and you'll receive the same but a thousand times worse.'

The threat chilled the air in the room.

'You're lying.'

Ten minutes left.

'Hardly. And you're correct: the three of us are going to take a walk outside. Then I want your phone from whoever you handed it to before you came in here. Once I've checked to see who you have on this covert operation, I want all their communication devices and the keys to all their vehicles.'

She ran it through her mind again to make sure she hadn't forgotten anything.

'And if I don't comply?'

She pulled up the chair opposite Davis, sat in it and crossed her legs, placing the blade on top of her knee.

'You've studied my work, read through the files, correct?' Davis nodded. 'So, you know what I'm capable of. I shouldn't have to spell it out for you.'

'This won't work, Snow.'

'Let's go,' Astrid said to Laurel as she grabbed Davis by the arm and dragged her towards the door. She caressed the sharp steel against the director's flesh as they went, curious as to what would be waiting for them when they stepped outside.

Five minutes left.

THE LAST ONE WAS ENJOYABLE, but it was merely a distraction, something to soothe my new urges on the return home. I'd been away for three weeks and missed my comforts. And of course, there was my guest all alone in the basement.

I'd left enough food and water, plus access to an en suite bathroom; better facilities than most hotels I'd stayed in. Not as nice as the house I'd taken him from, but much better than my original plan. He would have been floating with the others if I hadn't changed my mind. It would be better if she had to watch him die.

I was surprised he let me into his house when I arrived; his natural caution, his unease at somebody turning up at his secret abode, withered away in a flash when I mentioned the magic words.

'Astrid Snow is in trouble.'

It wasn't a lie, and he recognised the truth in my voice. He couldn't get the door open quick enough to usher me inside. Before he could say anything, I had the syringe in his neck, pushing the ketamine deep into his bloodstream. The effects were immediate, his flesh relaxing as the chemical buzz swept through his body, his legs going weak as his mind slipped down into the abyss which was the K-hole.

I caught him by the arm as he dropped, moving him over to the sofa and laying him down as his eyes glazed over. I'd come prepared, taking out the zips to tie his hands and feet. Once I was confident he was safe and secure, I scoured the rest of the house. It only took an hour to place the cameras and listening devices in each room, then another five minutes to install the spyware on the laptop.

Then I sat as he hallucinated, rambling on about lost loves while I waited for the approaching darkness to spirit him out the house and into the car. Anyone who may have witnessed the kidnapping would assume he was drunk as I propped him in the back seat.

And now he'd been my unwilling guest for three months, a pregnant pause in his new life. He was sleeping when I returned. In the first month of his captivity, he'd kept up a daily exercise routine in his room. But for the last few weeks before I left, he'd given up and resigned himself to sleep and reading books. I slipped in and administered a sedative into his arm, ensuring no resistance while changing the sheets on the bed. He'd lost weight while existing under my strict regime, so it was easy to lift him and place him in the chair in the corner. I was beginning to understand how people felt when looking after an aged or infirm relative.

'Won't be long now,' I said to him as he slept. 'She's being led where I want her to be, but I'm still not sure what to do with you.'

There were a few options, none of them pleasant for him. I finished off in his room, leaving fresh food and water, and locked the door behind me.

25 ESCAPE

The dogs had stopped barking, leashed and panting at the feet of their owners. Astrid pushed Davis towards the chav with the hipster beard, his lips quivering in sympathy with the canine desperate to escape its confinement. A propitious sky, marbled with pearly white dashes, shimmered above her head. A flock of seagulls drifted by, glancing down at the scene unfolding below them. She was jealous of their effortless grace and ability to fly from danger.

Her plan was meticulous, depending on her former colleagues doing everything she was about to tell them; doing everything they should to keep their director alive.

'Whoever is second in command, get them now,' she barked at the chinless wonder.

She glared at him, recognising his reluctance, seeing new troubles dawning on his thickening mental horizon. He ignored her and stared at his director.

'Do as she says,' Davis said through shaking teeth.

As he hurried away, he let go of the leash and left the dog sitting there in confusion, unsure whether to follow its fake master or jump at the two new humans in front of it. Laurel solved its canine dilemma by striding forward to kneel and pat it on the head.

'Good boy,' she whispered into its ear.

Astrid furrowed her eyebrows at the sight before turning to the figure coming towards them. Even from a distance, she recognised who it was.

'How unpleasant it is to see you again, Agent Lincoln.'

'The feeling is mutual, Snow. Now let the director go.'

He mustered as much assertiveness as possible, but Astrid dismissed it out of hand.

'Or what?'

He had no reply and could only stare at the small trickle of blood congealing on Davis's skin. Laurel picked up the dog, worrying Astrid she might want to take the mutt with them during their great escape.

'Give me the director's phone,' Astrid demanded. Agent Lincoln hesitated, staring at his boss again. Davis nodded. Lincoln reached into his jacket and offered Astrid the device. She peered into his irritable eyes, seeing his dull mind working overtime as he handed it over. 'Now bring me all the keys to the vehicles you have for this operation and every agent's phone.'

She spoke as she held the device to Davis's face to get a retinal scan to unlock it. Then she scanned through the operational data. Lincoln didn't look for advice this time, speaking into his phone to fulfil her demand. In fewer than five minutes, a dozen agents trooped forward with keys and communicators in their hands. They were restricted to Agency issued mobiles while on duty, so what they brought to her were the only ones they had. They came from all directions, giving her a good idea of their positions. The map in her mind grew organically, but she still waited for the strategic escape points to appear. The sight of Laurel with her new animal friend bothered her, and she didn't know why.

The agents scrutinised her as Lincoln spoke. 'There's no way out, Snow. You're only making things harder for yourself.' He peered beyond her. 'And for Agent Lee.'

She ignored him. 'Get them to give their keys and phones to Lee.'

As they did so, she was thankful to see Laurel putting the dog on the ground. Astrid had always preferred cats to dogs.

Laurel held out the bag she'd brought from the house and collected the plastic and metal. 'Which car are we going to use?'

'None of them.'

Astrid took the bag from her and checked the keys and mobiles matched all the vehicles logged in for the operation the Agency had tagged as CROSSFIRE. As she sped through her choices, her eyes scanned every inch of the environment. Most of the residents were pensioners, people who'd ended up there for a quiet life. She'd met a few of them when George threw the occasional party.

'How long have you been watching George's house?' Astrid asked Davis as she dragged the director towards the end of the street and away from prying Agency eyes.

'Not long enough.'

Davis gasped as she moved. Astrid allowed herself a smile as she gazed down the next street at the few cars parked there.

'You know how to steal a car?' she said to Laurel while returning her focus to Agent Lincoln. He and the others stood in the middle of the street, trapped motionless like balloons stuck in a tree. A summer breeze drifted in, delivering the aroma of fresh bread from some nearby bakery. The smell only made Astrid's hunger worse. She never enjoyed working on an empty stomach. It made her think of the recent breakfast she'd had, of Frank Delaney standing there full of hate and desperation.

'I might do.'

She kept her back to Laurel, the blade still pressed up underneath Davis's chin, the older woman between her and the furrowed eyebrows of Agent Lincoln and Astrid's former colleagues.

'Take the silver Vauxhall on the right and bring it here.' Laurel didn't reply and ran towards the vehicle. Astrid checked the data on Davis's phone again. 'I'm surprised you haven't got helicopter surveillance for this soiree.'

It was another basic mistake which would have had competent agents cringing with embarrassment. She relaxed her arm against Davis's throat, allowing her captor to speak.

'Too much activity in the area would attract unwarranted attention, especially from the media.' The director's voice crackled with pain.

'Don't you get sick of wallowing in a world of secrets and lies?'

'Is that why you convinced Cross to break Agency rules and make you disappear?'

Astrid stared at her while the sweet smell of cakes and bread floated around them.

'How did you know about our plans?'

'We're the Agency, Snow. It's what we do.'

Astrid ignored the scorn in her voice and peered down the street to see Laurel. She brought the car up to them as Astrid switched to stare at the agents in the distance, making sure they were unmoving. She opened the Vauxhall's back door and shoved Davis onto the seat, moving next to her.

'You need to head out of the city as fast as possible.'

She emptied all the car keys onto the floor as the car sped down the road. A mile later and the bag of phones disappeared over a garden wall.

'Am I part of your villainous gang now?'

Davis spat the words into the air, summoning a vestige of courage missing since Astrid had grabbed her by the throat. Astrid swivelled her head to one side to make sure nobody was following them. They had five to ten minutes at best to put some distance between themselves and the inevitable pursuit. Then she returned her attention to their captive.

'Sure, if you can come up with a fancy name for the three of us.'

They were leaving Brighton in the distance as Laurel kept her foot on the edge of the speed limit.

'Did you kill Frank Delaney because of his sister?'

Davis was like a dog with a bone with her crackpot theory.

Astrid shook her head. 'Who do you think broke us out of the van?'

Her eyes narrowed with apprehension, happy but cautious to ensure they were the only vehicle on the road. 'I don't believe you.'

The words slithered out of Davis's mouth with a painful croak. Her throat was now a vibrant shade of purple, reminiscent of a sizeable leathery grape.

'It's true,' Laurel said from the front of the car.

Astrid peered deep into Davis's eyes and confirmed what she'd suspected after spending the first five minutes with the other woman: she didn't care about the truth; she just wanted to hurt Astrid.

'What have I done to make you hate me so much?'

The outside world whizzed by as she waited for an answer, her mind looking for the best spot for them to pull over and deal with the belligerent director. Davis shifted in the seat as the car slowed to a halt at a set of red lights.

'You're a murderer, Snow, and we catch murderers, even when they're one of our own.'

Astrid sighed at the futility of trying to get any sense out of her, deciding it was time to put her out of sight and mind. They approached an industrial part of the city, which was the perfect place to stop.

'Laurel, turn left and head for the alley beyond that derelict building.'

She did as instructed without question. Astrid leant forward to put her hands on Laurel's shoulders, resting them on the bright red silk scarf she wore. Tiny yellow stars dotted the material, which glittered in the gloom.

'Did you find this in one of George's cupboards?'

It was as dazzling and distinctive as he could be when he wasn't working.

'It was draped over a chair in the kitchen looking lost and lonely, so I liberated it for myself. I hope you don't mind?'

'Of course not; but I need it now.'

She slipped it from Laurel's neck with gentle precision, careful not to disturb her movements as she pulled the car into the shadows. As they stopped, Astrid tore the scarf in two.

Laurel grimaced. 'What are you doing?'

She ignored her and reached for the director.

'We don't have long, so I'll make this quick.'

SHE WAS RUTHLESS, but she was getting sloppy, and it warmed my heart. It was nearly twelve hours before she'd realised there were agents around the house; that would never have happened if she'd been thinking straight. I sat across the street from them all, well hidden in the bungalow I'd rented three months ago. Everything happening inside Cross's home played out on my laptop.

The sex infuriated me for more reasons than one. She should have concentrated on the plan, but she couldn't help herself. I could have turned away, but didn't, becoming more annoyed when it was impossible to see what was happening inside the shower. My frustration dissipated in the steam when I made a mental note to make her suffer even more.

But there was much to do before then, as long as she escaped from the house. It was a curious gambit by Davis, to go into the place on her own. Her agenda, whatever it was, had been a happy coincidence for me, helping my plans along in ways I didn't imagine possible. It was a shame what happened to Frank, but I didn't want to dwell on that. It was the one kill I didn't enjoy. I needed to feel the rush again to wipe him from my mind.

As soon as the three of them came out of the house, with the blade pressed hard against Davis's throat, it was apparent what she was going to do. I quickly formulated my response, leaving the house through the back door and slip-ping into my rented car. I drove down the street parallel to them as they completed their scenario. I waited at the bottom of the road as Agent Lee broke into the silver Vaux-hall. After that, it was a simple matter of keeping my distance as they left the town.

I thought they'd dump Davis at the first available opportunity, was surprised when they pulled into the industrial estate and the director fell out of the car and hit the concrete hard

I observed from a distance, hoping she'd snapped and was about to murder Davis with what appeared to be the prettiest of scarves.

She kicked Davis from the car, the director rolling through dirty water on the ground, scattering a murder of crows into the derelict factory ahead. Astrid followed her into the industrial wasteland, pulling on the scarf in her hands. They didn't have much time, so she had to get this done quickly.

Davis crawled through the dirt, scrambling as Astrid reached for her. She had one hand close to the director as a shout forced her to glance backwards. Laurel jumped out of the car, her arms shaking and face flushed. She stumbled towards the women, mumbling something Astrid couldn't hear. She was distracted as Laurel tripped over a piece of wood hidden underneath the pool of water she'd stepped in.

Laurel hit the ground with a thud and rolled towards Davis. Her shoulder smacked against the concrete, letting out a loud cracking sound. The cold water covered her face, the smell of industrial waste drifting in the air. She lay between Astrid and Davis, a human barrier of crocked flesh. It was all the director needed to grab the wood which had felled Laurel, push herself upwards and strike Astrid across both knees.

Astrid's legs gave way. An electric current shot through her knees, turning her bones to lead, before rushing through the rest of her. She peered at her reflection in the muddy water, observing the pain painted into her distorted face. She grabbed her knee as she tried to stand, finding Laurel next to her. The air around them was a stagnant engineering waste pool, with an aroma of festering grease and rotting chemicals.

Astrid grasped her legs while Davis sprinted away.

'Shit,' she shouted as Laurel stood and pulled Astrid with her. Davis disappeared into the shadows as if she'd never been there at all. They were the only things moving in the wasteland, surrounded by abandoned concrete structures and gloom hanging in the air.

'Do we look for her?' Laurel stretched down to examine her feet.

'No point,' Astrid replied. 'I was only going to gag her and dump her in the boot, but now she can run to wherever she wants. She did us a favour, but I could have done without the agony.' She was also embarrassed at how easily she'd been distracted and knocked to the ground. Her concern for Laurel when she'd fallen over had outweighed her desire to deal with Davis. 'We need to get back on track before they catch up with us.' A quick look at their surroundings confirmed they were in an isolated spot on the road to Worthing. 'There isn't anything residential here, so she won't find a phone anytime soon.' Astrid ignored her discomfort and focused on Laurel. 'Are you up to driving with your bad foot?'

Laurel brushed water from her face and flexed her leg.

'Yeah, it's only numb. I'm more annoyed by my stupidity. How are your legs?'

They dragged each other along and back to the car, feet swimming through substantial puddles and discarded nuts and bolts. Laurel returned to the driver's side while Astrid slipped in next to her.

'It's like a thousand tiny fists punching away inside both kneecaps.'

Laurel drove away, reaching the main road and searched for a sign pointing towards Portsmouth. 'I thought you were going to strangle Davis.'

Astrid rubbed at her damaged knees. 'Strangled like a victim of the Reaper, you mean?'

Laurel shook her head. 'No, not like that; I know you're not the Reaper. But after what Davis said about your niece, I saw the hate in your face. I guessed anything was possible then.'

Astrid dismissed Laurel's concerns and returned to the death of Delaney. 'Somebody followed us to Frank's house.'

She tried to stretch her legs as she spoke, little twinges of sharp pain sprinting through her knees, more so on the right, which had caught the majority of the blow.

'Not somebody; the Reaper,' Laurel said.

'Frank's murder means they're probably following us now.' She didn't bother to check, but Laurel gazed into the rearview mirror. 'They're too good to be spotted.' Astrid tried to massage the fire from her bruised knees. 'Let's see if we can put enough distance between them and us, but it's good to know they're there.'

'Why?'

Laurel focused on the road. The discomfort started to wane in Astrid's knees, her back sinking into the seat.

'Always keep your enemies nearby, and if they're close,

it'll be easier to find them when we get to Portsmouth.' She twisted her body in the car, struggling to get comfortable.

'And then?'

'I get her to confess to her crimes while you record it. We need to buy a cheap phone when we get there.'

'Buy a phone with what money?'

Astrid squeezed a hand into her trouser pocket and pulled out a shiny plastic credit card. 'George kept this for emergencies. There should be enough for what we need. It's not in his name, so the Agency won't be able to trace it.'

'You make it sound so simple.'

'I have many powers of persuasion.'

'What about your father?'

Astrid peered into the darkness outside the car. 'What about him?'

'Davis said he'd gone missing years ago. Maybe he's spent all this time planning this for revenge on you. You could've been wrong about it being a woman. All those things you said about who women would trust and the Reaper having to push the men down as they killed them could apply to an old man as well as a woman.'

Astrid's eyes shrank as she listened to what the younger agent said. 'You're comparing an old man to a woman?'

'That's not what I meant, and you know it.'

Astrid clicked her knee to ease the pressure. 'I suppose it's possible.'

If one person in the world truly hated her this much, it would be Lawrence.

'Are we still heading for Portsmouth?' Astrid nodded, painful thoughts flooding her mind. 'Does this mean the agent in Portsmouth, Anne Dvorak, is not our suspect?'

'We can't rule anything out, Laurel.'

'Of course. Plus, the Reaper might be more than one person.'

Astrid closed her eyes and recalled her time with Sophisticated Annie: a fierce intellect, permanently sarcastic, with anger fuelled by volcanic lava. She had the temperament for murder, and the history, but this type of vengeance appeared beyond her. Or perhaps it was all part of some murderous artistic project she was creating.

Annie was frustrated because her creativity was unfulfilled by the world. Initially, it was the rejection of her paintings, mocked by the art world she was desperate to be part of. Astrid tried her best to console her, reminding Annie her prime purpose in life was working for the Agency. Then Annie tried her hand at writing the great contemporary novel, which also ended up in disaster and a multitude of cruel rejections. So perhaps those rejections could have tipped her over the edge. Or the blow on the head with the mini shark had brought out all her evil proclivities. But it hadn't all been arguments and violent encounters with poorly made works of art. There'd been an attraction between them on their first meeting, staring at the *Astarte Syriaca* in Manchester Art Gallery before finding each other's eyes.

'Annie worked undercover for the Agency for a long time, so we'll have to be careful about how we approach her.'

Astrid's mind returned to the present as they continued along the A27, and Farlington Marshes passed them on the right; they were fewer than ten minutes from the city.

'You don't have a home address for her, just where she works?'

'That was all the information George had in his database.' Weariness seeped out of her in great waves, her voice struggling to keep pace with her brain.

'We better find a hotel then, get some rest for the morning.' Laurel stretched her hand away from the wheel and intertwined her fingers with Astrid's.

'Head towards Gunwharf Quays; the gallery is nearby, plus there are plenty of places where we can get a room for the night.'

Astrid had only visited Portsmouth a few times, but her mind hadn't forgotten how to get to Sophisticated Annie's art gallery. Laurel drove by the tourist sights, past the turnoff for the Mary Rose Museum, seeing the sign for an express hotel and heading towards it.

'How long before the Agency knows we're here?' Laurel pulled the car into the first free parking spot.

'They have little idea as to where we went, plus they'll be more focused on finding Davis before getting to us. We should have enough time for some sleep and what we need to do.'

Astrid wanted it to end here, to get it over and done with so she could return to Olivia and make sure she was safe. There was no doubt in her mind she'd find this Reaper and clear her name, but she needed to rest. As keen as she was to keep things moving, she was all too aware tiredness would lead to mistakes, and mistakes would get people killed.

It was early, but as Astrid got out of the car, lethargy leaked through her legs. It was more emotional than physical, as if the sun slipping from the sky had settled onto her shoulders, weighing her down to the point of discomfort.

Laurel put a hand on her arm. 'You need to sleep.'

She shrugged her off. 'You wait here, and I'll book a

double room for one. There's no need for them to know two of us are staying in case the Agency comes sniffing around.'

She stepped into the building and waited in reception. A news channel blared from the TV in the corner, and she stared at it as the camera focused on Frank Delaney's house. She dug her nails into her palm and pushed all thoughts of his death from her mind. It was a success, but all it led to was the image of Davis scampering inside that darkened alley.

It didn't take long before Davis crept from the dark corner concealing her from the kidnappers. She was nervous at first, cautious in case it was them coming back for her. As soon as Davis grasped it wasn't, she couldn't wait to scramble towards me. I must have appeared an unusual sight in the impending gloom, wearing dark glasses, a large hat and the floppy blonde wig I'd borrowed from Cross's wardrobe. But she didn't care or notice, grateful I wasn't one of her abductors.

'Can you take me to the city?'

The bruises on her throat were visible even in the dark, her voice more rasping than when she'd smoked twenty cigarettes a day. I moved closer to her, seeing the finger marks embedded in her flesh, smiling at the thought of her trying to strangle Davis. It was another indicator of how her mind was slipping from its usual precision, which was precisely what I'd wanted.

'What did you do to upset her?' I asked.

My right hand was clenched, not for a punch because it was possible I could break my hand on her face, but to lift my arm and catch her on the neck. But not yet; I wanted to hear her speak first. There was no rush to get to Portsmouth. The spyware on the laptop meant it was no secret where they were going, and they wouldn't be heading to the gallery before it opened in the morning. I knew how her mind worked better than she did; how could I not?

'What?'

Davis stumbled towards me, splashing through puddles and dirtying those nondescript shoes she always wore. She hadn't seen me in some time, but recognition stole out from behind her eyes, then something else: anxiety. She was in the grip of silent panic, face growing wild, pupils dilated large enough to fall out of her eyes, internal organs throbbing at a thousand beats a minute. The place stank of chemicals and petrol fumes, the alleyway darker than my past, surrounded by the sour relics of abandoned buildings. I put my hand onto the fresh pain on her neck and forced her to the floor, until she was kneeling at my feet in agonised supplication.

'There is misery in this country, desolation and gloom glued to the insides of all its citizens. It has seeped out of its industrial heritage in great waves, washing over the majority of the population to the point where most of them don't even realise they're drowning in mediocrity and despair.'

Davis stared at me as if I was mad, looking like she wanted to be back in that car with those that took her. The phone was in my hand as I snapped away at her.

'Who are you?'

'The misery is endemic and everywhere, transforming good people into bad, the hopeful into the desperate. The only respite from their pain is a flickering screen like this digital device which present the trivial and mundane as modern religion. Is it any wonder we believe the only way to fend off the unknown abyss is to find solace in someone else's pain, in someone else's death?'

I didn't expect her to answer or understand; I just needed a body to talk to. I brought my forearm down into her right cheek, knocking her to the floor, not quite unconscious as her lips dripped blood into the water.

There was damp in her eyes, but it wasn't from the splashes of the puddle, her face grasping the truth as I removed the plastic bag from my pocket, pulling it over her head and caressing the bruises on her neck. Her eyes grew larger as I squeezed the bag tighter. It was only as her orbs popped that she truly understood who I was.

ASTRID RUBBED the sleep from her eyes as excited birds chattered outside the window. It hadn't been the most comfortable of beds, but it had done the trick when they'd collapsed into it. The gallery didn't open until midday, giving them time to get refreshed.

'How come artistic types never get out of bed in the morning?' Laurel said without humour when she returned from getting breakfast.

Astrid stared into the phone Laurel had picked up during her early morning excursion outside the hotel. The first thing she did was access the hotel's free Wi-Fi service, checking the latest news, pleased to find no updates on the Reaper or their escapade in Brighton. The talking heads were more concerned with another Royal baby, and some celebrity's extra-marital activities caught on video and posted online.

She dropped the phone on the sofa bed under the window.

She needed the bathroom.

'I'll get a shower, and then we can have a wander around the Quays.'

Laurel emptied her bag onto the table against the back wall, moving the cups and tatty looking kettle to one side as she retrieved the fresh sandwiches. Astrid resisted the temptation to invite Laurel into the shower, having noticed tension from the younger woman during the night. She'd put it down to the stress of escaping from George's house and their interrupted excursion with Davis, plus the news of Frank Delaney's murder.

She'd fallen asleep as soon as they'd hit the bed, while Astrid had to go through her usual routine of clearing everything from her mind before she could get any rest. It was a process which took some time, during which it was amusing to hear Laurel snoring like a baby pig and watch her sink into a delicate dream state. Every once in a while, Laurel would mumble some incomprehensible words, all apart from one: Reaper. She'd stroked the younger woman's hair until she fell asleep.

The hot water covered her head and ran down her back, reinvigorating her senses as she examined the map in her mind. The Reaper had followed them from the Agency to Frank Delaney's house, that much was clear.

They must have been tracking me since the park.

It seemed likely considering they'd followed her during the trip to Europe and in Manchester. Astrid bent her neck so the water flowed down her head, grabbed her hair and covered it with shampoo. She'd forgotten how good it was to get a shower every day, to cleanse her body of unwanted thoughts and villainous memories. She thought again about who hated her so much, returning to the seven names from the list. What if she'd been wrong all along and it wasn't an individual woman tormenting her? What if it was some-body inside the Agency? It made more sense, with all the resources they had at their disposal. What if it was Lawrence? What if someone from the Agency was working with him? The thought sent a shudder down her spine. Davis said she knew him, so maybe other agents did as well.

She turned the shower off and shook the damp fog from her head. She wrapped a towel around her waist and draped another over her hair. As she stepped out of the bathroom, Laurel was putting the finishing touches on their morning meal, pouring cheap coffee next to two sandwiches long enough to feed a small family. Astrid snatched the bread from the table, biting it in half as the water slid down her chest. She expected Laurel to smile at the sight, but she devoured her food while looking miserable.

Astrid placed the sandwich on the table and dried the rest of her hair. She let the towel around her waist slip to the floor as Laurel licked her lips and grinned.

'We've got some time to kill before the gallery opens.'

They left twenty minutes later, striding past the recep-tionist with the patent leather face, and headed towards the DV8 art gallery Annie Dvorak had run for the past five years.

'That's a pretentious name for the place.'

Laurel stared at the website on the phone as they headed towards the sea. Noisy gulls hovered overhead as the finest retail stores, cafes, restaurants, and bars sailed past them on both sides.

'Be careful when you meet her. She's rather choleric and rises to insults quickly.'

'You won't be there?'

Astrid grinned, remembering how much of a rookie Laurel was when she was out from behind a desk. 'You'll need to have a word with Annie before she sees me; prepare her for the shock.'

She grabbed Laurel's hand as they made their way to the gallery, both sets of eyes dragged towards the giant stuffed animal coming in their direction. It wasn't every day somebody waddled towards her dressed as a humongous furry frog. The creature was a light shade of blue, no green anywhere, with eyes bigger than its head and a mouth which could have swallowed them in one go.

Laurel nodded in acceptance of Astrid's request. The tall frog marched past them as a group of school kids ran behind it, giggling and screaming in its wake. Astrid found a bench next to the clock and opposite the art gallery. She sat, staring at the kids as they disappeared into the distance. Olivia was never far from her mind. So much so, she'd started to create a second escape map inside her head, but this one was for her niece and her options to get her away from Courtney and, potentially, Astrid's father.

'I have a niece. That's who Davis threatened when I grabbed her.'

There was a longing in her voice which hadn't been there before. They held hands as if they were kids waiting for their first day at school, staring at the unassuming entrance to the art gallery, with its plain white curtains draped against the inside of the window and an ordinary-looking door. If there hadn't been an intricately designed business logo sitting above the front, she would have believed it was another run-down residential property.

'You love her.' Laurel gripped her hand as the clock ticked closer to twelve. 'She loved you.'

'Who loved me?' There were another five minutes before the gallery opened.

'Annie Dvorak.'

'I didn't know what love was.'

She stood, took in a large breath, and prepared for another reunion. Laurel got to her feet as well.

'And you do now?'

'Yes,' Astrid said as she strode forward. 'It's very much like hate.'

I scrutinised them from the other side of the quay. How funny it would have been to walk past them inside that frog suit, even though the outfit appeared uncomfortable. The sea air created an overpowering desire for ice cream and candy floss. A dense mix of sugar drifted over from the vendor behind me. The sweet fragrance brought a memory of fresh blood, threading ecstasy through my body and reminding my fingers of when I pulled plastic tight against cold skin. I dipped my hand into my pocket, clutching at the desire hiding there. What had started as a redemption journey had transformed into one of discovery, unfurling the creative artistry living inside me.

IT HAD GONE TWELVE, and the art gallery hadn't opened. Nobody else but Astrid and Laurel approached the building. An artistic vacuum surrounded them as Astrid pushed her face against the window, its coldness providing a welcome relief from the midday sun frying the back of her head. There was nothing inside but the outline of a man lying on the floor. His face was obscured by a bright red cloth, while a large sheath of dark metal split his body down the middle, spilling shrivelled organs out of his manicured suit and all over the floor.

'I hate modern art,' Astrid said as the clock struck fifteen minutes past the hour.

She strode from the entrance, down the side of the long, narrow building and around the corner towards the back of the DV8 art gallery.

Laurel hurried behind her. 'Will we restrain her first?'

'If you want to and you like that kind of foreplay.' Astrid's face was unmoving apart from the tiny glint of humour trickling from the corners of her lips. Laurel's eyebrows curved upwards in surprise. 'She's not our target.'

The rear of the retail area was bereft of any other sign of humanity. A black cat scampered across their path, prompting Laurel to reach for the cross around her neck.

'What is she, then?'

'I hoped she'd be the bait.'

Astrid jogged forward, with Laurel keeping pace by her side.

'Bait for what?'

Astrid kicked some empty beer cans to one side, regret creeping inside her.

'For whoever is following us; the one you like to call the Reaper.' As they approached the back of the art gallery, Astrid's heart sank. 'This isn't a good sign.'

They stepped over a surprising amount of trash at the back of the property.

'You think Annie's hiding or has left because she knew we were coming?'

'No, but somebody got here before us.'

Astrid grabbed the broken lock hanging from the handle of the door. She swore at herself for being so lax; if they hadn't rested, or if she hadn't been distracted by her desire for Laurel, they could have gotten there earlier and prevented this. They slipped inside through the open door. Laurel stepped into the storage room at the rear of the gallery as Astrid barged ahead, pushing boxes to one side and making for the front room.

'Shouldn't we wait?'

'If this Reaper wanted to kill me, they could've done it numerous times over; this is about more than murder. They wanted to do something here...' her voice trailed off at what greeted them.

IT WAS EASIER to get the two of them inside the gallery than I expected, helped by the emptiness waiting for me when I arrived there early in the morning. The lock on the door was no obstacle, the metal snapping like a neck in the hangman's noose. It was a good job I had Dvorak's home address from the data I got from Jack Chill. Getting into her house was child's play, for who would suspect somebody like me of nefarious intentions? The gun helped as well, although I had to be inside the door first before showing it to her. She didn't protest when I injected her with the sedative, which was a shame because it would have been a treat to beat her around the face a bit. I was missing the excitement of murder. He was out cold in the boot. All I had to do was drive up to the back of the gallery.

THE COMFORT of the storage room, with its numerous stacked boxes and random pieces of artwork dotted against the walls, was replaced with a scene lifted straight from a Hollywood thriller: two bodies standing on tiptoes atop chairs, ropes around their necks and tied to the beams above them. The plastic bags over their heads obscured their features enough for Astrid to be unable to recognise them, but she guessed the woman was Annie Dvorak.

'Shit!'

Laurel moved forward to steady the trembling legs of the woman: if the chair moved, she'd snap her neck.

'Stop.' Astrid grabbed Laurel by the shoulder. 'Look at the ground.'

Wires and ropes crisscrossed the floor, intricate knots and connections running over everything, up the chairs and hanging bodies. They looped and spiralled above their heads along the rafters: coiled snakes of imminent death if Astrid and Laurel put a foot wrong. Not their deaths, but those of the two trussed figures in front of them. The woman was Sophisticated Annie. Astrid recognised Annie behind the plastic bag which was moving in and out as she struggled to breathe. She ignored the advice she'd given Laurel, stepping as carefully as she could between the cables to get a better look at the other hostage.

Laurel checked the rest of the room. 'It's clear.'

Astrid focused on the floor. She probed for any trap which might set the chairs to fall and the ropes to fly to the ceiling, killing the hostages before help could reach them. There was no free space left to move in. She stepped as close as she could to the wires, staring at Annie's agonised face, features contorted to resemble a reflection cast from a circus mirror. Then she peered at the other hostage and her insides turned to ice.

'George?' The word tumbled out of her mouth, lips trembling with shock.

'You can save one of us, Astrid; only one.'

There was no panic in his voice, his body unwavering on the chair even though the tips of his favourite hand-stitched shoes were just about touching the furniture and keeping him alive.

'What?' Astrid's heart pounded against her ribcage.

'Can't we grab one of them each?'

Laurel had managed to get close to Astrid's side without standing on any obstacles littering the ground. The low noise of the ticking coming from behind the hanging couple startled them both: it was the sound of numbers clicking over, the unmistakable echo of a countdown.

'There's a bomb under the window.'

Astrid pointed through the gap separating George and Annie towards two objects sitting on top of a cupboard. The clock ticked down from a hundred, with a large knife resting against it.

'Time enough to cut one of us down,' George said.

'Shit!'

Panic seeped out of Laurel, her eyes twitching in a frenzy, switching from the clock, to the bodies, and then to Astrid. Ten seconds had evaporated, and they hadn't moved.

'Save Annie,' George said.

The cogs inside Astrid's brain hadn't stopped moving since they'd entered the room. George pleaded with her again to save Annie, but she wasn't going to let anyone die. There was just over a minute left. Astrid ran around the threat on the floor, thrust the cupboard door open, and stared at the explosives inside.

'Can you stop it?' Laurel asked in desperation.

'Not in the time we have left.'

There were four sticks of dynamite, forty per cent nitro, ready to shoot out at fourteen thousand feet per second. There was enough to blow a hole in the wall and destroy everything in front of it. That included George and Annie, plus Astrid and Laurel if they didn't get out of the way.

There were fifty seconds before it went boom.

'You have to choose one,' Laurel shouted.

'Follow me.' Astrid sprinted into the other room.

Laurel ran after her. 'You're just going to leave them there?'

Anger and disappointment sat heavy in her voice. Astrid ignored the question.

'We need to move this piece of metal into the other room, between them and the device.'

She grabbed one end of the artwork, the metal splitting the plastic man down the middle. It was a large chunk of lead, at least an inch thick, which was good for what they needed, but was going to be a pain to move in the time they had.

Forty seconds to go.

'It's too heavy,' Laurel said.

Then Astrid got the first bit of good luck she'd had in a long time. Whoever designed such an unusual art piece had the good sense to place the large, heavy centrepiece on wheels.

'Help me get this in front of the explosives.'

Laurel dragged one end while Astrid pushed the other, placing it equally distant from the cupboard and George and Annie. Astrid didn't want the force of the blast to send the metal flying into the two of them, hoping it would be strong enough for protection.

Thirty seconds left.

Astrid ran back into the other room, scooped up the plastic man, and then returned to Annie Dvorak's feet. She lifted Annie's legs, making sure her neck was supported, before plopping her back down, so she rested on top of the shoulders of the plastic man.

'Grab the knife, and then get in the other room,' she shouted to Laurel.

She reached over to George and grabbed hold of his legs for support. Dismay gripped Laurel's face.

Fifteen seconds left.

'Leave me, Astrid,' George said.

'You need to be in there in case something goes wrong, Laurel.'

The calmness in her voice must have convinced Laurel to follow the instructions as she lunged for the blade and snatched it away from the concealed dynamite.

Ten seconds left.

Laurel scampered into the other room, both hands over her ears. Her vision fixed on Astrid, their eyes glued together like magnets.

Then the whole room shook.

29 REVELATION

Astrid thought about George and the times they'd shared; of how she'd missed him. Until she was eighteen, she'd had no real experience of love or kindness. It was Ramon and his gang of criminals who'd provided her first sense of belonging. She'd romanticised the experience, drawing a soft focus on the violence and intimidation surrounding her life then. He was the bad boy who oozed a magnetism which no girl could resist. In reality, he was ten years older than her, skilled in manipulation and deceit, which blinded her to his true self.

Eventually, Astrid grasped she'd fallen into a traditional role of girl attracted to the boy until she appreciated she much preferred other girls. She was on the verge of leaving him and the criminal underworld's confines when she was arrested and ended up in handcuffs, sitting opposite Joe Storm. He was her superior, but it grew into something much more: colleagues; equals. Once Director Cross entered her working life, Astrid found it possible to look up to somebody who was a parental figure. Now she looked up to him in a different and terrible way.

The explosion knocked the memories from Astrid; her ears shook so much, she thought they'd fall off. Vibrations rippled through her body as the chair rocked from side to side, teetering on the brink of sending her over the edge and snapping George's neck. It was like a huge hand was pushing against every inch of her until it travelled through and out the other side.

She held on to him with all her strength as the blast smacked into the lead sheet with enough force to topple it over and towards the dangling torsos of Annie and George. Astrid twisted her shoulder to one side, stuck her hand out, and took the full brunt of the lead as it staggered towards them. Shock jumped inside her wrist, and agony sprang through her like an electric current.

Debris flew into the air, not quite a mushroom cloud, but enough to obscure anything around her. Astrid used her shoulder to shove the wheels one way, moving the lead sheet away. Her right arm dangled to the side, parallel to George's legs as she continued to cling to them for dear life. Through the haze, she saw the plastic man had achieved what she wanted: supporting Annie so there was no threat of her collapsing and the rope ripping the life from her.

She peered through the vapour at the large hole in the wall, waiting for her hearing to return. The noise had been a deep rolling crack like the voice of God in a furious apocalyptic mood. Laurel staggered forward, putting her hand on Astrid's shoulders as she surveyed the damage in the room. There was smoke everywhere and the smell of burning metal fused with concrete.

'I'm going to push George up, keeping his weight as high as possible. Can you climb onto the chair and cut through the restraints?' Astrid shouted.

Laurel didn't need to reply, pushing her legs on to the furniture and reaching up with the knife.

'I'm going to cut the bag away first,' Laurel said to George as she held the plastic with one hand and pierced the bag with the blade.

'You must be new,' he said as she threw the bag onto the floor.

She turned her attention to the thick rope around his neck. It was tough to slice through the material, but she concentrated on nothing else, freeing him from his death trap in a couple of minutes. Astrid lowered him to the ground, her wrist throbbing as if it was in a pan of boiling water. She wanted to hang on to him, to talk to him, but she turned to Annie to release her.

'Same procedure,' she said to Laurel as she sat George in the chair.

Another couple of minutes and they'd finished, helping the hostages into the main room and counting their blessings. It had been fewer than ten minutes since the explosion, but nobody from outside the building had come to find out what had happened; now, they had to get away as quickly as possible.

'Come on.'

Astrid pulled George to the door with her one good hand as Laurel and Annie followed. As they stumbled through the front and into the afternoon sun, she realised why nobody had rushed over to them. A huge steel band had taken over the whole of the quay, made up of dozens of musicians and their drums belting out tunes, surrounded by hundreds of people screaming and shouting. The noise was louder than the explosion they'd survived.

She was glad of the distraction. The pain in her wrist focused her mind as she searched for the instigator of all her problems. The Reaper had to be there somewhere, basking in the confusion and pain they'd caused.

AS THEY STUMBLED out of the art gallery, I thought she was going to look right through me. But a large man dressed in the colours of Jamaica stepped between us, banging the drum so hard I thought he'd damage his hands. Some of his compatriots joined him, smiling as they wiggled their hips and created the sounds of a euphoric calypso. It was the distraction I needed to move to the side and watch as the four of them faltered into the open. My mind was a combination of emotions: a heady cocktail of disappointment nobody had died, but also joy at the prospect of installing more pain into her.

The cameras I'd placed inside George and Annie's clothes still worked. They'd allow me the perfect opportunity to watch her ingenuity in action once again. She wouldn't die. I didn't want her to die; that wouldn't have been sufficient punishment for her.

Watching them struggle as the clock counted down was a bittersweet joy. Her psychological suffering gladdened my heart as I worried she wouldn't have enough time to do the right thing and save one of them, and herself. Bringing the lead wall from the art installation as protection was a stroke of genius. That incredible mind of hers had lost none of its spark. I was glad she was safe, but disappointed Dvorak or Cross hadn't been mutilated, anticipating Astrid's horror as she stared at the scarred body of her only friend or ex-lover. How disappointing that was.

I continued to watch from the safety of the shadows behind the steel band, seeing the four of them stagger towards their car. I ran through the video recordings again, flicking through them on my phone, making sure they hadn't gone upstairs in the short time they were there. The shock of finding Cross inside the gallery and dealing with the danger they were in didn't leave them enough time to discover the other surprise I'd placed upstairs.

The photos stared at me from the phone, Director Davis sitting on the table where I'd placed her. Plastic bag obscuring her haggard unmoving face, legs and arms crossed as I'd positioned them. Head pulled backwards, the end of the bag tied around the large lamp in the room as if she was a normal part of the furniture.

And her DNA was all over the body. No matter what Cross would tell the authorities, the evidence pointed towards Agent Astrid Snow. All that mattered now was the next step of the plan.

I turned the cameras back on as the car drove away, wondering how long it would take before Cross revealed who kidnapped him.

GEORGE AND ANNIE were recovering in the back seat. Astrid's wrist was so bad, she left the driving to Laurel.

'How's your hand?' Laurel asked her.

Astrid couldn't hide the pain etched on her face. 'I'll survive. We need to head back to London.'

Frustration was mixed with agony in her voice as she stared out the window to see their way blocked by a vast crowd of revellers. Adults and children dressed in gaudy coloured clothes wandered in front of them. More people garbed in giant animal costumes danced in the streets, dragging unsuspecting members of the public into their wild kingdom; a colossal mechanical spider teetered on its eight legs and crawled towards their unmoving car. The four of them caught their breath as the insect strode by them.

'Why go back to London?' Laurel said.

'We have to get these two to the Agency so they can tell Davis everything they know. You can take them in while I wait somewhere safe.'

It was hard for Astrid to move her wrist too much as she thrust her good hand into the glove compartment, searching for painkillers. Before she could start looking, a female voice behind provided an unexpected distraction.

'Davis is dead. That woman dragged her up the stairs at the gallery.'

It was the first time Annie Dvorak had spoken since they'd found her trussed up and hanging from the ceiling. The car moved, weaving its way through the excited crowd. Astrid's shoulders slumped at the news of Davis's death. She turned her head to look at the passengers, her mind racing ahead, neurones travelling faster than the car as it made it on to the main road and Laurel hit the accelerator.

'No point going back to the Agency, then. They'll lock us all up and throw away the keys.' She dredged a smile from deep within her heart, gave it to George and gently took hold of his hand. 'How are you feeling?'

The familiar sparkle was in his eyes, overshadowed by a combination of sadness and fear. 'I have to tell you who did this, Astrid.'

They were travelling on the A3, heading through Queen Elizabeth Country Park.

'There's no need.' She dropped her arm to the side, the discomfort growing the faster the car went. 'I already know who it is.' Laurel's hands nearly slipped from the wheel, her eyes torn from the road, fixed to Astrid's unmoving face. 'Think about it.'

'How do you know who the Reaper is?'

'Somebody who loves me so much, their feelings have transformed into hate.' There was no joy on her face as she spoke, just the utter disappointment with herself for not realising it sooner. But then again, it had been the perfect smokescreen.

Laurel kept the car moving forward while she waited for Astrid to continue. 'We've all been fooled right from the very start.' The sign to London whizzed by them. There were fewer than sixty miles to go. 'Who loved me the most? So much so, when that love disappeared, their life collapsed.'

Laurel shrugged. 'Your sister?'

'It was some woman I'd never seen before,' Sophisticated Annie said from the back of the car.

'It was Cara Delaney,' Astrid and George said in unison.

Silence engulfed the car, an oppressive vacuum hanging over them. Annie Dvorak stared at Astrid, her face weary and dotted with bits of ash from the explosion. After months of imprisonment, George seemed happy to be in the open again, even if it was inside a car. He held on to Astrid's arm and squeezed. Traffic had stopped, and Laurel's face was frozen at the moment. The car wasn't going anywhere, and with her hands riveted to the wheel, she spoke.

'You think Cara Delaney is the Reaper?'

Astrid's mind sprinted through all the times she'd spent with Cara, thinking about their life together and those things they hadn't shared with anyone but each other. Outside, it was a complete gridlock of metal cans designed to go somewhere, but stuck to the concrete. Red and blue flashing lights were behind them before being joined by a cacophony of sirens. Her arm hung down her side, numb to the point where she'd forgotten about the pain. The tension increased in the car, with sighs of relief when the emergency vehicles whizzed past. She squeezed at the discomfort in her wrist.

'You might as well turn the engine off, Laurel. We might be here for a while.'

Astrid rolled down the window as everything in front of them stopped. The cold air whistled between them, disturbing the silence, prompting Laurel to speak.

'Cara Delaney is dead.'

George didn't attempt to hide his anger. 'Then she must be a pretty solid ghost or have a twin sister.'

'Do we need to get you two to a hospital or doctor?'

Astrid peered into the back of the car, appearing to have no desire to expand upon the bombshell she'd dropped. George leant forward, putting his hand on her cheek as the tension coursed through her body.

'I think you're the one who needs medical attention.'

'I'm fine, George. I need to get a bandage around this and take some of the pressure off. And painkillers would help.'

'Cara Delaney is dead,' Laurel said again.

'No,' Astrid said. 'She fooled us from the start; a classic case of misdirection.'

I wanted to believe Cara was dead.

George's skin shivered as he relived his ordeal. 'I didn't recognise her at first when she came to my door. I was half-awake, expecting a delivery, and she wore a disguise. She mentioned your name, Astrid, and before I could react, she was inside the house, and I fell to the floor. Then I was locked in a room, forced to listen to her tirades against the rest of the world. The hate she has for you, Astrid. She kept me there for months.'

Astrid grimaced at the sadness in his voice, his normal assertive tone eaten away by his captivity until it was a thin, wispy imitation of what it used to be. His eyes had shrunk into their sockets, so it wasn't easy to see the vivid hazelnut shade of brown which lived there. She placed her hands on his, clasping his fingers, determined to bring his spark back, to reignite the vivacity she'd always known. She ignored the ache in her wrist, holding on to his hands until Laurel spoke again. Then she turned to face the woman driving the car.

'What about the body discovered in Berlin?'

The lights flashed ahead of them, but the sirens had stopped wailing. Annie Dvorak breathed heavily in the back, her gaze fixed on the younger woman.

'Cara was, is, the most resourceful person I've ever met. She'd suffer as much as she needed to complete her objectives.' Astrid rested her damaged wrist in her good hand. 'She must have planned this for a long time. It wouldn't have been hard to find somebody of similar weight, height and facial features. Then she snipped her doppelganger's fingers off and dumped them somewhere. While we all thought it was a serial killer collecting trophies, she used this to hide behind everyone believing she was dead.' There was admiration in Astrid's voice, regardless of how much pain it had cost her and those murdered agents. 'And Frank covered up anything out of the ordinary in the autopsy or from the coroner.'

She remembered how much Frank Delaney hated her and how he said he'd do anything for his sister.

'She killed her brother?' Pain lurked in Laurel's eyes.

'They had a complicated relationship.'

Astrid opened the door and stepped onto the side of the road. Up ahead, the traffic was jammed as far as she could see. Laurel got out the car, walking around to stand next to her.

'What aren't you telling me?'

Astrid stared beyond the flashing lights, wondering how many were dead or injured. These feelings of concern and empathy were both wondrous and crippling, but she didn't want them hampering her in the pursuit of Cara Delaney.

'Cara is damaged. I'm damaged. It's what drew us together.' The slight tremor in her lips betrayed the calmness in her voice. 'She was already broken when we met. I just created more pieces that she couldn't put back together.'

'Damaged, in what way?' Laurel said.

The drivers on the opposite side slowed down to gawp at the accident before accelerating towards Portsmouth. The sun was low in the sky, with vast shards of yellow shooting through the blue and white canvas, warming them both as they stared at the destruction ahead.

'I was twenty-three when we met. She was twenty-one. I was the first person to say "I love you" to her.'

Astrid stood at the roadside as the lights went by on the other side, her mind a jumble of sights and sounds of Cara Delaney: Cara's eternal sobbing when she told her it was over; her anguished face when Astrid ignored all the pleading. The memories were as if she gazed at an alternative version of herself which didn't exist anymore.

'You ended the relationship, I get that, but why would it create such bitterness in her?'

Astrid turned to Laurel and told her about Cara Delaney's early life.

'Cara grew up in a household where she believed she was invisible. She was a non-person to her parents and her brother. Mother and father showed her no emotions, took no interest in her life beyond food, clothes and shelter. Whether intentional or not, they denied her the one thing she desperately needed. All her life, she cried out for love, and then she thought she'd found it with me. It was different for me. My parents were violent and abusive; nothing but negative emotions.'

Sorrow, remorse, sadness and regret saturated Astrid's words. There was a stone in her heart, and she feared the weight would drag her into an inescapable abyss. 'When Cara unburdened herself to me, I was struck by the similarities between us. There were many differences, but the emotional wreckage was the same. I thought Cara's revelations would release my feelings from the crippling burden oppressing me, that they would produce a spark of empathy for the woman I wanted to love. But it was the opposite, forcing my memories back into the void at the centre of me and pushing Cara away. I knew I'd hate her for it if I didn't get away from her.'

'And that's why you ended it in Berlin?'

'I had to. Cara was starting to unravel, and I couldn't help her. It had taken me a long time to get control of my past, and I wouldn't let her problems resurrect mine; especially when she became obsessed with things beyond the reach of her memory.'

'What things?'

'She believed something terrible happened to her when she was a child. Cara didn't know if it was real or if it was a false memory. Either way, it messed up her head at a time when she needed love and support from those who didn't provide it. And that confusion never left her.'

'What about Cara's brother? What about Frank?' The vehicles started to move ahead of them, and they would have to get back into the car soon. 'Why would she kill him?'

'Like I said, it was a complicated relationship. In the Delaney household, both kids were ignored, bereft of love and any encouragement. Frank handled it better than Cara, six years difference between them in age. She blamed him for not looking after her, forgetting he was only a kid himself and that the adults in the house never took any responsibility themselves. I think she resented him all her life, while he loved her, but was incapable of showing it.'

'She was waiting for someone like you to come along and give her everything she'd wanted but never had.' Laurel laid her fingers on Astrid's right cheek.

'And then I took it from her again.' Astrid turned away and slipped into the car. Laurel got inside and switched on the engine as Annie and George sat silently in the back. 'We need to get you two safe.'

The pain receded in her wrist, allowing her to move it a little. She was wishing she had more time to get reacquainted with George when something caught her attention. A tiny light flickered on his shirt, a few inches below his neck, and there was something similar on Annie. She reached across to him, placed her fingers on the top button, and found the miniature camera hiding there. She pulled it away in one go, turned her head to the front of the car, and held the device up to the light. She peered straight into it, knowing Cara was at the other end.

'That's an Agency surveillance camera,' Laurel said.

'She's been spying on us the whole time.' Hidden fingers clawed at Astrid's gut as the car passed the debris of the accident. She stared at the device, hoping her piercing gaze would travel down the connection and smash Cara straight between the eyes. 'This is good for us. George can take these into the Agency and they'll be able to trace where she is, or perhaps retrieve some of what came through both cameras.'

Astrid clasped her fingers over the lens, obscuring anything Cara could see. She turned back to Annie, reached over and removed her camera. With both devices in her hand, she fixed on the windscreen. They were thirty miles from London, and the road was clear. She was about to drop the cameras into her pocket when they started vibrating inside her hand: sounds hummed from both of them.

'What's that music?' Laurel asked.

Astrid opened her fingers, recognising the song as soon as the noise hit her ears.

'It's *Suffragette City*.'

The colour drained from her face, the pain returned to her wrist, and her voice trembled as if she was about to collapse.

'The David Bowie song?' George said. 'What does it mean?'

Astrid had no doubt.

'I have to save Olivia.'

My first memory is from age five. My mother dragged me to the nursery, and then abandoned me there. No warning of what would happen, no idea she would be leaving me. All I remember from the rest of the day are cold stares and harsh words, the pain of being ignored joined by resentment and ridicule. It was an alien and inhospitable place, so like the home I'd lived in since birth, only now there were people my age around me.

Two years of blankness followed before the next recollection entered my brain, agony shooting through my seven-year-old leg when I knelt into the long grass growing at the back of our house. The broken glass cut through my knee like scissors dissecting paper. I screamed before help arrived in the shape of the old woman from next door. She kept a thousand cats in the house, creating an aroma of living death. She scooped me up in her fleshy arms, which were bigger than my whole body. Her smile was crooked, unbalanced to the point it was about to tumble off her face.

'Let's get you home,' she said with a mouth full of yellow teeth. She whispered something in my ear, I can never remember what it was, giving me a taste of her breath, which had a fragrance of week-old fish. I still feel her arms around me, squashing my bones, putting her hands where she shouldn't. Her smile grew wider the more she touched me. The scar on my knee is still there. And the other scars.

Things didn't improve after that, my teenage years spent in isolation, both inside and outside the family home. I was ostracised at school, with no friends and only enemies. It was a hostile environment which led me to abandon any attempt at education, skipping lessons so truanting became my specialist subject. Stealing became my new hobby. It started at home, taking coins from the pile my father dumped in his bedroom when he staggered home from the pub. I stole for attention, but he never noticed. Then it was stealing from my mother's purse. If she comprehended what I did, she didn't care.

That was my apprenticeship before moving towards the bigger shops in our insignificant town. It was too easy. My small frame and angelic face deceived all the shop assistants and retailers. How could someone so perfect do something so wrong? This was my secret life until the police caught me stealing cigarettes. Taking me to a dirty back room at the station, three of them tried to scare me into going straight. Then they took me home and dropped me off at the front door and my mother's stern look. The police nodded at a job well done. As soon as they left, she asked for her cigarettes.

I left home at sixteen. That's not strictly true; I was thrown out of the family home by my father because I went to a party when I was told to stay at home, his indifference towards me transforming into anger. It was the last time I saw him, and the only time I witnessed emotion of any kind from the man who called himself a parent.

The memories never went away, always present in my

mind. They all came back in a flash when she mentioned my name for the first time in years. Hands wrapped around my heart when she said it. There was no emotion in her voice, no anger or hate, but she had to feel something for me. You can't be that much in love, and then feel nothing after it's over. Not that it's ever been over for me. All I had to do was wait for her to come to me.

***

'DRIVE TO MILE END PARK in the East End of London,' Astrid shouted.

All she thought about was Olivia and her safety. She had to get there immediately, panic ripping her insides apart with the sound of the Bowie tune coming from Cara's secret cameras, knowing it could only mean one thing: the conclusion for Cara's revenge meant hurting Olivia. Anger replaced the panic, with thoughts of what she'd do to Cara when she got hold of her. The blood vibrated in Astrid's veins, her arms trembling as she tried to stay in control.

'She wants you upset,' Laurel said.

Astrid was aware of what Cara wanted; to see her angry and confused when she confronted her. She'd planned it to the finest detail to chip away at everything Astrid was good at. To take away her liberty, isolate her from all support; to weaken her physically and emotionally, make her a fugitive from justice, and force her to sacrifice one life to save another. Then, and only then, would Cara threaten her with the thing she cared about the most: Olivia.

'Cara might not like getting what she wants.'

'Would she kill a child?' Laurel asked.

Astrid couldn't answer the question with any certainty. Cara's time with Astrid had only buried her childhood pain, not erased it. Once Astrid broke her heart, it all resurfaced, apparently multiplied a thousandfold, sending her over the edge of sanity.

'She won't get the chance.'

Astrid's mind whirled. The invisible scars returned on her back as she felt the whip again.

And again.

'We need to prepare,' Laurel said as she stared at the protection on Astrid's damaged wrist. They'd dropped George and Annie close to an Agency safe house before picking up medical supplies from a pharmacy.

'I'm always prepared.' But she didn't feel like it.

'You need somebody to have a proper look at this.'

Laurel had packed Astrid's wrist as tightly as she could. They'd picked up a temporary plaster cast which was easy to apply. It gave her hand extra support.

'No time.' Astrid swallowed more painkillers. 'We need to get to the park.'

Her voice was high-pitched, her eyelids flickering at the same rate her lips trembled. Laurel slowed down as they came to a red light, the blazing neon a perfect symmetry to the frustration burning inside Astrid's eyes.

'Will she be there at this time of the day?'

Laurel appeared as calm as Astrid was panicked. Astrid placed her hands on the dashboard, letting the cold of the plastic seep into her body.

'You're right; it's too early for the nanny to have taken her to the park. We need to go somewhere else.'

'Should we go to your sister's place?'

Astrid shook her head and sat back in the seat. 'No; she won't be there, either.'

'Cara could be playing with you again.'

'Of course she's playing with me.'

She spat the words out, her anger reaching a crescendo, knowing it was precisely what Cara wanted. She closed her eyes and attempted to control her breathing, focusing on Olivia's face, telling herself how she'd sweep the child into her arms and tell Olivia who she was. She didn't care how much her sister would protest. She peered into her mind and found all of her escape maps torn to shreds.

'Where shall we go?'

'Olivia won't be at home. She should be at the nursery before the nanny goes to collect her.'

It was a strange term to use: collect her. Astrid smiled inwardly, realising she'd slipped back into her traditional impersonal mode, changing Olivia into a thing, not a person. She was a target to be acquired, not somebody who needed saving. She felt good about it. It meant she was in control again, not blinded by emotions. She would be no help to Olivia or anybody else if she couldn't separate her feelings from the job she had to do.

They were fifteen minutes from the nursery, some posh building Courtney had decided was a better place for her daughter to spend those critical early years instead of with her parents. She found it ironic her sister had learnt nothing from her childhood. It was a torturous drive there as Astrid struggled to rein in her emotions.

'She should be safe in the nursery,' Laurel said. 'All those places have added security now.'

'I sent people to watch over Olivia.' Suburban life trickled outside the window.

Laurel seemed surprised. 'How did you do that?'

Astrid moved the fingertips of her damaged hand, cringing at the pain. 'I did it at George's house after Davis appeared. I used the laptop to contact someone I worked with a long time ago.' She didn't elaborate on who it was.

'So, she should be safe.'

'She better be.'

'Who was it?' Laurel drove across a roundabout and past a bunch of shops.

'The leader of the gang,' Astrid said vaguely. It didn't take Laurel long to work out who she meant.

'Ramon, your ex? The leader of the gang the Agency recruited you from.' Astrid nodded, memories of their fractious relationship haunting her mind as the desperation of relying on him punched her hard in the gut. Ramon had blamed her for betraying him and the gang once she'd left prison and started her new life without them. 'How do you know your message got through?'

Outside the window, the adults and children moved in the opposite direction. The nursery had closed earlier than Astrid had expected. A sea of people came down the street in waves.

'I don't, which is why we need to get there now.'

The nervous alarm rang through Astrid's voice, all semblance of control vanishing once more. They were stuck at a crossing, watching children smiling and laughing as they moved from one side of the road to the other. It was another ten minutes before they got to the entrance of the nursery. She jumped from the car before Laurel could turn the engine off.

'Wait for me,' Laurel said.

'Olivia Snow?'

Astrid shouted at the teacher standing outside the entrance. Laurel wasn't far behind. Astrid's panic forced her to lunge at the woman. Laurel stepped between the two of them before Astrid could grab the teacher by the arms.

The teacher gazed into Astrid's bloodshot eyes. 'She left early today. The nanny brought Olivia a treat.'

'What type of treat?'

'It was a special surprise, a first-time visit from one of her relatives.'

She could only think of one person: her father. Lawrence, had taken Olivia away. An idea too terrible to contemplate crossed her mind as she thought of Cara and Lawrence working together to hurt her, and to hurt Olivia. Only the pain in her wrist stopped her legs from collapsing. Her voice shook like an ancient steam train crossing a wooden bridge.

'Was it her grandfather?'

'Oh, no.' Astrid relaxed with a massive sigh of relief. 'It was her aunt.'

The air froze around her. She held her breath, pulling her fingers so tightly into her palms, her skin started to bleed.

'Which aunt was it?'

'Why, it was Olivia's Aunt Astrid; such a polite woman. Do you know her?'

Astrid turned away before the question reached her, running as fast as she could, with the throbbing in her arm seeping into her whole body.

32 DOWN IN THE PARK

'We need to get to the park.'

Astrid sprinted to the car. Searing pain sped up her arm, jumping from her shoulder and straight between her eyes. Inside her head, it split into a thousand sharpened pieces and eviscerated the rescue map she'd devised for Olivia. Blood was in her mouth as she bit her tongue, the warm liquid dripping down her throat, but unable to fill the emptiness consuming her.

Laurel shouted something to Astrid as she threw the door open and jumped into the car. Fear surged through her as she strapped herself into the passenger seat, and Laurel got behind the wheel. Cara was one step ahead of them again.

'I'm sure she's fine,' Laurel said.

The traffic was as slow getting to the park as it had been to the nursery. Astrid gripped the seat all the way there, her fingers turning a dark shade of apple red as a journey which should have taken ten minutes ended up lasting thirty. It was an eternity for her. A million terrible permutations swam through her head as a multitude of kids ran around outside.

She stared hard at the children's faces; so intent was her gaze that each one of the kids transformed into the image of Olivia, real-life shimmering into Astrid's worst nightmare until dozens of duplicates of her niece ran on either side of the car. They tormented her with their wide mouths, expressive eyes and cheeky grins absorbed in laughter. She could take no more, closing her eyes in search of the comfort of the dark, but instead finding her internal gloom saturated with the vision of Cara Delaney placing a plastic bag over Olivia's head.

'This is my fault.'

Astrid whispered into the hands scratching at her face. She snapped out of her nightmare as Laurel pulled the car up to the entrance to the park. Astrid was unmoving, eyes glued to the topiary which greeted them.

Was it only a couple of weeks ago when I was here last?

It appeared like another lifetime and another world away. She held on to the pain in her wrist and focused her mind.

'You can't blame yourself for this, Astrid.'

But she did. 'Only one thing matters, and that's Olivia's safety.'

'Of course.'

They stepped from the vehicle and moved through the park. Astrid flexed her fingers as she walked, ignoring the throbbing in her hand, kicking at stray lumps of grass and petrifying a Chihuahua which got too close. They strode past the pack of dog walkers congregating at the entrance and beyond the pair of ice cream vans competing for the families enjoying the last haze of summer. They kept going along the path running parallel to the lake until the suffragette statues and the playground appeared. The sky was overcast with the promise of rain, dark clouds lingering above and scaring most of the visitors away, leaving the area short of people. Discarded branches crunched underfoot as they entered the playground.

'I thought you'd have been here sooner.'

She heard the voice before she saw Cara, sitting in the middle of the swings as if she'd returned to a childhood she never had. Astrid ignored her and scanned the rest of the area. Olivia was nowhere in sight.

'Where's my niece?'

'Don't worry, Astrid, she's safe. I brought some friends along to play with her.'

Astrid held her breath when Olivia stepped from the shadows behind Cara. But she wasn't alone. Holding on to her shoulders was someone she'd seen before in the same surroundings: the tattooed neo-Nazi she'd warned off so long ago. And he wasn't alone, joined by four figures she didn't recognise. They weren't the lumbering drug addicts from before.

On the right was a large man with an immense afro haircut obscuring the sun. His physique was impressive, like he couldn't find any clothes to fit him, his shirt ready to burst if he moved too soon. On the left were two bald blokes who must have been twins considering they had the same piercing blue eyes and sculpted cheekbones. Between their laughter, they insulted her in German. The last of the quartet was a heavy-set man with outlandish eyebrows, manicured and cultivated to the point they were extra appendages on his body, stretching up and out from his forehead like mandibles on a peculiar insect.

'Never underestimate the stupidity of the ignorant,' Astrid said to Laurel as she did as he commanded.

Cara stopped moving on the swings, watching as Astrid stepped towards Olivia. The kid seemed more confused than frightened. Astrid scanned the area, searching for the nanny, seeing a body on the ground behind the tattooed thug.

'She was just for practice.' He reached down to his side and brought up a cricket bat Astrid recognised. 'Do you remember this?' A smile crept across his face like a slug slithering through mud. 'Now get on your knees.'

She strode towards him, concentrating only on her niece. She ignored the tattooed man and dropped to her knees, close to Olivia; she resisted the temptation to reach out and touch her.

'Hi, Olivia. It'll all be over soon, and you'll be back with your parents.'

'You got that right, bitch.'

The tattooed fascist grunted the words through his twisted mouth, raising the bat high before bringing it down towards her skull. It whooshed through the air, mixed in with Laurel's scream and the tattooed man's triumphant laugh. His movement was fast, dropping his arm at a hundred miles an hour, but Astrid was quicker, raising her arm so the temporary cast blocked his attempt to crush her head.

The wood cracked against the cast, which protected her wrist as she pushed her other hand into the ground for stability, fighting back against the vibrations rippling through her body. She used her momentum to move upwards, forcing him back and away from Olivia. They crashed into a tree, tumbling to the ground as she shouted to Laurel.

'Get Olivia out of here!'

His hands struggled for her throat; her knee pushed up against his chest to keep him off balance, the bat lying half in the shadows and out of their grasps. His fingers gave up trying to reach her neck, looking for her eyes instead. Her arm throbbed with tremors from the blow as she brought her hand into his Adam's apple, jagging into his throat with her nails. He gurgled, spitting blood and phlegm as she rolled from him.

A gust of wind brought leaves swirling up from the ground as Astrid stood and kicked him in the head, knocking him unconscious with one blow. She held on to her aching arm as she sought out Laurel and Olivia, finding them only a few feet from her. She ignored her natural urge to hide her emotions, stumbling forward to throw her good arm around her niece.

'Are you okay?' Olivia said to Astrid.

'I'm fine, kid.'

Astrid ruffled her niece's hair, grinning as Olivia smiled at her. All she wanted was to scoop the girl up and get out of the park, but she knew she couldn't leave yet.

She let go of Olivia.

One side of Astrid's body ached as if cast in iron, while the rest of her was on the verge of exhaustion. Olivia's smile sparked her into action, dampening how every muscle screamed out for rest. She imagined the inevitable meeting with her sister, but she pushed that to the back of her mind and strode towards another unwanted reunion.

'Is this what you wanted, Cara?'

Delaney was motionless on the swing, her gaze focused on the woman who approached her.

'What sort of welcome is this for the love of your life?' Cara said with curled lips and flickering eyelashes.

'I never loved you.' Astrid said it with enough venom to feed a thousand snakes.

'I wasn't talking to you, Snow.'

Astrid froze for an instant before the cricket bat collided with the side of her head, and everything turned dark.

33 ISLAND OF DREAMS

Astrid's vision returned in erratic bursts, watching her legs floating effortlessly over grass before she drifted into a troubled dream state. She was on a pirate ship, the Jolly Roger fluttering over her head, Olivia running just out of her reach, laughing and smiling. She chased her niece across a giant treasure map. She clutched at her chest as Olivia sped across a rickety wooden bridge; it swayed close to the jaw-snapping crocodiles leaping from below. Pain rippled through her bones, her skin sparkling with anxiety.

The two of them ran into the jungle, Astrid struggling to catch up with Olivia, the words refusing to leap from her throat and reach the attention of her niece. An icy dagger clutched at her chest as green-skinned monsters lunged at them. Two bald doppelgangers with orange teeth charged at Olivia, but she dodged them by jumping over their claws. A sword appeared in Astrid's hand, the weight of it hurting her wrist as she swung it in an arc and decapitated the twin beasts in one go. Olivia made it out of the jungle to the other side, Astrid's invisible voice failing to catch up with the kid.

She increased her speed, desperate to catch up. Leaving

the jungle, she saw Olivia frozen in time, staring at the glowing golden city in front of her. Astrid relaxed as she reached forward to put her hand on her niece's shoulder, the sword having mysteriously vanished. As she did so, something swooped from the air and snatched Olivia from the ground. Astrid's heart ached as the kid screamed and the creature swung back around, snakes protruding from its body like poisonous hairs. A giant yellow-skinned serpent rested where its tail should have been and on its shoulders were three enormous skulls. The beast headed straight for her, as Olivia struggled inside its claws. The faces of the three heads, two female and one male, glared at Astrid; she recognised each one: Cara, Laurel and Lawrence. They grinned as they bared their teeth, breathing poisonous fumes in her direction. She stretched her mouth wide to scream as the darkness crashed down on her again.

WHEN SHE WOKE, cold metal was pressing against her skull. She didn't need to see the length of the gun caressing her skin to know she could be dead without anyone hearing.

'It's amazing the things people will ignore so they can stay safe in their little bubble, never realising until it's too late how terrible isolation is.' Cara's voice slipped into her ears and brought Astrid back to consciousness. 'We hauled you here while Laurel held on to the cricket bat and I dragged the kid behind me, and not one person batted an eyelid.' The wind caressed the water, so it rippled in the dark. Astrid found herself on the small island in the middle of the lake. 'Do you remember the first time you brought me here? You liked the danger of outdoor sex then.'

Cara stepped backwards, moving the gun away from

Astrid's face. Astrid pressed her hands into the dirt as she pushed up.

'Where's Olivia?'

'I sent Laurel off to dispose of her.' Astrid's breath froze inside her. 'It's for the best, really, for the kid. She'd only end up heartbroken when she discovers you never really loved her.'

'Laurel wouldn't hurt Olivia.'

Bitterness dripped out of Cara like water from a leaky pipe. 'You think you know her because you've rolled around a few times?'

'You did all this because I broke up with you?'

The sneer matched the scorn in her voice. Cara peered at her victim, pressing the barrel of the gun into Astrid's cheek before pulling it away.

'You give yourself far too much credit, Snow. You were the trigger, of course, but what I am now was already inside me. I just didn't know it.' Cara smirked as she swept the damp from her lips with her free hand. 'You still have to pay for what you did to me, though.'

'Why don't you kill me and get it over with?'

'Because you have to suffer as I did. You won't die, but you will feel pain.' Cara fired the gun before she'd finished talking, the bullet flashing into Astrid's shoulder. She fell backwards, pain spreading through her like hot lava eating at her insides. She froze on the ground, unable to move or breathe. 'My veins are full of other people's diseases. My parents and brother; the extended family; so-called friends; work colleagues; the woman who said she loved me. I've had to clear out the ailments of others before they overwhelmed me. It's been cathartic, allowing me to find my true love in life.'

Astrid crawled through the grass as a thousand piranhas

ate through every part of her. She couldn't let it overwhelm her, focusing on getting up and finding Olivia. She needed to keep Cara talking, hoping she wouldn't fire the gun again.

'You mean Laurel?'

'God, no,' Cara said with a raucous laugh ripped from an asthmatic hyena. 'Inflicting pain on others is what I love; it's the only thing I can thank you for teaching me. Laurel is a means to an end. I'll admit I had some pangs of jealousy when I saw the two of you together, but I dismissed them when I appreciated how little she means to me.' Astrid glared at Cara, hoping to find a relic of the woman she'd once shared a life with. There was mania behind those eyes, making her unpredictable. 'I've discovered I enjoy killing people.'

Delaney's calm voice belittled the obsession pouring from her eyes. She ripped the long blonde wig off and tossed it into the lake, revealing the short black bob Astrid had always loved. There was a tinge of grey which hadn't been there before, surprising for a woman her age.

'What did you do with all the fingers you snipped?'

Astrid's lids were heavy as if the weight of her past had deposited itself above her eyes. The brown inside Delaney's eyes swirled around like fresh coffee poured into a human vessel. She shrugged as Astrid wriggled in pain.

'I might have dumped them somewhere or eaten them. I can't remember which.'

Her voice was velvet, rubbing against the back of her throat. Astrid was about to faint, but the image of Cara feasting on human flesh shocked her back to alertness. She didn't believe a word of it, knowing Cara was still playing with her mind.

I have to get inside her head.

It was a low whisper trickling inside Astrid's skull. She

reached deep into her gut and found the last remnants of her strength.

'You hate me for not loving you, transferring the resentment you feel for your family towards me, and yet you've turned into the same type of person. You pretended to care for your brother, used him for your ends, and then killed him.'

Astrid pushed all the pain into one spot in her mind, the corner she'd gone to when she was younger after he'd hurt her so many times.

'Frank owed me a great debt. He was keen to sacrifice his life so that mine would be better.' There was no sense of guilt or sorrow in her voice.

'And now you've done the same with Laurel. How did you manage to drag her into your twisted world?'

'She fell into the Agency and my arms. It was fate.'

'She was vulnerable, and you took advantage.'

'Did she tell you what happened to her in the army? I helped Laurel to recover from her ordeal.'

'You helped by lying to her?'

'Telling somebody you love them when you don't? That's rich, you, of all people, criticising me for that.' Cara removed a scarf from her pocket, knelt next to Astrid, and grabbed hold of the arm below the bullet wound, the weapon pointed towards Astrid's chest. 'I can't have you dying on me from blood loss.' She put the gun down to tie the scarf around the wound.

'You must have spent a long time planning this.'

She ignored the stinging in her shoulder and contemplated throwing herself on top of Cara while the weapon was on the ground.

'I think I've been heading towards this all my life. That

moment of realisation that inflicting pain on others is what truly makes me happy.'

'You've turned into your parents.'

'That may well be true, but I'll achieve so much more. You did me a favour, Snow, so I'll grant you a request. Which leg do you prefer? And eye?' Cara laughed as she moved the gun closer to her victim. Astrid considered the odds of overpowering her while the blood dripped from her shoulder. They weren't good. 'I'm going to shatter one of your kneecaps and blind you on one side. I know you'll come looking for me once this is done, and I'll need an advantage.'

Astrid tried to ignore the discomfort leaking from her body, ready for a desperate leap towards the woman who once loved her.

'You've lost your mind, Cara. I feel sorry for you.'

'I'm going to make sure you're never whole again, dissemble you physically and emotionally, so the rest of your life is in a constant state of despair.'

There was unbridled joy in her voice and a spark behind her eyes.

'You seem happier than when we were together, Cara; maybe you should be thanking me for starting you on this path to ecstasy.'

The agony in her body was nothing compared to what was in her mind: images of Olivia and how she'd let the kid down. Her brain worked through the distress, computing how to disorientate Cara as much as possible. A sly grin crept across Cara's face as the shadows dripped from the branches, tipping their fingers into the water surrounding them and searching for the light hidden below the lake.

'You mean I should thank you for breaking my heart?' Cara's laugh was loud and aggressive. 'Only love can cut so deep,' she snarled at Astrid. 'You killed everything good inside me, ripped me apart and then ignored the results. You were witness to my failing sleep, observed the desertion of my appetite, feeding off my pain, increasing your cruelty as I withered away into nothing.'

Cara's voice fluctuated between weakness and strength. Astrid stared at the woman whose life had descended into such emotional chaos.

The only way she could save herself was by hurting others.

'You murdered your brother.'

Astrid searched for anything to help her, a weapon to even the odds. The tranquil waters of the lake whispered in the air, urging her to do something soon, to run and find Olivia before it was too late.

'He deserved it. He should have protected me, but he didn't. His lack of action brought its consequences.'

The mud slipped through Astrid's fingers. She searched for the strength to get off the ground, fingers sinking deeper into the slime. The grime and dampness slithered into her skin, sucking the life from her flesh.

'You couldn't have done any of this without him.'

A bird fluttered down from the sky and landed near where Astrid knelt in the wet grass. It was searching for food, walking close to her.

Grab the animal and toss it into Cara's face. You can do it. Move forward. Reach for it.

Cara spoke as the bird crept towards Astrid's fingers. 'It was his guilt which drove his dedication to me, a desperate attempt to redeem his soul.'

'You keep blaming everybody else for your failings, Cara. He was a child in the same household as you, with as much power and influence as any kid surrounded by domineering adults. You used his regrets to manipulate him into helping you murder five people. He didn't sacrifice himself to help you, but to save his soul.'

Cara strode forward, pulling her foot back before launching it and kicking the bird into the lake. It screeched as feathers flew everywhere.

'You always did have a knack for rewriting history, didn't you, Snow?' Cara raised the gun and caressed the trigger. 'Is that what you did with our relationship, told yourself it was all my fault and you had to get rid of me?' Cara lowered her body so she was looking straight at Astrid, the gun pointing towards Astrid's right eye. 'Don't worry; I'm not going to shoot you in the face. When Laurel returns, I'll use the knife she used when slitting your niece's throat.'

As the words left Cara's mouth, the desperation reached a crescendo within Astrid; she tightened her fists as much as possible, fresh mud sticking to her palms and slithering between her fingers. She ignored the pain and lunged at Cara.

'I'll kill you, Delaney.'

'That's the spirit, Snow.' Cara moved to one side and laughed as Astrid missed by a mile, hitting the grass with her shoulder. Cara knelt so she was close to her face. Astrid's breathing came in substantial clumps, along with a desperate desire to bury her head in the ground and sleep, hoping all the agonies would vanish if she only closed her eyes. There was wet mud on her face, the stink of the dirt rushing into her lungs. 'Think of poor Olivia and how you failed her.'

Cara was enjoying herself, dragging out Astrid's torture for as long as possible. She was about to lunge at Cara again when a shadow approached them. At first, she thought one of the trees had uprooted itself and was marching to her rescue, branches pointing outwards like bayonetted rifles. Cara stood as the footsteps approached.

Astrid blinked and focused on the woman who strode towards her.

'Help me, Laurel.'

Cara grinned. 'This is excellent timing, Laurel, just when I need the knife.'

Astrid's eyes widened as her former partner stepped forward. Laurel's arms were outstretched. Olivia's unmoving body rested there; a gift Laurel laid down next to Astrid's body, which had taken root in the ground.

A slight drizzle of rain joined them from the sky as Astrid's tears flowed in waves.

34   THE END

Olivia's frozen eyes cut through Astrid's heart. All her terrible childhood memories flooded back, images of her battered and bruised face glaring at her through the years.

Drizzle settled onto Olivia's cheeks while tears swam down Astrid's. All she saw was her niece's head, the rest of her covered by the blanket Laurel had wrapped her in. Astrid's body gave out, her neck hanging low before her hands sank into the shroud covering Olivia. The coldness of the fabric transferred ice into her skin, penetrating deep into her flesh. Olivia was frozen, with icicles of agony piercing Astrid's chest.

'In all the years I spent planning this, lost in the times when I pictured this moment, never did I think it would be this perfect.'

Cara hovered over her victims, a malicious dark presence sucking the life from everything in her orbit. Astrid gazed at Olivia's flawless face, her youthful blonde hair moving in the wind as the rain caressed her skin. She wanted to pick her up, but was helpless both physically and mentally, her fingers digging into the earth in search of something miraculous. She stretched her head up to the moon and wanted to scream.

'She was innocent, Cara.'

'Do you see now, Snow, how debilitating and destructive love is?'

Cara was a vision of cruelty, ugliness stretching through her skin as if a thousand scorpions crawled inside her flesh.

'Whatever I did to you, Cara, however painful it was, none of it was intentional; none of it was as vindictive as you've become.'

The words slunk over her lips, tears mixed in with the rain, her heart shrinking as she curled up on the ground. She wanted to return to before she was born, before all the hurt consumed her life. But instinct fought against it.

'You've lost everything important to you, Snow, all thanks to me. I was surprised to see you could love another human being, shocked at your emotions for your niece, but it was the perfect final addition to what I'd spent all these years preparing for you. If you'd kept away from her, I never would have known you could be so fragile, which makes things even better as you only have yourself to blame for her death.'

Cara was reaching her end game. There was little time for Astrid to do anything.

'What did you do with the knife, Laurel?' Cara turned from Astrid and switched her attention to her partner. 'I need to relieve Snow of one of her eyes. Which one did you find the prettiest when you gazed at them? I'll let you keep it as a souvenir.'

Laurel held on to the blade at her side, the moonlight reflecting in its steel. 'Did you mean what you said?' she asked Cara, who reached out for the weapon.

'Which part, my love?'

Astrid found strength from somewhere, taking her hands from the grass and wiping the wet mud across her shirt. Part of her needed to look into Olivia's eyes for the last time. She was only vaguely aware of what the other two women were saying to each other.

'I heard you talking to Astrid when you told her you didn't love me, that you were using me.'

Tension fell from every syllable in Laurel's words. Grief surged through Astrid like spilt ink across a piece of paper, but she had enough awareness to see something was wrong with Laurel. Astrid tore her gaze from Olivia as Cara took hold of Laurel's free hand.

'That was all lies, my sweet, to confuse Snow. Now hand me the blade so I can give her one final kiss; unless you want to do it? I know how much you enjoyed sucking on those lush lips.'

The taste of death was in Delaney's words. Something about them sparked the last surge of adrenaline Astrid had hidden deep inside her, strength returning as she dismissed the agony screaming through every inch of her. She had to decide what to do with the last of her energy: a futile attack on the women standing over her or a final embrace of Olivia. There was no choice to make. Astrid reached over to her niece as Laurel raised her voice.

'I don't believe you, Cara. I see you for what you are now, somebody incapable of love, only driven by the pain you cause for others. Astrid was right: you used me like you used your brother.' Her voice was serene, determination in her eyes.

'You're confused, Laurel.'

'Are you planning the same fate for me as that you dished out to Frank?'

Astrid heard everything, but she didn't care anymore. She could only stare at Olivia's cold flesh. The weight of it was too much, so she twisted to glare at the designer of her misery. Cara had let go of Laurel's hand, looking at the younger woman with pure disdain across her face.

'Well, my sweet, I can't leave any witnesses to what I've created. I thought about hanging on to you a bit longer, but you've turned into such a whiny bitch. Now would be a good time to dispense with your services. I can arrange it to look as if Snow killed you as well as all the others.' Cara raised the gun and pointed it towards Laurel. For Astrid, this would be her last chance to leap at Cara and drag her into the lake. 'Snow couldn't help herself since she was so distraught about you murdering her niece. Yes, that would bring things into a nice, neat ending.'

'Perhaps,' Laurel said. 'But I didn't kill Olivia.' She smiled as Cara's grin sank. 'I may have loved you, or thought I loved you, but you must be mad to think I'd kill a child for you.'

Before Astrid could react, there was movement below her and Olivia coughed.

Laurel didn't wait for Cara to fire the gun, lifting the blade in one swift arc of her arm and bringing it down on Cara's wrist. The knife wasn't sharp enough to go through flesh and bone in one go, but it cut down halfway, blood spraying out in a shower as Cara screamed and dropped the pistol. She plunged to the ground, rolling towards the edge of the lake.

Laurel kicked the gun into the water and moved to Astrid as the rain continued to fall.

'Can you stand?'

'I think so.' Astrid slipped Olivia from the blanket and took her hand. 'Are you okay, kid?'

Olivia yawned, wiping the sleep from her face and staring into her eyes. 'Aunt Astrid?'

Astrid smiled as if she'd never known happiness in her life; her lips stretched so far up her face, they nearly covered her nose. 'Yes, Olivia, it's me. How did you know?'

Astrid pulled them up. Laurel went to the unconscious Cara.

'She's fainted from the shock. I need to tie this off before she dies from lack of blood.'

Laurel removed a cloth from her pocket and wrapped it around the wound. Astrid recognised it as the rest of the scarf Laurel had taken from George's house. She didn't care if Cara lived or died, with only one person on her mind now.

Olivia answered her question.

'I knew she wasn't my aunt when she came to the nursery. I've seen pictures of you when you were younger.'

Astrid was stunned, not only by Olivia's strength, but the knowledge Courtney had shown Olivia photos of her.

'Why did you go with her?' Astrid said.

'Because she'd hurt others if I didn't.'

'That's some brave kid you have there.' Laurel tied the cloth around what was left of Cara's wrist. Her voice brought Astrid back to the present and what to do next. She stared at Laurel, for once lost for something to say. 'I gave Olivia a mild sedative. I needed time to think while Cara spoke with you.'

'If you hadn't overheard Cara say she didn't love you, what would you have done?'

Astrid held on to Olivia's hand and never wanted to let go. The lines on Laurel's face appeared inked from a mixture of emotions: regret, shame, embarrassment and sorrow, all of them the consequence of her love for the woman lying at her feet.

'Honestly? I don't know, but I could never hurt a child. They took my child from me; I couldn't do that to anybody else.'

Laurel gazed at Olivia as she spoke. Astrid wanted to spare her niece any potential bad memories, knowing how childhood trauma could screw up the rest of your life. But she needed to know what was going on inside Laurel's head.

'Who took your child?'

Astrid put her arms around Olivia as she waited for the reply.

'That's a story for another day, Astrid, but you were right when you said something terrible happened to me in the army.'

A river of sadness poured out of Laurel as she stared at Astrid holding on to Olivia.

'You knew Cara's plans and what she'd do to the other agents; what she'd do to her brother.'

'No.' Laurel sputtered with resentment and anger. 'I didn't know what would happen to Frank. She kept that from me.'

'But you knew what she'd planned for the others?'

There was pity in Astrid's heart for the woman she could have loved. Laurel bent closer to the sleeping Cara Delaney and stroked her hair as only a lover would.

'I did, but they all deserved it; some more than others.'

Astrid knew from experience Laurel had persuaded herself everything she'd done had been righteous. 'What about the woman in Berlin, the one she convinced everybody was her?'

Laurel turned her back on Astrid and Olivia, her voice so low it verged on whispering.

'I don't know who that was. That's when my doubts started.'

Laurel removed her hands from Cara's cheek, gazing down at her as Delaney's eyes flickered into life.

'Shame you didn't have them sooner.'

Astrid continued to hold on to Olivia as she searched for a way off the island.

'There's a row of boats further along the edge and behind us,' Laurel said as Astrid walked away. 'What do you want me to do with Cara?'

'Take her to the Agency, confess everything to them.'

Astrid found their transport on the water. The rain had stopped, and she smiled at Olivia as she helped her into the boat. She didn't care about Cara Delaney and Laurel Lee anymore. The only thing that mattered was getting Olivia home and her reunion with her sister.

How strange that's going to be.

Astrid picked up the oars, struggling with both of them because of the damaged wrist on one side and the bullet hole below her shoulder on the other.

'This may take some time, Olivia.'

She managed a smile as she spoke. Olivia moved forward a little, putting her hands on Astrid's legs.

'Don't worry, Aunt Astrid, take as long as you want.' Astrid grinned. 'And you can call me Liv.'

AN HOUR LATER, Astrid was in a hospital cubicle getting patched up. Olivia sat opposite her, sucking on a lollipop one of the nurses had provided. Astrid was wondering who would turn up first, the Agency or her sister.

Then Courtney arrived.

She rushed to Olivia as the doctor finished stitching Astrid's wound and left. Courtney threw her arms around her daughter and squeezed the life from her. They stayed like that for two minutes before Olivia wriggled free from her mother's embrace.

'Aunt Astrid saved me, Mum.'

Courtney smiled at her daughter before turning to the sister she hadn't seen since they were teenagers.

'Are you hurt?'

Was that genuine concern she heard in Courtney's voice or just a show for her daughter?

'Why didn't you call the police, Courtney?'

'That woman said she'd hurt...' she glanced at Olivia, 'well, she told me not to speak to anyone, especially the authorities.'

Astrid flinched as she got off the trolley, a shiver of pain jumping from her shoulder and rushing down the rest of her.

'You better get the kid home. She's had a hard day.'

Courtney grabbed Astrid's arm, pulled her from the cubicle and out of earshot of her daughter. A sharp stab of electricity surged through Astrid's bones, and she bit her lip in an attempt to ignore it.

'What the fuck did you do?'

The concern hadn't lasted long. Astrid allowed her sister to keep on digging her nails into her arm.

'More than you ever did for me, Sis.'

Courtney pushed away from her and placed one hand over her face.

'Fuck, fuck, fuck.' She dragged two fingers over her cheek. 'I haven't slept since God knows when.' She peered over Astrid's shoulder at her daughter. 'Is she okay?'

'She needs to rest, but I think she'll be fine, Courtney.' Astrid moved a foot from her sister and noticed the dark-suited agents entering the hospital ward. 'You should take her home now.'

Astrid was stepping from her sister, ready for another unwanted reunion, when a small hand grabbed her arm.

'When will I see you again, Aunty Astrid?'

Astrid glanced down at her niece. 'You've got my phone number now, kid.' Then she looked at Courtney. 'You'll just have to get your mother's permission to call me.'

She left her sister grimacing and stepped towards the dark suits.

ABOUT THE AUTHOR

Andrew French lives amongst faded seaside glamour on the North East coast of England. He likes gin and cats but not together, new music and old movies, curry and ice cream. Slow bike rides and long walks to the pub are his usual exercise, as well as flicking through the pages of good books and the memoirs of bad people.

Find out more at www.andrewsfrench.com

Facebook:

https://www.facebook.com/A-S-French-Author-150145625006018

Twitter:

www.twitter.com/andrewfrench100

Instagram:

www.instagram.com/andrewfrench100

And replies to all his email at mail@andrewsfrench.com

If you have the time, please leave a review at Amazon or Goodreads

Thank you!

ACKNOWLEDGMENTS

Many thanks to my wonderful wife for all her support and patience.

Don't Fear the Reaper edited by Alison Jack.

Cover design by James, GoOnWrite.com